I Thought I'd Be Happy

The world is beyond us even as we own it.
It is a hugeness ... we climb toward.

- Jack Gilbert -

I Thought I'd Be Happy

a novel

JIM NASON

Tightrope Books Inc.
167 Browning Trail
Barrie, Ontario
Canada L4N 5E7
www.tightropebooks.com

Editor: Jeffrey Round
Copy Editor: Amber McMillan
Cover Design: Deanna Janovski
Cover Photo: Herbert Tobias:
          Berlinische Galerie; copyright VG Bildkunst, Bonn
Author Photo: David Leyes
Typesetting: David Bigham

Produced with the support of the Canada Council for the Arts
and the Ontario Arts Council

Canada Council   Conseil des Arts
for the Arts   du Canada

ONTARIO ARTS COUNCIL
CONSEIL DES ARTS DE L'ONTARIO
50 YEARS OF ONTARIO GOVERNMENT SUPPORT OF THE ARTS
50 ANS DE SOUTIEN DU GOUVERNEMENT DE L'ONTARIO AUX ARTS

Cataloguing data available from Library and Archives Canada

Printed in Canada

Contents

Prologue

"How long has it been?" asks Bernd. "You know…" he says, taking his hand off Marco's knee.

"Almost three years. It's hard to believe."

Bernd folds his arms across his chest, falls back into the sofa. His good looks still unsettle Marco—the green eyes and square jaw, the wavy blonde hair and taut, muscular body. "I guess I still don't have a place in your life?" he asks.

"Don't go getting weird on me," says Marco. "You and I hardly had two weeks together."

"All right, all right," says Bernd. "Moving on. Do you think that as the writer of the script you are also capable of directing this movie? Directing takes incredible control, concentration and collaboration. From what I know about you…" he says, placing his hand on Marco's knee again, "…these aren't your stronger qualities."

"I know the story," says Marco, lifting the hand off his leg, standing and looking down at Bernd. "I know the feel of it, its colours and tones. I have watched every *film noir* ever made. Twice. My soundtrack plays over and over in my brain—every string, each note of sax and blast of trumpet across every scene. I know the shadows that cross the walls, and I hear the rumbling of every single subway train that cuts through the tunnels of London, Berlin, Toronto, Paris, New York…"

"Whoa!" laughs Bernd. "I believe you."

"He deserves this," says Marco, sitting down.

"*Film noir* is about subtlety and it's easy to screw up," says Bernd.

"Oh, I won't screw this up," says Marco, looking Bernd head on. "My feet are on the ground and I know what's in front of me. But this isn't about me; this is for Andreas."

The doorbell rings and both men look in the direction of the screen door where Bernd stood naked the day they met. *One more peek*, Marco had convinced himself as he circled the house. "You like coffee?" Bernd asked, holding open the door with his foot as Marco walked in.

"You'd better get it," says Marco, pointing to the door. And as Bernd walks across the living room, he adds: "How's that for direction?"

Manya comes into the room first—tall, fit and gorgeous—followed by Brent Kingford, who will play the leading male role. "Where's the coffee?" he asks. "Whose idea was a seven a.m. start?"

The doorbell rings again. A cameraman enters, followed by the costume designer and the editor. Before long, the living room fills with extras, technicians and props people. Marco inhales and stands as Bernd's assistant hands out copies of the script. This is the first readthrough and Marco wants everyone to get a feel for what he has in mind for the movie. He nudges past the crowd, kisses Manya on the cheek.

"Are you happy, Mister Neuroplasticity?" she jokes, touching his forehead with her finger.

"I'm happy to see you," says Marco, clearing his throat. "All right, everybody," he says, in a strong, confident voice. "We're ready," he shouts. "Let's get *Steam* rolling."

1
FLYING

It's not immediate. Sometimes it takes seconds, some-times it takes minutes, but he feels it, the tug and twinge under his skull—old brain shrinking under, new brain swelling up—*I am happy. There it is.* Marco rubs his head and smiles at Andreas, who doesn't see him because he's still focused on the obituaries he started reading in the *Globe* while they were waiting to board. He takes his cam-era out of his backpack and pans it across the silver-blue lake. There's a line of smog hanging over the downtown core, but the sun has emerged and the Toronto skyline is camera-ready. Tall and sexy, the Royal Bank building glit-ters gold. Next to it, topped with its enormous red crane, the Trump Tower inches up day by day between the exist-ing high-rises.

He loves the airplane's warm leather seats. He's ready for this: three weeks in Greece and they'll both come back refreshed. The flight attendant places two glasses of wine on the armrest between them.

"The brain is a sex organ." Andreas puts down the paper, leans closer and places his hand on Marco's leg. He has a solid, booming voice. A passenger across the aisle looks over. For once, Andreas notices. "The largest in the body," he adds, lowering his voice a notch.

The airplane banks left. The Fasten Your Seatbelt sign flashes.

"Since when did an ophthalmologist become an expert on the brain?" Marco returns the camera to his backpack and passes Andreas a piece of chocolate. 70% Cacao. Organic.

"Probably at the same time the cameraman did," says Andreas, poking Marco in the ribs.

Marco's brain imagines where his tongue goes—over the curve of Andreas' gorgeous butt, up the muscle-tight spine, around the suntanned neck, across the chin to the full, enticing mouth. He wants to hold and kiss him.

"What's on your mind?" asks Andreas, removing the lid from a bottle of pills and shaking a small tablet into his hand.

"You," he says.

"Nice thoughts, I hope."

"Very nice thoughts," Marco says.

"Are you happy?" asks Andreas.

"I worry about you and those pills," says Marco, nodding at the bottle in Andreas' hand.

"We've had this conversation before, Marco. It's a low dose of Effexor."

"Well, I want bliss in a pill too," he says. "This brain stuff is hard work."

Andreas looks at the book that Marco has tucked in the seat pouch in front of them: *I Thought I'd be Happy: Wired and fired, plugging your brain into bliss.*

"What's 'wired and fired'?" asks Andreas.

"Well," says Marco, sitting up in his seat, "this neuroscientist, David Lowell, refers to something called neuroplasticity—the idea that neurons that wire together, fire together. "And..." he adds, waving the book in the air, "Lowell takes those theories and adds a pinch of happiness into the scientific mix. And he describes our ability to influence the way the brain molds itself around thought patterns. And...if a person is unhappy, it just means that they have neurons out of sync with each other. And...if he really tries, a guy can *always* be happy and get those neurons back into sync again. And..."

Andreas playfully places his hand over Marco's mouth.

"*And*, a person needs contrast – a sense of grief to understand joy; loss to appreciate what he already has. This medication doesn't change any of those things; it simply keeps me on an even keel, that's all. I'm not high or *blissful*."

"The neuroplasticity stuff works," says Marco. "We're on vacation for three whole weeks. Let's think only good thoughts."

"I'm in," says Andreas, squeezing Marco's hand. "Turkey, Greece, climbing Mytikas…Who has time for negativity!"

They are on their way to Mount Olympus, via Newark and Istanbul. *I am happy*, Marco thinks as the plane levels out.

"That was a nice take off," says Andreas, leafing through his new Journal of Ophthalmology. "This pilot is good."

"Don't kid yourself," says Marco. "This aircraft stays airborne only because all hundred-and-fifty passengers will it to."

Andreas laughs, pulls his table out of the armrest. The flight attendant is out with drinks. "She seems like a genuinely pleasant human being," Andreas says, after she walks past their row.

"Uh-huh," Marco says, picking up his glass of red wine. "She looks like something off the set of Casablanca in that retro uniform."

"Do you remember the time we flew to Chicago and that older flight attendant crawled through the cabin on her hands and knees as if she were looking for a lost earring or something?"

"Her announcement was hilarious," Marco says. "*Good afternoon ladies and gentlemen. I suppose you may be wondering why I was crawling through the cabin on my knees just now? Well. I was looking for the glamour. Today is my last day on the job, and I'm still looking for the glamour that I was promised when I started this job twenty-five years ago*."

"Cheers," says Marco, holding up his glass.

"To Mytikas!" Andreas says, washing back the pill with a sip of Shiraz.

2
MEETING

The cyclist rode alongside the streetcar. At the traffic light, Marco slid the window open for a closer look. He was handsome, with black, wavy hair, and judging by the size of his legs, Marco could tell the guy spent a lot of time on his bicycle. But more than that, beyond the fitness and Mediterranean good looks, Marco wanted to meet him because of the way he rested his hand on his chin as he rolled to a stop at College and Euclid; because of his indifference to the scorching sun and the rush-hour traffic trying to muscle past him. He oozed intelligence and sex. A philosopher jock. A thinking hunk. Just before the light changed, he looked up at Marco, who was looking down from the streetcar window, and winked. He leaned over the handlebars, and cupped the elbow of the arm where he rested his chin. He didn't move his hand away or roll forward when the light changed. The guy waited on his bicycle while Marco ran back.

Twenty minutes later, Marco was naked on the hardwood floor of an Annex apartment. The bike lay on its side in the middle of the room. His helmet sat on a wingback chair piled with sheets and towels. It was raining hard outside.

"My plan was to finish the laundry before having

guests in," the cyclist said, straddling Marco's chest, while he attempted to light a joint.

"You're hung," Marco said.

"Why thank you, sir," the cyclist said in a fake Southern drawl. "What did y'all say your name was again?"

"Marco. Marco Morelli."

"I'm Andreas," he said, inhaling and passing the joint. "Andreas," he coughed,

"Triandaphyllo."

"You're Greek," said Marco. "A philosophical Greek with a lovely…uh, hmm…body."

"Yes. And you're an adorable Italian."

"Italian from Montreal," Marco said. "But let's not go there right now."

Andreas talked about his parents, Anastasia and Andreas senior, who lived on the Danforth. He talked about why he became an ophthalmologist—most of it having to do with his father becoming blind in an accident in the restaurant he owned. He got excited about Zeus and Athena and all kinds of Greek mythology. He hugged and squeezed Marco and, before long, he lit another joint.

"What do you do?" Andreas asked. "What are your parents like?"

"I'm a cameraman for MBTV. And…" he hesitated, "…I'd rather not talk about Franco and Antonietta right now."

"Okay," said Andreas. "We won't talk about your parents," he added, passing Marco the joint. "What a great job you have."

"Not really. I do the morning show and I'm not big on getting out of bed before ten."

"Oh," said Andreas. "What's the show?"

"Mad Breakfast Television," Marco said. "If I hear that theme song one more time I'm going to throw my camera through the Queen Street window."

"Oh, I've seen it. *MBTV: The Wake Up Show For The Working Joe.*" He did a bad imitation of the theme song, *"I'm a maniac, maniac and I dance..."* then took a long draw off the joint and continued, *"maniac, maniac ..."*

"Stop!" Marco said. "You're killing me."

"What song would you rather hear?" asked Andreas.

"*Both Sides Now,*" said Marco.

"I love Joni Mitchell," said Andreas.

"Clouds are my friends," said Marco, looking out the window at the rainy sky. "I float on them, sink and fly with them. I wander away."

"Have clouds always been your little imaginary friends?" Andreas teased. "You're soooo serious!"

Marco hesitated before answering, but decided to be honest. "Yes," he said. "I think they were my only friends growing up. My dad was kind of obsessed with Greek mythology," Andreas said. "He used to call my mother Harmony. And Harmony's parents were Aphrodite and Ares, the gods of love and war."

"Sounds eccentric."

"Eccentric, yes," said Andreas. "But my father really believed in living life to the fullest—not always playing it safe, living with the consequences, good and bad."

"My parents weren't the philosophical type," Marco said. "But they were smart, I guess, and loving, in a white trash way."

3
KITTEN

"The cat was white, but its fur was dirty, probably from living under cars and porches. Watching out for the swollen belly and ignoring her hissing and growling, Franco put her out of her misery by dropping a stone on her head. He stepped on the stone with his dress shoes, being careful not to get blood on the cuffs of his good grey pants. He was on his way home from work. He wasn't disturbed by the sound of the cracking skull, the way the bottom teeth stuck out. He had to move fast to save the babies. Franco sliced her belly with his red Swiss Army knife. Only it's not a belly beneath the fur, it's called a litter sac. He had to be steady and watch the pressure, the blade not as sharp as it could have been. They came out in a lump, six little sausages strung together. Wet and slippery, with squinty eyes like apple seeds. All grey. None were moving, except for the smallest one. Grey with a white face and two white paws, one in the front and one in the back. He kept that one. The others went down the sewer drain with her. That's the way it is in nature. One lives and that's better than none. That's the way it is in nature, he says again. Do you like her, son? I named her Kitten."

Marco didn't understand his father's need to tell the story over and over, each version slightly different from the one before. Clearly, there was a feral cat and at least one kitten, but Marco knew his father had never had a job that required dress shoes or good pants with cuffs.

The mother cat was difficult to pick up, so Franco said. All messed up like that, and the other five kittens like brain mush or porridge. In order to get Kitten, he'd had to use his knife to cut the cord. It was bloody and strong like plastic-coated wire. He'd had to breathe into Kitten's nose and mouth to get her lungs going. "It was like breathing into a wet rat," he said.

4
ANASTASIA

The house on Logan Avenue is on the side of a hill. Tobogganing in the winter, soccer in the summer, Anastasia has it all thought out. It's big for three people—one of them only seven years old, but she knows that soon enough there will be more children; friends for Andreas, grandchildren and neighbours' kids stopping in for a visit. That's what she dreams of, anyhow.

Andreas plays with his cars on the floor, pretending he's an Indy driver. Her stubborn child, named after his father and his grandfather, with his beautiful eyes, the same pale green of the leaves on young olive trees, his curly hair black as the ripe olives themselves. He will be envied and desired. Whenever admirers come to the house, she ties a red ribbon around his leg to ward off the Evil Eye.

The house smells of cooking oil. It smells of mint lamb and tarragon chicken. These are the meats her husband brings home from his restaurant to find her asleep in bed with their son by her side—there's no point in telling him that it will spoil. There's no point in trying to hide her excitement those nights when he comes home with his arms free of plates, smelling of roses he bought on the way.

"Business was good?" she asks him.

"I ran out of lamb and chicken," he says.

This afternoon, the house on Logan feels empty.

"*Pedhi mou!*" she yells, hating her own quick temper. "Don't push the car so hard across the floor."

Everything is wood and red brick in this country. The toilets flush and the lights work, but everything feels empty and cold.

Anastasia stands at the kitchen sink staring down last night's dishes. The grass in Withrow Park is scorched brown from a dry summer. There are children playing on the hill. Several people let their dogs race in the leash-free zone. She drops her cigarette into the dishwater. Maybe she can convince Andreas to play outside.

"Put your car in the bag. And a ball. And a hat. And put on your sandals with the straps in the back," she tells him before hearing the harshness in her voice.

"Don't give me the eye," she says. "You are Greek," she says. "You were born for the sun, now let's go."

He will not talk to her when they are alone. He will not play outside with the other boys. He hates to go to the restaurant with his father. He hates Greek food and he hates his father's talk of the old country. She should worry about this, but she doesn't. For the most part, he is a happy child and as he grows, his good looks will draw plenty of women to his side.

"Come, *Pedhi mou*," she says. "Cindy is there. Come to the window and see for yourself."

Cindy is a loud girl with red hair who is eight or nine. Her young mother is Italian, but the father must have been Irish or some other pale species, Anastasia thinks. She is always outside. Every time they go to the park, Cindy is playing on the swing or in the sand. Sometimes she's skipping along the sidewalk by herself.

"Where is your mother today?" Anastasia asks her, unpacking Andreas' cars and a plastic shovel, placing them alongside him in the sandbox.

"Over there." Cindy points to the green building with the toilets and a small room where they have yoga and drawing classes.

Anastasia has to squint to see the woman against the sun, but soon she can just make out Cindy's mother leaning against the building, arms crossed, smoking a cigarette. The mother waves, and Anastasia turns back to the children. She does not know this woman. She does not care to know this careless girl who has a child and no husband.

"She doesn't think I know," says Cindy, wise beyond her years.

"About what?" Anastasia asks, knowing perfectly well what the child is referring to.

"The cigarettes," Cindy says, skipping in circles pretending to blow smoke from a twig she has stuck in her mouth.

"It's not funny," Anastasia tells Andreas, who is rolling in the sand laughing. "Where's the hat I asked you to put in the bag?"

Andreas does not answer. He ignores her when his father is not there.

"Don't look at Cindy," Anastasia says. "Your face will get burnt from the sun."

Andreas shrugs his shoulders, digs his shovel into the sand.

"Let's build a castle," he says to Cindy. "A castle with dragons and monsters and a guard dog with three heads and burning red eyes!"

Cindy steps into the sand. She looks at Anastasia and smiles.

"Okay, Miss Anastasia?" she asks.

Anastasia nods. "Sure," she says back, worried about her son's reference to a guard dog with three heads and burning red eyes.

She sits on the bench under the shade of a sickly maple and lights a cigarette. There's no point hiding them, the boy isn't stupid. The years will pass, and like every teenager in the world, he too will be smoking cigarettes.

The temperature rises quickly. The children have fallen asleep in the grass with Cindy's mother. The girl is curled close to Andreas. She has her small hand on his shirtless shoulder. Her mother sleeps on her back, her arm shading the sun from her eyes. Anastasia hasn't moved from the bench. She is lighting her third cigarette when she sees her husband on the far side of the park. Like a mirage of the man she married eight years earlier, his head is high and he walks slowly. He carries two large shopping bags and takes measured steps in her direction. He knows where she sits by now. Her daily routine doesn't change much and the path goes directly past the swings and sandbox.

He sets the bags down at her feet.

"Come, Harmony," he says to her, feeling her face for her lips. "We are off to the soft, white sands of Kuofonissi."

"But it is only Wednesday," she says. "You have no staff to run the restaurant."

"I do now," he says. "And you smell like cigarettes."

She drops her freshly lit cigarette on the sidewalk, rubs it out with her foot.

"I have one a day, Andreas," she lies. "One cigarette in the fresh air of the park."

"Where is my little Polydorus," he says. "Where is my earth-born spirit?"

He had always referred to the world in terms of mythology, but since the accident, things are worse. It's as if their existence together has shifted to an ethereal plane. Nobody has a real name anymore. She is Harmony. Their son is Polydorus, the only son of Cadmus and Harmony. Lake Huron is Koufonissi, and their car is a silver chariot.

"Over there," Anastasia nods. "Sleeping."

"Let's go," he says. "You drive."

"Very funny," she says.

***

She takes the Don Valley Parkway north and gets off at the very last exit. She drives west to Highway 9. She likes this part of the trip. Rolling hills and green pastures. Cows and sheep, and field after field of tall corn. Rich and peaceful. Young and prosperous, Canada.

"What did you pack for lunch?" she asks him.

"Keep your eyes on the road," he says. "It wouldn't be so easy to pull this beast out from between a row of corn."

She'd kill for a cigarette. Pay a million dollars if just once he'd let her listen to something decent on the radio.

At Station Beach she finds a clearing in the sand and lays down the pink blanket she always uses for picnics. She finds the two bags of food in the back seat of the car and feels under the seat for a bottle of red wine.

Andreas holds his son above the water. The child kicks his feet and screams. She hates it when he screams like that. Un-boy like.

Andreas does not mind. "If you ever fall in and can't stay on top," he says to his son, "count your steamboats and head for the shore."

Each time they go to the beach, Andreas gives his son the same lesson.

"One steamboat. Two steamboats. Three steamboats…like that," he says. "Now practice, Polydoros. Give it a try."

Anastasia always has the same interjection.

"You're teaching him to drown, Andreas. Why don't you teach your son to stay above the water?"

"Let him celebrate the underworld," Andreas says. "Soon enough he'll be a defeated old Skylos."

By the time his sentence is finished the boy is underwater.

She lights a cigarette and pours herself a glass of wine. She looks out at the lake and the perfect blue sky. Almost heaven. Almost heaven, so why the tears? She wipes her cheek and kicks off her sandals. She puts her feet in the lake and sips her wine. Andreas sniffs at the air and shakes his head disapprovingly. She drops the cigarette into the water and waits for the sizzle. She picks it up, wet and limp, and smiles back at her husband who will not see the red of anger in her face.

***

They came to Canada because of the washrooms. That's what his father always tells him. *Toilets you can flush and a door you can lock.*

They came to Canada because of the perfect weather. That's what his mother says when she's being sarcastic. *Too hot to move in July. So cold in December that you have to run to the market in layers of sweaters and coats.*

He goes with his father to the restaurant some Saturday evenings.

"It's okay to stay awake late on weekends," his father tells him as he stuffs a handful of bills into a small green bag. "Feel," he says to Andreas. "The weight of hard work."

"How do you know the big dollars and the little dollars?" Andreas asks his father.

"By the way they feel," he says. "You try."

Andreas closes his eyes. His father puts a single bill in his hand.

"Fifty," he says.

"Nope."

"Five?"

No matter how hard he tries, Andreas gets it wrong.

"Go slow, *Pedhi mou*," his father says.

"Ten!"

"Perfect. You can see from deep inside."

***

He knows something is wrong by the acrid smell when he walks through the swinging doors to the kitchen, but he is late and there are customers waiting for food. He opens the windows and the back door. He walks into the cooler and carries out the two long trays of kebobs he'd prepared the night before. He sets them on the counter next to the stove and returns for cucumbers and tomatoes. He lines them along the back of the cutting block and takes his sharpest knife out of the drawer. He opens the oven door. The air is still a little off. He holds his apron to his nose and strikes the match. The force of the explosion knocks him across the floor. It happens fast, but it's all in slow motion—the fireball that covers his body, the mop and the bucket of water that he crashes into. He cannot see. He cannot breathe. *Drop and roll. Drop and roll.* This is what he remembers from the television, but he cannot—every inch of his being tells him to run for water. There is searing pain inside his head—he can feel his hair on fire. He bangs against the sink and feels for the tap. He is burning and cannot breathe. *Water. Dear God, water please.* He cannot find the tap. His hands are on fire. *Water please. Water.* He pushes through the swinging doors to the dining room, his hair and his hands and his face on fire.

***

What is the smell of burnt flesh? Who is the God of Flames? What is the taste of his lips and his tongue? Who is the God of Words? What words to describe unbearable pain?

"Anastasia?" he asks. He feels the weight of her against the hospital bed.

"Does this hurt?" she asks, gently picking up his bandaged hand.

The tears fall. Not through the bandages and down his cheek, the tears fall inside. They fall from the orbits that once held light. They fall grey, like water tinted from smoke, down the back of his throat. They pool inside until he feels like he's drowning. He tries to sit up but cannot move. He cannot breathe, cannot call out.

"Nurse," Anastasia calls. "I think my husband's in pain."

"Press the morphine pump," she tells him. "You'll feel better."

The nurse gently rolls him to his side. She pulls back the sheet and slowly lifts his legs, places a small pillow between his knees, does the same with his arms and feet.

"Try to sleep," she tells him. "You'll feel better tomorrow."

He holds up his hand and shakes his head.

"Where's the boy?" he attempts to speak. "Where's…"

She has not brought him. Anastasia was not sure what she would see. She was not sure that she should allow Andreas to witness his father like this. The curls are gone. He has bandages over his eyes. He is blind now, his burnt body blistered and peeling—her husband taking small breaths, hanging on to life.

"He's at school today," she says. "I will bring him next time."

***

One steamboat. Two steamboats…

Andreas was seven years old. Four more sleeps until he turned eight. Every summer he went to the lake with his mom and dad. *Not as nice as the water at home*, his father told him, *but almost*. He swam away from his parents, but there was no danger, the water didn't get deep until a long way out.

…Four steamboats. Five steamboats…

He opened his eyes underwater and watched the minnows swimming above the sand. They were small and fast, hundreds of them. His mother told him not to open his eyes underwater because he would get bad things in them. His father said to keep counting.

…Six steamboats.

He came up from under the water, glad for air. Glad that his feet could touch the bottom.

"I did it!" he yelled. "Six steamboats."

He couldn't hear his father, but could see him on the beach standing next to his mother. He was waving his cane above his head.

His mother did not move. No cheering or waving hands. She called Andreas in for lunch, but in a lazy voice, the lazy voice that she got after drinking wine.

He kicked his feet in the water, swam back to them.

It was the same picnic every time. Corn on the cob. Feta and black olives. Tomatoes and cucumber. *Spanakopita* and *moussaka*. *Baklava* for dessert.

"Why can't we have ice cream like normal people?" he asked his father.

"Because honey is the nectar of the gods," he said.

"Wine is the nectar of the gods," his mother laughed.

His mother wrapped a towel around him and lifted him up. Andreas liked it when she did this. He liked it when she smiled and tickled his feet.

"You're a tiny boy for seven," she said. "You're shivering, *Pedhi mou*." She dried his hair and wrapped him in a giant towel that was warm from the sun.

"What's nectar?" Andreas asked.

"It's thick," she said. "Thick juice that's very concentrated."

"What's concentrated?" he asked.

"Eat," she said, handing him a paper plate heaped with food. "Never mind."

She was not looking at him anymore. His mother was watching his father who was adding branches to the fire.

"You're too close," she said. "Too close to the flames."

"You think I don't know the feel of fire?" he said. "Leave me be."

"I'm not hungry," Andreas said as he handed the plate of food back to his mother, ran across the sand, and dove into the cool, clear water.

5
JERSEY

The sun shines and then it rains. The sun shines and then it rains again. The sun shines and the rain starts and doesn't stop, all within the fifteen minutes it takes to ride the train from the Newark airport to the subway. They've decided to take a quick trip into Manhattan; Marco wants to go to the top of the Empire State Building.

"Something's wrong with the weather," says a small boy to his mother.

"There sure is," says the mother, frowning at Marco, who has inadvertently slid his arm through Andreas' as the train rumbles through the New Jersey wasteland. Rusting oil drums. Abandoned cars piled and crushed. Vacant lots and falling down buildings. Marco considers removing his arm from Andreas', but decides to hold tough.

"We're from Canada," he says waving his wedding band at her, aware how childish he sounds, feeling Andreas press an elbow into his ribs.

Marco loves the US. Even the massive American flag that dominates the baggage area doesn't offend him. It does, however, make him feel sad. *Life, Liberty, and the pursuit of Happiness* seems to have been replaced by something urgent and desperate. Like the bully in the playground, it's big and tough and yet beat down. *Life, Liberty and the pursuit of indebtedness.*

But there's hope, Marco thinks. This is the land of the Sears Tower and the Empire State Building.

"What's your dinosaur's name?" Marco asks the little boy.

"He doesn't have a name."

"How about Barney? After all, he is purple."

"I hate Barney," says the child. His mother leads him by the elbow to a seat at the back of the train.

6
MANYA

Waiting in the boarding lounge at JFK for their con-
nection to Istanbul is uneventful. Marco is frustrated
and a little tired after the trip into the city. *I am happy*,
he tries again. Andreas has nodded off with his laptop
balanced on his knee. More and more, Andreas seems
obsessed with checking e-mail. The young woman in the
chair next to him stands and walks around the waiting
area. She sighs and looks at her giant wrist-watch. She's
probably twenty-five, but dresses sixteen. She's wearing
silver platform shoes—at least a size ten—and a short,
short skirt. She's gorgeous and has muscular legs, like a
tennis pro or a runner. Her t-shirt is really only a half
t-shirt; it completely leaves her flat stomach and pierced
navel exposed. Her long, straight hair is black and the
skirt mauve. She's wearing silver bangles. She drops into
the chair, stretches her legs, crosses her ankles. The silver
shoes stick out like glistening cartons.

"The flight is two hours late," she says to Marco.
"That means we'll be getting into Istanbul just as the
sun rises."

Marco looks over. The girl leans forward, searching
for something in her bag. She's wearing a brightly coloured hair-band.

"How long will you be staying there?" Marco asks.

"Just a few days," she says. "I'm en-route to Greece."

"Us too," he says.

"I just did the Boston marathon. I'm still pumped," the girl says, opening a bag of chips and offering them to Marco.

"Wow," he says. "That's impressive."

"Now I'm training for Olympus," she says, pointing to a tattoo on her ankle. "I'm running for my grandmother."

The tattoo is a small red circle with a line through a burning cigarette: *Ashes to Ashes,* it reads.

"I take it your grandmother was against smoking?" Marco asks.

"Not really," the girl says. "I'm a teacher and an artist and this is my project."

"And what does this have to do with your grandmother?" he asks.

"My grandmother was a famous Greek actor who died of cancer in New York," the girl says. "She died of lung cancer and I'm taking some of her ashes to the top of Olympus. My mother always dreamt of doing it, but wasn't well enough."

"Ashes to ashes," Marco says, suddenly filled with grief. "That's kind of sad."

"Yep," the girl says. "That's why I took on the anti-smoking campaign for New York Health. That's why I'm running Olympus."

"What was her name?"

"Maria Meltiades. She sang and acted, but her true obsession was getting the Elgin marbles back to Greece, they're still in the British Museum."

"I know her," Marco says, hardly able to contain himself. "Everyone knows Maria Meltiades!"

The girl grinned. "She was a force. I don't remember her too well."

"Have you ever been to Greece?" Marco asks.

"Nope. But I'm told that there's a beautiful marble statue of my grandmother in the heart of Athens."

"My name is Marco," he said extending his hand. "And that's Andreas over there," he adds, nodding his head in Andreas' direction.

"My name is Manya. Not to be confused with Mania," she says, extending her arm with silver bangles.

"Nice to meet you," Marco says, feeling an instant affinity with her. "That's very interesting," he adds, pointing to her head-band.

"Thanks," she says. "It's from my Suicide Series."

"Suicide series?" he laughs, feels a tingle and drop inside his skull. He reaches his hand out. "Do you mind?"

"No problem," she says removing the band and handing it to him.

Across the arc of the band there are pieces of a puzzle, varnished and glued on. There's a puzzle-piece gun, and a puzzle-piece photo of a woman, a puzzle-piece razorblade and a puzzle-piece bottle of pills, then another puzzle-piece woman, a puzzle-piece stove and another puzzle-piece woman, a puzzle-piece martini glass and a puzzle-piece man.

"A stove?" Marco asks.

"Sylvia," she says. "The razor and pills is Diane Arbus. The gun is Penelope Delta; an amazing writer who shot herself the day the Nazis arrived in Greece. The other woman is Marilyn. There's debate about overdose, suicide or murder … whatever … I like having her here. And the poet, he's Frank O'Hara. He didn't really commit suicide, but he drank too much, and that counts too."

"What a great idea," Marco says.

"When I was a kid, I would make these with my father's friend, Gary," she says.

"Do you have others?" Marco asks.

"Well," she says, pulling the bag up onto her lap. "I have the Glorious Illuminator," she says. "My favourite. I love having this much energy near my brain."

"Let me see that!" says Marco, hardly able to contain himself. The band consists of various hand-drawn light bulbs, moons, suns and surging wires. It's a simple black and silver design, but it glows like a neon arc.

"Fantastic," he tells her. "You should create a pleasure band…" he says. "…pieces of puzzle that fit together to make your brain happy."

"What do you think this is?" she says, showing him her Sex band. "I love the way the pieces are interchangeable," she adds, winking at Andreas, who has joined them.

"You mentioned that your mom wasn't well before, is she all right now?"

"She died," Manya says. "Diabetes."

"That's too bad," Marco says, sitting down. "And your dad?"

"My dad," sighs Manya. "Ben isn't dead, but let's just leave it at that."

"Ouch," says Andreas.

"It's not that bad," she says, looking at Andreas then back to Marco. "Just a little weird to talk about, it's a long story."

When she hears the boarding announcement a few seconds later, Manya looks relieved.

"We're off," says Andreas, bending to pick up his carry-on.

"Enjoy your trip," Marco says to Manya, regretting that he'll probably never see her again. "Maybe our paths will cross in Greece?"

7
MANYA

Ouch. Ouch. Ouch. I hate this. I hate this. I hate this.
Coasting. Coasting. Coasting.

I can do it. I can do it. I can do it. Burning. Burning.
Burning legs. Look at me go. Look at me go. Look at me
run Chicago. Boston, in the dust! Olympus, here I come!
Coasting. Coasting. Coasting. I love this. Love this. Love
this. Coasting. Coasting. Coasting. Love this. Hate this.
Love this. I can do it. I can do it. Do it. Coasting. Coast-
ing. Coasting. Ouch. Ouch. Ouch. Doing it. Doing it.
Doing it. Phew! Done.

Every other morning for three hours, Manya ran from
Millennium Park, under the Lakeshore to Navy Pier,
north along the bicycle path to Lincoln Park Zoo and
back again. She ignored the downtown Chicago skyscrapers on her left and focused on the lake—the waves
splashing over the pier, the fishy smell of Michigan. She
never got used to the ache in her calves, the shortness of
breath, the throbbing under her ribs. But she loved the
solitude of running. During her runs, she composed the
key elements of her painting—red, green and gold oils,
an abstract she called *Fall Canyon*. She knew from the

first thick brush stroke of red that she would be painting capital J for *joy*. Her professors at SAIC criticized her for unreasonable optimism. Just like George. They called her painting "Romanticized" and "naïve." She ran along the water's edge until she was exhausted. In her brain, she continued to dive into her painting—stroke after stroke, her feet splashing along the wave-slapped pier, whatever it took to run through the hurt.

8
MARCO

Awake in bed, Marco wanted to be alone. He smelled toast and bacon, knew Andreas would show up with coffee and a newspaper any second. Andreas could never just relax; he was obsessive and restless, always on the move, always wanting to please. They were seven years apart, but it might as well be seventy—Andreas was extremely old fashioned, especially about relationships.

"Ours will be a great love," he said, after only a few weeks of dating. "A blue-eyed Capricorn," he said. "You're perfect. Let's move in together."

Andreas was everything he saw from the streetcar window and more. He was loving and playful, generous and decent. But Marco also craved solitude. He wanted the peacefulness of a darkened room. He pictured himself at the top of an imaginary tower. He imagined living in a high-rise with a view of city towers and water. For reasons he can't explain, in his fantasy apartment, he always lives alone. He has tasteful furniture and amazing art on the walls. He listens to *Both Sides Now*, Joni whispering from an expensive stereo while he sips champagne. He pictures King Kong hanging off the Empire State building defiantly pounding his chest as aircraft fly through the sky and attempt to gun him down. He smiled and thought about how, in his fantasy condo, he can sleep in late, only bring out his camera to make edgy, solitude-inspired movies.

"Hey mister," said Andreas, as he stood at the foot of the bed with a steaming mug of coffee and an armful of roses. "Come down from the clouds, I've made omelets."

"I'm not hungry," Marco said. "But thank you," he added, reaching up to take the flowers.

"That's not very Italian of you," Andreas said, setting the coffee on the bedside table. "Skipping breakfast is not a good idea."

"You should know by now this Italian's not big on breakfast."

It was raining hard and branches from the linden tree in the front yard tapped against the window. They'd bought a house together, a bungalow on Victor Avenue with a backyard and a fireplace. They had planned on taking a bike ride through the neighbourhood to celebrate one year of living together.

"Would you like the anniversary special then?" asked Andreas, slipping out of his underwear, crawling naked into the bed.

"You're squishing the flowers," said Marco. "I'd rather just relax."

"But you're such a turn on," said Andreas. "The brain is a sex organ."

"There are other uses for a brain," said Marco, as he turned away.

Andreas got slowly out of bed and went back to the kitchen. Marco watched him go, waited a beat till he felt the guilt coming on, then he did what he always did.

"But if you insist," he called out, throwing the blankets onto the floor. "I feel a swelling in my head right now."

After sex, Andreas massaged his back.

"I love your big hands," Marco said.

"I love my little sweetheart," Andreas said.

Marco rolled over. "So do I," he answered, the way he always did.

Andreas let things go. He was even-tempered and usually didn't need a lot of reassurance about the relationship. But that time it felt different...

"Can't you say, just once, say: *I love you too, Andreas*? Saying, *So do I*, every time, is ridiculous and annoying."

"You get the drift," Marco said, shrugging it off. "You know how much I care. Do you remember the name of the street where we met?"

"Of course," said Andreas. "I remember every detail of meeting you. We met at the streetcar stop on the corner of Euclid and College."

"Who was Euclid?"

"Euclid is the numbers guy. He was a Greek mathematician. The father of geometry."

"So why do you think we met on Euclid Avenue?" Marco asked, knowing Andreas lived for this kind of mystery-probing discussion, knowing he'd be off the hook for the *love* thing.

"I don't know, Marco. Maybe because of his Theory of Optics. Or maybe it's just where the streetcar stopped that day."

"Maybe," said Marco.

"Let's have a nap," said Andreas, clicking off the bedside lamp. "It's dark and rainy. Let's stay in bed all day. I love my little sweetheart," he said.

"I love him too," Marco said back.

Marco closed his eyes and imagined being alone. High above a city. Not necessarily Toronto or New York, but another big city overflowing with buildings and people. Big enough for him to get lost in. Far away from the work loop that keeps playing inside his head, *you're a maniac, maniac...* Marco cared for Andreas, and had a feeling that they were going to be together for a long time, but he also imagined how happy he would be with freedom. Andreas couldn't stand to be without him. Marco looked across his imaginary horizon. In his mind, it's a lakefront view. His balcony extends out over the water. The waves are high as he watches a solitary gull fly against the gentle rain. He feels peaceful, floats into the grey.

"What's ya thinking?" Andreas whispered.

Marco pretended to be asleep.

"Talk to me, baby," Andreas said, gently shaking Marco's shoulder. "What movie is playing inside my beautiful cameraman's head?"

"Well," said Marco, sitting up, flicking on the bedside lamp. "It's a noir, black-and-white period piece with plenty of fog and rain, sex and mirrors."

"Why noir?" asked Andreas.

"I love *The Big Combo* and *Night and the City*," said Marco. "I like mood and mystery. Desire, betrayal, all that good stuff."

"You *are* all that good stuff," teased Andreas. "Do you have a script? Who's the director? Who's the producer? Where's the money coming from?"

"Enough questions, already," said Marco, kissing Andreas lightly on the cheek. "I don't know yet," he added, and flicked off the light.

The two men didn't speak, but Marco sensed that Andreas was awake. He refused to give in, though. He wouldn't be the ice-breaker or feed into Andreas' notion that he wasn't capable of making a movie.

"It's not that I don't think you're capable," Andreas finally spoke. "It's just that you can't make a movie on your own."

"You think I didn't learn anything at Ryerson," Marco said. "I'm not an idiot."

"You certainly aren't an idiot," said Andreas. "But collaboration isn't your strong point," he added, rolling over to face the wall.

9
TUMOUR

They started right after his thirtieth birthday, the headaches and blurred vision. His doctor said the symptoms were probably the result of carrying a heavy camera around all day. He gave Marco a note to take a few weeks off work. He recommended a low-carb diet and suggested that he drop the large volume of chocolate he consumed each day. However, the headaches got worse, as did his vision. One day, walking with Andreas along Danforth Avenue, Marco's hands started shaking, and then his legs. He didn't remember falling to the ground or Andreas packing a sweater around his head after he hit the sidewalk. The seizure lasted several minutes. When he regained consciousness, he was at St. Mike's Emergency.

After a CAT scan, an MRI, a million blood tests, and sickening worry, Marco received a call from the neurologist. *I need you to come into the office. As soon as possible,* he'd said.

It was a primary brain tumour. Still, the prognosis was good.

"It's a small, benign tumour in the occipital lobe," the neurologist said. "We'll bring it down with radiation then they'll pluck the sucker out."

Who talks like that? Marco thought. *Pluck it out.* I'm a cameraman, not some wild turkey.

10
ISTANBUL

The traffic is moving slowly along the Sea of Marmara. Marco is not exactly won over by his first impressions of Istanbul, but he's trying to remain positive.

"We've arrived!" he says. "In the land of *Midnight Express*."

"Yes," says Andreas. "Prisons, palaces and mosques across two continents."

I am happy, Marco tries, but quickly gives in. "The air's stifling," he says to Andreas. "Do you think the driver will put out his cigarette?"

"Why don't you ask him?" says Andreas. "Most people here speak English."

But before Marco can open his mouth the taxi driver throws his cigarette out the window, blasts the air-conditioning, smiles at him in the rearview mirror.

There are thousands of people picnicking along a narrow strip of park between the highway and the sea, creating an unbelievable amount of litter, mostly plastic bottles and bags, the detritus of the tourist trade. Hammocks are strung between eucalyptus trees, blankets spread over the water-starved grass. Straight ahead, the Theodosian walls rise like grey waves in the heat.

I am happy. Marco tries again, then waits for the drop, the shift in his brain. Air begins to circulate in the taxi, the traffic moves a little faster. Finally, there it is—the tug and pull on his brain: *I am happy.*

He smiles at Andreas. "I like that woman, Manya, we met at the airport," he says.

"Me too," says Andreas. "Talk about a force of nature—even the goddess Athena would be envied!"

Andreas' energy has picked up since the beginning of the trip; Marco hopes that he will return to his passionate and funny self. As they arrive at the Hippodrome, Marco is aware that taxis, rather than chariots, crowd the oval.

"We should have found out where she is staying in Greece," Andreas says. "She seems like a lot of fun."

"Who knows?" says Marco. "I have a feeling we'll see her again."

Andreas leans toward Marco and risks a kiss on his cheek, as the driver navigates the traffic, lights another cigarette.

Eventually they make it to the Empress Zoë, a small hotel with no more than twenty rooms and a wonderful garden courtyard. Marco is comforted to learn that the staff at the front desk speaks English.

Through the window. Through the dark and across the humid air, the Call to Prayer.

"It's five a.m.," Marco says, looking at the bedside clock.

"It's kind of awesome and eerie, isn't it?" asks Andreas.

Although he knows it's only prayer, only an ancient and sacred ritual, Marco finds it frightening. "The North American equivalent would be like being wakened in the middle of the night by Jerry Falwell preaching over loud-speakers."

"It's not the same thing at all," says Andreas. "Sleep. We have a big day tomorrow."

***

Tilt-tip, tilt-tip. Seasick on the Bosphorus. It's eleven in the morning, and they've decided to take the water route to the far side of the city. They've hired an old man in a battered boat to take them to the city for three Turkish Lira. Andreas and Marco can't resist the deal until they step into the boat. It sinks to water level. The old man introduces himself as "Baba Cap." He starts the motor. Somehow, unbelievably, the three of them move across the water. Baba is wearing a cap and dirty white pants and shirt. His belly, girdled by a blue vest, bulges out. His white beard is long and curly. His old hands seem strong as he steers the boat, silent and calm, through the rough water toward the city.

"Write in your journal," Andreas says, trying to distract Marco. "You need to stare at something that isn't moving."

"I feel bad for those feral cats roaming all over the city," he says. "And I feel like throwing up."

"Because of the waves or the cats?" asks Andreas.

"Both," says Marco, hanging his head over the side of the small boat.

Marco is constantly thinking about the cats under cars, next to bags of torn-open trash, stretched across the round roofs of the abandoned Turkish baths, inside store windows, hiding behind the walls of the Grand Bazaar. His own cat, Kitten, would have died in a minute on these streets: she'd lived a very pampered life.

"We're almost there," Andreas says. "Keep writing. And for goodness sake, stop thinking about the cats."

Although he doesn't usually get seasick, the side-to-side motion of the small boat overcomes him. *I am happy.* But it is too late. Marco vomits once into the water, a second time on Andreas' sandaled feet. Both Andreas and the old man act as if nothing has happened. Marco attempts to bale handfuls of water to clean up his vomit.

He's grateful when they finally reach the dock. The old man inches the boat between two other small boats. He motions for them to step across one of the boats beside them. "Is okay," says Baba. Marco takes his word for it. He trusts that the driver does this dozens of times each day. Besides, he desperately wants to be on solid ground. Before crawling out of the boat, he gives the old guy a tip. His toothless smile breaks Marco's heart.

They walk through the Gate of Felicity past rows of rose bushes and up to the quarters of the Black Eunuch in the Harem of Topkapi. To distract Marco, Andreas explains how eunuchs were the masters of the girls. Marco struggles to take in the gold mirrors and tile mosaics, the long marble slabs with drains for the dishes, the bath of the concubines where enormous marble slats were heated by fire underneath. Next door to the harem hospital, caged and gilded, he explained, the favourite of the four wives lived. There are bars across the chamber windows, a domed ceiling with glass, like a beehive. Along the walls, a belt of verse from the Koran is inscribed in white letters on a blue tile background. When the favourites became pregnant, Andreas says, they assumed the powers of the official consort. Here, the light is soft. The rooms are cool and sad.

"Someone lived a happy, decadent life here," says Marco. "And I don't think it was the concubines."

They take a taxi back to the Empress Zoë. Painted blue, yellow and white—on the car window in front of them, the Evil Eye: **BACK OFF** written in bold letters under. Although it originally struck him as comical, Marco worried about the Evil Eye all the way back to the hotel.

After a long nap, they decide to make a trip to the Turkish Baths. The desk clerk tells them the Cemberlitas Baths are no more than a twenty-minute walk.

It's more expensive than either of them thought, but they agree that a good, relaxing massage is in order. In the center of a steamy, circular room is a large marble platform. Around the edges, large attendants are scrubbing men in towels. One of the attendants directs Andreas to the showers. Another approaches Marco. He's big, hairy, and heavy. He smiles and directs him to the shower as well. When Marco comes back to the central room, the man directs him to lie on the marble platform. It's hard and warm. Marco closes his eyes and submits. The attendant pulls him to the edge of the wet platform. Marco keeps his eyes closed tightly to avoid getting soap in them. Assaulted by soap and hot water, his arms and legs are thoroughly scrubbed. More soap and hot water.

"Sit," the attendant orders. When Marco sits on the edge of the platform, his head is pulled forward and his neck and back are scrubbed. "Turn," the man says. "Stand," he directs, pointing Marco to a sink where his hair will be washed. His head is turned and his face scrubbed. Before Marco can take a breath, the attendant pours a bucket of hot water over him. "Back on platform," he says. "Sit. Turn. Finish."

Marco feels weak—not relaxed. He feels beat up and bruised.

"You like?" the attendant asks, holding out his hand for a tip.

***

Marco stands in the square between the Hagia Sophia and the Blue Mosque.

There's a line up for the bank machine, but he's in no hurry. It's a gorgeous warm evening and he has fifteen minutes to kill before meeting Andreas back at the Empress Zoë for dinner. When his turn for the bank machine comes, he debates how much to withdraw. He has a budget and he needs to stick to it. He cups his hand so the two guys behind him can't read his PIN. They're a little too close for comfort. Marco is certain that he's entered 100, but the machine dispenses 1,000 Turkish *liras*. For an instant, he's worried—there's no way he has that much left in his account. Then he remembers that it's the first of June—payday. He feels two hands on his back pushing him forward, hard and fast. He sees a man reach for the cash, but he hangs on to it and is shoved up against the machine. There's no time to yell, he barely has time to catch his breath. Marco can't know it's a piece of pipe that crashes into the back of his skull. He doesn't know what happens until he hears a woman talking to him in French. "Monsieur?" she says worriedly. Marco struggles to get up. He feels dizzy. He touches the lump and sees blood on the pavement, squeezes his hand where the money had been. He wonders where the French woman came from, but he can't speak to thank her. He feels sleepy. Blood pools like darkness over his brain.

Back at the hotel, Andreas holds an ice pack to the back of his neck. The owner of the Hotel Zoë is in their room as well. "This is rare," he says. "Istanbul is a very safe city."

When the hotelier leaves, Marco looks at Andreas and says, "This is the last thing my head needs right now. I hope it's not an omen. So far, Istanbul has been like *Midnight Express*, only without the rough-trade prison sex."

"You'll be fine," says Andreas, kissing him on the forehead. "We'll be in Athens tomorrow."

I am happy. Marco smiles, tries to reassure Andreas. *I am happy.* He waits for a pleasant feeling. Instead, there's darkness, like a black sheet over his head.

11
ANDREAS

Andreas understood that knowing how to perform this procedure was expected as part of his clinical training. He knew he'd be happy when the deed was done. The man on the table was eighty-four years old. He had died of natural causes.

He was introduced to the coroner who would supervise the extraction and a nurse clinician named Nancy who would read him step-by-step instructions.

"I'll be right by your side," she said.

Andreas stood straight, tried to emanate confidence.

"Perfect," he told the nurse. "You read. I'll cut."

The coroner stepped back.

Andreas was surprised that there were no unpleasant smells. He had expected ammonia or perhaps even cleaning fluids. Instead, he smelled Nancy's mint gum and a subtle lilac perfume. She handed him the retractor.

"Step one," she said. "Pull back the eyelid."

Andreas' hands were sweaty and he didn't like the scratchy sound of the coroner scribbling notes onto a clipboard. He rolled the first eyelid back with his fingers and inserted the top of the retractor. The eyeball was white and firm, the pupil pinpoint black. *This guy is dead*, he had to remind himself. He rounded the instrument around the lower part of the ball.

Nancy handed him a pair of bladed scissors.

"Cut the superior oblique," she said.

Andreas took a deep breath. He tried not to think of the man's past. What those eyes may have witnessed—his wife's body the first time they'd made love? The inside rooms of their comfortable house? The beauty and violence of his son or daughter's birth?

Shake it off, he told himself. These eyes can no longer see.

"Done," he said, not liking the *snip* of scissored flesh.

"Now the inferior oblique."

"Got it."

"And finally," she said, "cut the lateral rectus."

"That can't be it?" Andreas asked, doubting it could be that simple.

"That's it," she said snapping her gum from behind her mask.

Andreas exhaled and tugged, but the eyeball wouldn't let go. The eyes are everything. The personality and vision of a person. The soul's younger brother. He probed around with the curved scissors. Perhaps there was something he missed? He tugged gently, careful not to cause any damage, still no release.

"Read it again," said Andreas. Aware of the sharpness in his voice, he added, "Please."

Nancy reluctantly flipped back to the first page of the instructions. The coroner lowered his clipboard and stepped closer.

"Oh, my god," she said. "I did miss something."

Andreas was both angry and relieved.

"Yes?" he asked.

"The optic nerve," she said. "You have to cut that first."

The second eye went quickly. He dropped it into the kidney-shaped dish. The eyes were already taking on the silver shine of the bowl before he could ask Nancy to let the donor clinic know that two beauties were ready for pick up. *Never. Never again*, he told himself.

***

"What do you see when you look into someone's eyes?" Marco asks.

"In the obese diabetic, I see pooling blood. In the old woman who lives alone, I see cataracts and near blindness. In the crack-addicted prostitute with AIDS, I see CMV."

"Wow," says Marco, pulling him closer. "What else?"

They have just had sex. Over-the-top passionate sex. Athens has inspired passion and truthfulness in both of them.

"Well," says Andreas, cupping Marco's face in his hands. "When I look in your eyes and tell you how much I love you, I see that you look up at the sky rather than back at me."

***

Marco works on his movie script. The best time is after Andreas has gone to sleep. Images take shape before the words. He imagines flying over a skating rink with blue ice. Then another image takes shape, he sees a wheat field, gold and swaying in a prairie breeze. Sometimes he sees Montreal during a blizzard—snow swirling down a spiral staircase or piling against a frosty window. Other times he hovers over Chicago and observes its bright colours reflected in the nighttime lake. Sometimes he imagines a musical number set in the streets of New York—various scenes come and go—graffiti, subway trains, and people dancing in choreographed rows. He keeps his eyes closed, tries not to disturb Andreas. If something fantastic comes to mind, a brilliant plot or an idea for a scene, he will slowly lift the blankets and slip into the bathroom to write it down. Tonight's vision comes in a rush of close ups, probably inspired by the Athens Market—a pig's head looking startled and half-alive; several sheep, skinned and bleeding, hanging by their broken necks; a liver dangling from a calf; a row of goat heads on ice. Surreal movies annoy him, but in this case, he respects the power of images to move the plot forward. There will be death and plenty of it. The audience will learn, by contrast, to value life. Close-up after close-up, glorious and grotesque, the living, breathing market. It will premiere at Sundance. They will have to find a replacement for him at *Mad Breakfast Television* that week. He will be a featured guest, the distinguished writer-director with a clipboard of stunning reviews, the smug guy on the *other* side of the camera for once.

Andreas wraps his arm around Marco's waist. "Go to sleep sweetheart," he says.

"It's all wrong," mumbles Marco. "None of these ideas make any sense."

***

"Zeus has no eyes," Marco says. "I can't stand looking at him."

"He has no eyes because he was underwater for a few centuries."

"I don't care," says Marco. "I love the details—the muscular body, the legs and ass, the thick masculine neck, sexy lips and strong, chiseled nose—they're all gorgeous, but I can't stand looking at a life-size man without eyes."

"What's with you and eyes these days?" says Andreas.

"Eyes are everything," says Marco.

"They have a function. Yes …" says Andreas. "… And, sometimes, eyes are beautiful," he adds. "But in ancient art you have to appreciate that sometimes wood or bone didn't wear too well in water. This bronze Zeus was found at the bottom of the sea!"

"Whatever," says Marco. "It creeps me out to look into his face and see only darkness. No life or light in the eyeball sockets. No sign of joy or hint of real-life sadness. No lightning-struck soul to show the world he'd lived and fought and loved."

"You expect a lot from art," says Andreas smiling.

"More of art than life," Marco says, turning his back on Zeus.

***

Andreas had gone with his mother to his father's restaurant. There was plenty of snow to walk through. He'd sliced the tomatoes, being *very, very* careful with the knife. He kept her company as she folded napkins at a table near the swinging silver doors while his father set up the kitchen. *There will be no noise, Pedhi Mou*, she'd said. *People come to restaurants for peace and quiet.* He heard the bang like a whole house exploding. He saw his father running from the kitchen with his head on fire.

***

Andreas believed superheroes could do anything. As a child, his imaginary siblings included Batbrother and Catsister. They played cops and robbers with him and they sat between him and his mother on the nights that his father was at the restaurant. As an adult, Andreas refused to eat alone. His first cooking class was called *Wokking for Health*. He couldn't wait to have friends over to show off his skill with Chinese cuisine. The next class was called *Thai Chi Chef*. He learned how to use lemongrass and coriander in one-hundred-and-fifty different recipes. But his favourite of all was called *A Week of Nights at ElBulli*. This is where his love of food met his love of science and philosophy. The students were taught the delicate art of fusion—ice creams that fizz and foam in your mouth, salads that tingle and bite. Andreas soon became notorious for his elaborate dinner parties. He never ate alone.

Between dinner parties, Andreas ate out. He would drive to the Gerrard Square food court and sit beside a stranger or go to Kensington Market and eat among the chaos of cars and bicycles, pigeons and people. Anything seemed better than being alone. That's when he took up riding his bicycle. Up and down Euclid. Through the bumpy treed streets of the Annex. Behind the College streetcar as it headed downtown.

On hot days, he would park his bike in the shade next to the giant griffins of the Palmerston Street library. In awe of the bronze wings, the claws and muscled shoulders, Andreas would sit in the shade and imagine the museums in Greece with their thousands of mythological animals, the marbled statues of Icarus and Zeus.

Rested, he would take a long sip from his water bottle and ride back out into the heat.

12
TRUMP

Trump: a verb. Overriding; a hindrance or obstruction.

Marco put the dictionary aside and went back to his keyboard. He sat at his computer imagining the drive to the Trump Tower—Bay Street winding south, away from the glitzy shops of Bloor, around the chaotic markets of Chinatown, along the curve of Old City Hall into the concrete grid of the business district. He googled the Tower's progress:

October 12, 2007, Donald Trump arrives with his golden shovel at 311 Bay.

The Trump International Hotel and Tower, Canada's largest residential building, is underway at the southeast corner of Bay and Adelaide.

September, 2008. First concrete pour of the Trump Tower foundation.

There's a blog on the site. Marco wrote: "I want to live on the top floor. The view will be spectacular!"

Somebody blogged back: "Hope you're a billionaire!!"

February, 2010. New floor every 6 days. Windows are being installed.

May 5, 2010. They're building at a rate of two floors a week now. They are at floor 27. The green granite curtain walls are going up.

April 3, 2011. It's towering above the other buildings now, tall, sexy and slick.

"I can't do it," said Andreas. He had stood behind Marco and pointed to the photograph of the Trump Tower on the computer. "On sheer principle, I just can't move into that man's building."

"You think all the other condos in this town aren't owned by some equally ambitious comb-over capitalist? This building's going to be brilliant!" said Marco.

13
MANYA

Manya stands in front of the statue. Finding the monument on Leoforos Andhrea Syngrou wasn't as easy as the guide-book made it seem.

Directly across from Hadrian's Arch, it reads, *sits a large marble bust on a pedestal. You can't miss it.*

Well, it isn't directly across, the streets go in circles and never seem to meet; it took Manya a good hour of walking before she finally found the statue. Her grandmother is depicted as an intellectual, carved in white marble, handsome and beautiful with long hair, solid jaw and large nose. She is wearing a coat and scarf. The sculptor has given her broad shoulders. Manya wants to touch her face, the lips and eyes that capture her beauty. Full of longing and grief, her one memory of her grandmother is of a visit to the hospital where she died. She sat in a wheelchair and Manya lolled on her lap as she finished her cigarette. Manya had no way of knowing then that grandmother Maria would leave her so much. Her money. Her bravery and determination.

Manya touches the statue and hopes that somehow the marble will yield to her touch. *Just ten minutes*, she whispers. *Ten minutes with you listening would mean everything.*

His name was George. They met at a restaurant across from the college on her nineteenth birthday. He sat at the window table with a woman and another couple and, when Manya got up to go to the washroom after a big fight with Ben and Gary, George followed her through the lobby. They talked for a long time and agreed to meet for breakfast in the morning. She saw the ring on his finger and he didn't lie to her.

No regrets. No shame, but plenty of trouble.

Manya didn't feel that she could talk to her friends about George. She knew they would side with the wife.

Still, they continued to meet whenever he was in Chicago. Manya had been studying art history at SAIC. Even though she had an apartment on her own, they always went back to the Hotel Felix on Huron Street. The room wasn't spectacular and the view wasn't so hot either—they couldn't see the lake or the river. The only interesting site from their window was the shimmering silver Chicago Trump Tower. She is now convinced that they were trying to relive the morning they first met for breakfast.

Manya had made a point of dressing casually that first morning—no makeup, hair tied in a knot at the back of her head, with jeans and a blue cotton blouse from the GAP. She sat on the edge of the bed doing up her blouse. Naked, he sat next to her, put his hand over hers.

"You're everything she's not," he'd said. "Unpretentious, fun, and bloody hot in bed!"

They had been standing in front of Hopper's *Nighthawks*.

"I'm a true-blue night person," Manya had told him.

"I love love *love* this painting!"

"It's kind of cold and green looking," he'd said.

"Cold! Are you kidding? Look at those people," she'd said. "They're relaxed and cozy. The curved glass window wrapped around the warm yellow interior, four friends spending a night together talking over coffee. It's bliss."

"You know," he'd said, slapping her ass hard enough that the noise caused the couple on the other side of the gallery to turn around. "You're amazing! The most optimistic person I know."

"And I plan on staying that way," she'd said. "I'm not going to rescue you from your alleged *lifeless* marriage. Get out of it on your own, if that's what you really want."

It was the last time they spoke.

Manya takes her hand off the marble statue of her grandmother and looks up. *Thank you*, she whispers, leaning closer. *I knew you'd understand.*

14
MARCO

Marco started film school that September. His father disliked the French and made no attempt to speak the language.

"Good for you for getting out of this province, away from these ignorant people," Franco said.

"You're a bigot, dad," Marco said. "But I love you, and that's not why I'm going to Toronto."

His mother, Antonietta, kept busy in the kitchen.

"Is ham and cheese okay for the train?" she shouted. She wasn't really waiting for an answer, Marco knew. He didn't respond.

"She's pretty upset," his father said. "You're the last one."

There were six of them. Three girls and three boys. They all shared one bedroom growing up—boys on one side, girls on the other. Marco had the bottom bunk bed on the boys' side.

"Her runt kid is off to university," his father yelled in the direction of the kitchen. "He got the brains in the family," he said. "Imagine if a famous movie maker like that guy who made *The Maltese Falcon*, ends up coming from this poor-excuse-for-a-neighbourhood!"

Ville-Émard was a mix of French, English and Italian. Their house was one floor and the kitchen and both of the bedrooms had doors into a room in the middle. There was a pot-belly stove that they used most of the winter, and brown linoleum that his mother waxed, even though his father said that plain old water and soap worked just as well. Although six of them had to share the one bedroom with Kitten, it was a big room and pretty warm in the winter. At night, sometimes one of the others would crawl in bed with him if they had peed the bed or had a nightmare. Sometimes one of the others would tease him just because he was little. Sometimes they would tease Kitten too, just because. Marco spent a great deal of time finding places to hide when he was young, but close to the house so he could hear his mom. He had never had the experience of living alone, but he knew that's what he wanted when he grew up. To be alone. To have his own apartment high above the city.

He didn't want to play hockey with his brothers. Just think, his father would say, Mario Lemieux lived right on the corner of our street. Sometimes Marco would play dress-up with his sister Aurora and her dolls, but that wasn't allowed so they did it in secret. It was easy because hers was the bottom bed on the girl's side of the room, and he could sneak over in the dark.

The house was painted white. The two wooden stairs leading up to the front door were always loose. The house was pressed into a row of other falling-down houses with peeling paint. The air smelled gassy from the oil refinery and the streets were grey from the salt and gravel spread there for the ice.

"I suppose he's going to get uppity now," said his father, directing his voice to the kitchen. "Like those Westmount people or the ones from Hampstead."

"Don't start," shouted his mother from the kitchen. "He's got a train to catch in a few minutes."

There was never enough light. Their bedroom was up against the house next door, and the one small window in the front only let light in for a few hours each day.

"Look at that," said Marco, pointing to the floor. Kitten was on her back, purring, rolling from side-to-side. "She always could find the one ray of sunlight that squeezed through that window."

"Did I ever tell you how I got her?" his father asked.

His mother closed the kitchen door.

Marco stood and put his hand on his father's shoulder, kissed the top of his head. "Tell me dad," he said. "How you saved her and how you've kept the same knife all these years."

15
ANDREAS

Marco and Andreas walked from their house on Victor Avenue to the Tim Horton's on the Danforth every Saturday morning. They picked up a *Globe & Mail* from the Alpha Variety along the way then kept walking up Logan past the house on the hill with the *For Sale* sign on the snowy lawn. The old men sat at tables of sixes and fours. They smiled and nodded when Marco and Andreas came through the door, a gust of cold air following. The line for coffee moved quickly and they sat at an empty table close to the window. Marco took off his gloves and jotted down their list—cheese from Alex's; avocados from Fruitland Market; *baklava* from Athena Pastry; the Quentin Tarantino biography from Book City.

"Hermes is missing today," Marco said, nodding at the empty table by the door.

It wasn't his real name, but they had a nickname for everyone in the shop.

"Yes," said Andreas. "That guy never lets anyone into this place without a full look-over."

"Maybe he has that flu everyone has?"

There were posters above the tables for Tim's *Hockey and Homestyle* soups. The environment was cold, no com-

72

fortable chairs or ambient lighting; the wealthier people who lived on the north side of the Danforth, were at the Starbucks two blocks east. But they both agreed that the crowd was more interesting at Tim's. The customers were people who lived in the neighbourhood—the family of three, with bags from the Dollar Store; the four young girls from the group home on Pape; the homeless guy who came in to use the washroom and buy something with the change he had panhandled in front of the liquor store; the perpetually bent-over bag lady with dreadlocks, known to Andreas as Medusa.

"Hermes must be nearly dead to not be here," Andreas said. "Do you know who he is in Greek mythology?"

Marco did know, but he was going to hear it again whether he wanted to or not.

"He's the psycho-pomp, guider of souls, messenger of the gods."

"Interesting," Marco said, stirring his coffee.

Andreas talked about the gods as if they were living, breathing people. Sometimes in the past. Sometimes in the present.

"He's a bit of a character," said Andreas.

"Why don't we go?" asked Marco.

"Go?"

"To Greece. In honour of your parents. Climb Mount Olympus. See the country that inspired your dad's stories!"

Andreas hung his head. Marco had never seen him crying. Not at the funeral. Not even when they went back to the empty house. He tapped Andreas on the shoulder.

"Come on, Andreas," he said. "Olympus Travel is right up the street."

"Hey, there's Kronos," he said, avoiding eye contact with Marco. A man with an eye patch hits the chair legs with his white cane, feels his way downstairs to the washroom.

"Andreas?" Marco said. "Between the sale of your mom and dad's place and what we get for the place on Victor, we'll have a little extra money. I can bring my camera, might even get inspiration for a movie!"

The house on Victor had always been a bone of contention. Andreas loved it. Marco tolerated it.

"Stupid birds," he'd say when they woke on summer mornings. "Why do they need to start their nattering at five a.m.?"

"Be grateful." Andreas always had the same response. "Some people would kill to live in a neighbourhood with this many trees and birds."

"I'd take a penthouse with a view over birds and raccoons in a minute," was Marco's pat answer.

"Okay. Let's look," Andreas said. "This city brings me down these days."

Down was the operative word. Andreas never came back up after his parents died in the crash.

***

They'd waited forty-five minutes before calling Andreas' parent's place. There was no answer. There was no answer on the cell phone either.

"They're never late for anything," Andreas had said. "Something's wrong. I know my parents."

"They'll get here eventually," Marco tried to reassure him. "The traffic on the 401 is insane and sometimes they don't even bother plowing the side roads near the cottage."

"Yes," said Andreas. "The traffic is insane and the roads are icy. And my mother hates driving in bad weather. It was stupid of us to plan the dinner on the day they were driving all the way from Kincardine."

"Remember?" said Marco. "It was your father who'd suggested that it would be a treat to have a homemade Greek meal after a long day in the car."

They didn't show. After another half-hour the *spanakopita* came out of the oven. The salad was put into the refrigerator along with the *baklava*. The napkins were folded and put in the drawer. The candles were blown out.

Marco was the one who took the call. The one who drove while Andreas folded himself in a ball in the back seat, refusing to put on a coat, ignoring the blanket Marco draped across his legs.

16
ANASTASIA

Anastasia is pinned against the steering wheel. She digs into her purse—only an eyeliner pencil and the back of an envelope.

Pedhi mou. Your father is gone.

I am crushed in metal. Please

don't dwell on our passing.

She thinks about her marriage, the house on Logan, then the explosion and blindness; her husband lost his sight. She became invisible.

She loved watching little Andreas pushing his toy car across the floor—his happiness and the tantrums, even the unpredictable dark moods. He grew into such a handsome teenager. When he became a doctor, an ophthalmologist, he would spend hours with his father on the telephone each day. They were so proud of him. Then the disappointment and horrible silence when Andreas first brought Marco to their house. She watched as the years passed and Marco brought her a pink begonia and a movie for her birthday about an independent woman, a beautiful Greek woman beaming with life. She began to ignore her disappointment about her son and Marco, settled into the joy of the two of them together. She was over-the-moon happy when they bought a house two blocks away.

The angel is coming, I see her wings. Keep swimming darling boy.

Remember what papa taught you—one steamboat … two steamboats

carry our love   xo mom

It's here in thirty seconds, life's quick rewind. Anastasia always said that the winter in this country would kill her. Funny how the brain works—she had never been big on puns and here she is at the moment of death, playing with humour and words. The truck loaded with animals couldn't brake and neither could she stop on the ice. She hears pigs squealing and smells fire. Dear god, enough fire. No more flames. No more pain. She wants to reach Andreas, but can't. Oh, to hold his hand one more time. Kiss his cheek. He is gone. His face on the air bag turned to the frozen lake. But maybe their son? Anastasia asks God to hold her until she can see her son one more time, his wise face and sad eyes. Marco is not who she would have chosen, but he is good. He understands and humours Andreas. He is sassy and like her, pretends to be strong, but she sees through him. Anastasia recognizes his tender soul, the love folded into the blanket of indifference. He accepts Andreas, who, like his father, has horrible fits of despair—her heart goes out to Marco for holding steady through the ups and downs. Like his father, Andreas inherited a capacity to live in two worlds at once, and along with that, the unsettled moodiness of divided loyalties—the hard, tangible facts of real life; and the ungraspable figures romping through the under-fields in his imagination. Anastasia resisted the two of them together. How wrong of her to judge. How stubborn. She is dying. She is numb. Her body shakes. It's as if she's drowning in this horrible car, a horrible amount of blood, the life force draining. She cannot breathe, can't catch her breath. She looks over at Andreas, imagines that he is holding her as she slides with him into the final darkness—under this knotted metal, through this tangled wreck.

17
ATHENS

There are no skyscrapers. No Empire State Building or Trump Tower. The structures are low and they flow across the sprawling landscape. As they walk down from the Acropolis, Marco thinks about Mount Olympus. It's hard to believe that the northern part of Greece is mountainous and that he and Andreas are going to climb the tallest peak, Mytikas. The two men stand for a few minutes among the crowds, mostly tourists with cameras admiring the memorial to Helena Gregoriou before taking the red line to Omonoia station to check out the meat market, one of the oldest in Athens.

"That was incredible," says Andreas, as they walk toward the market. "The Athens subway system is absolutely out of this world. It's transportation and ancient history rolled into one."

Marco agrees, but is immediately distracted by the heat and chaos of the market. Butchers shouting in Greek between the vendor stalls along the narrow aisles; sheep suspended upside-down from silver hooks; skinned goats, blood dripping into the clear tips of the plastic bags that cover them; the eyes like black and white marble. In one booth, a blonde woman in short-shorts and halter-top is the main attraction. She drops handfuls of meat into a grinder as the men gather round her, flirting and buying. Marco tries to take a picture, but he's constantly shoved by the shoppers pushing past him, anxious to buy a fresh leg of lamb or a piece of liver still attached to the carcass suspended from a blood-stained hook. There's an overwhelming stench of rotting garbage. Marco focuses his camera on a row of pigs' heads along the top of a cooler, but he is shoved again, this time by a large woman with over-stuffed shopping bags.

"Enough," he says to Andreas who is standing next to him. "This place is too much."

"Even for you, the one who always says, *gross is good for Art*?"

"Even for me," says Marco, packing up his camera. "It's not the dead, bloody animals that bother me. It's the living, breathing, shoving people that are driving me up the wall."

"Are you feeling okay?" asks Andreas.

"Yes," Marco says, watching the tone of his voice. Aware that Andreas has plenty to be concerned about— first the tumour, then the mugging in Istanbul. "I am fine."

"Not that you would tell me if you weren't," says Andreas. "You're so determined to climb Mytikas."

"No headaches. No dizziness. No weight loss or night-sweats. My energy is good. It's just too hot, let's get out of here."

18
CONCERT

After the market, they walk through side streets lined with orange trees, dusty with pollution. They sit on the doorstep of a torn-down building and drink from a large bottle of water they've bought from a corner store for five Euros. Like any side street in any big city, there is a sense of both regeneration and decay. Marco looks at an empty lot behind them. There's a broom handle and a construction helmet, a plastic water bottle, lumber and brick—a square between three buildings, vacant, but already the building permit has been posted on the stonewall above where he's sitting.

"It's good to be out of that craziness," he says to Andreas.

Andreas takes a sip from the water bottle and stares quietly into the empty lot.

By now, Marco knows how to read between the lines of silence. "I'm glad we're here together," he says. "Imagine. We're going to climb a mountain!"

**

Early evening, Andreas and Marco walk uphill through Kolonaki. Everything in Athens seems to be an uphill climb. At the top of the street, in a ground-floor apartment window, a plaster bust of one of the Seven Dwarfs.

"That's Happy," says Andreas.

"I don't think so," Marco answers. "It's Dopey."

"He looks pretty happy to me," says Andreas.

"Whatever," says Marco. "We'd better hurry or we'll be late for the concert."

The outdoor theatre sits on top of Lykabettus hill looking out over the city to the sea. It's a balmy, summer night. Rufus Wainwright, Canada's baroque pop diva, is about to come on stage for his European finale. Knowing Marco is a big fan, Andreas had bought the tickets as a surprise before leaving Toronto. A woman comes out and asks the audience, in Greek and then in English, to be silent during the first two numbers. Rufus comes on stage dressed as a black bird with long, soft feathers. A handful of people begin to applaud until they are shushed silent by the rest of the audience. Wainwright's eyes are painted black and, as he sits at the piano, a giant black eye appears on a screen behind him. Then another giant eye and another smaller, darkened eye. The eyes look out at them. The audience is silent, listening to a soulful rendition of Kate McGarrigle's "Walking". A giant eye on the screen behind Rufus opens and closes; twenty others stare back at the audience. The eyes open and close with the music, the small eyes disappear. The one on the bottom left and the one on the right of the screen also disappear. Then there is only one. A large eye outlined in black. Oily, black and teary, the eye looks out at them and a tear flows down the screen as Rufus belts out his mother's song.

When Marco hears the opening bars of *Cigarettes and Chocolate Milk*, he nearly falls off his seat.

"That's it!" he says, ignoring the audience who try to shush him. "That's the opening soundtrack to my movie!"

I am happy, he thinks, as Andreas puts his hand on his knee and Rufus hits the saddest note of the evening.

***

Marco dreams he's at the Fortress of Yedikule in Turkey. He is looking down into a deep cylinder of stone. As he stares into the dark, seven whirling dervishes float up in jeweled costumes. They're on hangers, arms stretched out like clothing on a line of red and green rubies. They are spinning and laughing, dressed in brightly coloured clothing.

Marco wakes and turns to Andreas in the dark. The concert had disturbed and inspired him; he's worried about climbing the mountain. He would never tell Andreas, but the headaches are there, subtle, but always present.

"Aristotle says that happiness is a virtue," he says to Andreas, whom he senses is also awake.

"Well," says Andreas, flicking on the bedside lamp and propping his head on his elbow. "The pursuit of philosophic wisdom, including happiness, was deemed a virtuous activity."

"But those guys had nothing better to do but stand around and think," says Marco. "They didn't have some crappy job in a television station to go to."

"It's more complicated than that," says Andreas. "Philosophers were deemed to be closer to the gods because of their natural inclination to reason."

"In that case," says Marco, pulling the covers over Andreas' head, "why don't you be a reasonable person and go back to sleep? It's four in the morning, and we have to pack up for Hydra in a few hours!"

"Hey," says Andreas, tickling Marco in the ribs. "You're the one who was getting all philosophical in the middle of the night!"

"And you…" says Marco, rolling onto Andreas, "… shouldn't start tickling me unless you're ready to be tickled back!"

19
LANDING

Manya is disappointed. She wanted to smell orange blossoms and olives. As unrealistic as it may seem, she wanted to hear the sound of a goat calling or be welcomed by the image of a goddess reading from an ancient scroll. But Eleftherios Venizelos is like any other modern airport—there are no bleating goats or statues of goddess, the terminal is bright and functional, her suitcase arrives on the carousel in a reasonable time.

As the terminal doors open onto the street, there are no warm fragrances and very little to indicate she has just entered a beautiful, ancient city by the sea. At street level, signs for the *Metro* are clearly marked—getting to the hotel will be easy. She crosses the street and follows more signs for the *Metro*. As she waits in line for tickets, she overhears rumblings: *Rotating strike. No subway.* Athens is famous for its chaos. The Olympics were supposed to change things. The IOC made it clear—smog had to be cut, transportation had to be timely and clean. The woman in front of her sighs and drops her backpack on the ground. The man beside her kicks his suitcase.

The suburban train will take her to the Metro, she is told by an exasperated attendant. The strike is rotating. The subway *may or may not* be running by the time she gets to Doukissis Plakentias.

When Manya finally arrives at Doukissis there are no trains and people are rushing to flag down taxis. This is worse than New York, she thinks, beginning to feel tired and a little disoriented. A Greek woman, slightly overweight with blonde hair, suntan, and too much makeup approaches her. Manya notices a large silver cross on her neck, gorgeous and gaudy.

"Can I be of assistance?" the woman asks.

"Oh," says Manya. "Thank god you speak English."

"Most Greeks do," she says.

"I'm trying to get to my hotel," Manya says. "It's near the Acropolis."

"You're American?" the woman says. "What do you think of the mess we're in?"

"I've just arrived," says Manya, "but things look pretty good to me."

"Well," the woman says. "The Greeks hardly notice there is a problem here! Life goes on. Misinformation, government ministers who feathered their nests for years, unsecured investments, greedy officials! *PO – PO.*"

"Thank you," says Manya. "Any idea how I can get downtown from here?"

"The government is letting so many immigrants have citizenship. It should be more difficult! There are immigrants, and then believe me, there are *immigrants*!"

Manya picks up her suitcase to leave. The woman doesn't seem to notice.

"The people from the former Communist countries: Russia, Romania, Bulgaria—what a bunch!" she says.

"Drugs and robberies and laziness, I tell you! You know it's dangerous to go out now! The people I know hardly ever go out. And it used to be so safe here! You never know what could happen to you. Homes are robbed and hotel rooms. Imagine, even in a good area like Glyfada where I live."

"Thank you," says Manya, her tone getting firm. "I'll figure it out."

"The people from Asia…" the woman keeps talking as they walk ahead, "…they're not the problem, they're different, and they work from morning to night trying to make a living for themselves and their families, trying to earn enough to send some home to their relatives."

"Taxi!!" Manya yells, but the driver does not stop.

"We have to think about who we let in and who can stay here! Did you know that Greece has the highest percentage of single ethnic lineage of all the countries in Europe! France is a mess! Germany too! You know, in the end, Greece is what? A wonderful place to visit. History and great weather, beautiful countryside, the islands, the sea? But it is a country of no resources, no products, and no future. In the case of the U S, Greeks go to America. Their kids come back, and are they Greek? No, they're Americans, not Greeks. Why would they be? Life is good in America, they tell us."

"Taxi!!" Manya yells. As it pulls away, she can hear the woman ranting about pushy, rude Americans.

Her driver is kind and smart. He takes routes to avoid the protests that are taking place in the core; he plays soft, classical music. Manya begins to feel better and by the time they arrive at the hotel, she is excited about her trip again. *Ashes to Ashes,* she thinks to herself, this is going to be an amazing journey!

Hotel Hera is a boutique hotel. Manya had decided to spend a little extra for this part of the trip. She took the Junior Suite with a giant balcony that faces the Acropolis. She drops her suitcase on the floor and walks out onto the terrace. With pen in hand, she writes down her first impressions of Athens—*monochromatic, flowing, sprawling white clay. A subtle fragrance in the air—not blossoms or sea-water, but something deeper. Subtle but powerful, like clay or blood.*

20
MANYA

Reach. Bounce. Step. Stride. Reach. Bounce. Step. Stride. Her bangles jingle; her hair band slips, her quads burn and her calves are in knots. *No problem*, she thinks. Reach. Bounce. Step. Stride. One fence post and then the next. The fire hydrant, the scaffolding alongside a townhouse; the bend onto the path past the Acropolis; she places one foot and then the next. Training is good. But the hills. You can't sprint through Athens. Hard to find her stride in the clouds, she keeps moving though, running Olympus isn't going to be easy.

21
MANYA

Cars are not permitted in Hydra, only donkeys and ponies on the cobblestone streets. And people, of course, the two thousand or so locals and a considerable number of tourists. Marco wakes up in the heat after a night of roosters crowing and donkeys braying and cats screeching and dogs barking, followed by a nightmare. The same nightmare he always has in which he is bending to pet a stray cat that appears helpless and then it sinks its claws and teeth into his leg and won't let go. The dream is so real that he turns on the light to see if his leg is bleeding.

"What's wrong?" says Andreas.

"Nothing," says Marco. "Go back to sleep."

A few seconds later, he hears Andreas snoring.

I am happy, he thinks, waits for the tug and twinge under his skull, waits for a decent dream to float down.

After a simple breakfast of thick yogurt, honey and toast, Marco and Andreas walk through the quiet streets. An old woman walking with a cane, her hair covered in a navy scarf, stops to check them out. Andreas says, *Yasou*, which seems to reassure her and she waves them along. They follow a stone and dirt path along the edge of the town. Marco hears an intense humming. The sound gets louder until they are standing beneath a eucalyptus tree. A cloud of bees swarms the branches. Every blossom seems to contain a bee. It's both terrifying and astonishingly beautiful. They stand there, mesmerized. Marco finds certain aspects of nature almost too perfect to comprehend.

The edge of town is crawling with cats, big and small, starving, and somehow surviving. Today is garbage day, and six or seven of them surround a black bag, tearing out its contents, fighting over scraps of fish and chicken bones.

Marco and Andreas walk slowly, taking in the gorgeous rolling hills and seascape.

"I had that dream about cats again," Marco tells Andreas.

"All these strays must trigger your fear of cats," Andreas says.

"I'm not afraid of cats," says Marco. "I don't think the dream is really about cats."

"What do you think it's really about?" asks Andreas.

"I don't know," says Marco. "All I know is that when I wake up, I'm scared shitless."

They continue walking along the cliff-side pathway, over narrow stone paths, worn by thousands of years. They haven't seen another person for over an hour and decide that it's safe to skinny-dip. They strip off their shirts and shorts and jump into the cool water. Marco can hardly find words for the beauty - clear, sparkling, small fish swimming between his legs, warm sunlight on his face—*Greece*, Marco thinks, *God's blue-white paradise*. Andreas slides under the water, and soon Marco feels tiny nibbles along his thighs, somewhat like the fish, only with teeth.

They fool around in the water for an hour or so, then get dressed and continue their walk until they find a small, hillside restaurant for lunch. From their table, high above, Marco can see down through the water ten or twenty feet. They share a large plate of feta, black olives and perfectly ripe tomatoes. Their waiter has disappeared along with the other two staff, to a table on the far side of the restaurant where a woman seems to be causing a scene. Andreas and Marco walk over to see what is going on, stand at a safe distance.

"You don't own this town," the woman yells in English.

"Some beggar being hauled off," says Andreas.

"That's no beggar," Marco says. "That's Manya, from the Newark airport!"

Marco and Andreas run over and push past the waiters. Manya jumps up and down. "I thought you were going to Turkey!" she says, hugging Andreas. "I thought I'd never see you guys again."

"I thought *you* were going to Turkey," he says.

"Turkey en route to Greece," Manya says. "How wonderful to see you both."

"You know?" the waiter asks.

"Yes!" says Andreas. "She is a friend."

"She cannot beg here," he says.

"I'm not begging," Manya says in a calm voice. "Jerk."

"She is with us," Andreas says to the waiter, handing him fifty euros.

The waiter frowns as Manya gathers up her hair bands and other handmade items from the table and places them into a large canvas bag.

"Too bad we're just running into you now," says Marco. "We're leaving here today on the ferry to Mykonos."

"The 2:15?" Manya asks.

"The 2:15!" Andreas says.

The ferry to Mykonos is fast and comfortable. Not a cruise ship, but it has all the amenities—two restaurants, a bar, televisions and comfortable seats. And, of course, everyone is smoking. Manya leading the way, the three of them climb the stairs to the upper deck in search of fresh air. The back section of the ferry is relatively free of smokers; Manya hands out her *Ashes to Ashes* brochures as Andreas and Marco stare down into the swirling water.

"Looks like those creamy blue popsicles we used to get as kids," Marco says.

"Greece truly is all about the sky and water," Andreas says.

"And the air," says Marco, taking in a deep breath. "Don't forget the white light and the salty air."

"Too much cigarette smoke," says Manya, leaning over the railing. She looks down into the trail of water churned up by the ferry. "I've had a sore throat since the day I stepped off the plane."

As she reaches in her backpack for another brochure, the couple standing next to them leaves.

"You're scaring away all the people," says Marco.

"I guess I'm being a little too pushy," says Manya, "with this anti-smoking thing."

"You got it," says Andreas.

22
LITTLE BEE

When Manya was eight years old her mother, Marina, took her to Washington Square Park. It was sunny and they sat on a bench close to the fountain. She was given a juice box and one of her dolls. Her mother unloaded a stack of papers from her briefcase and handed her a jigsaw puzzle. Manya liked the square shape of the park, the tall trees along the edges, and the round fountain in the middle. She liked watching the boys on their skateboards; she was happy to be with her mom away from the apartment.

"Does it hurt?" Manya asked.

"Does what hurt?"

"When you walk?"

Marina had always been a little heavy, but over the last year she'd put on so much weight that even the simple things became a challenge. Her body ached when she got out of bed. Her feet were swollen and they hurt when she walked the ten minutes to the university each morning, rocking from side to side. She rarely went to the park with Manya anymore.

"A little," her mother said. "But not today."

"What does my name mean?" she asked her mother, looking down at the box with blue fish and a pink sky on the cover.

"It means we have a deal, Missy."

"But what does it mean?"

"It means sit still."

"No, it doesn't."

"Manya," her mother said, raising her voice slightly. "I will answer this one question, but then I have to pay attention to these papers."

"Fine," said Manya, kicking her feet and shaking the box with the puzzle. "So what does it mean?"

"It means mania."

"What's mania?"

"Hyper. Fidgety. Bouncy. A pain in the ass."

"Why would you name me that?"

"It's not really your name," said her mother. "It's just what *he* called you."

"He?"

"Manya?" said her mother, sounding more agitated. "What was our deal?"

"It's still the same question," she said.

"Your real name is Melissa. It means Little Bee. But it didn't suit you," she said. "Manya suits you better."

"Melissa's nice," said Manya.

"It's too late. I've always called you Manya," said her mother. "Now why don't you play with your puzzle?"

Manya shook the pieces from the box onto the bench between her and her mother. She flipped the lid over and put the first piece down and then the next one beside it. She put the picture together in less than a minute. It was a school of fish. There were seven blue fish, numbered from one to seven. Floating above them in orange thought bubbles was the number seven, outlined seven times against the pink sky.

"Boring," Manya said to her mother, who was circling things and writing in the margins of her students' papers.

"Draw then," said Marina, sighing, and handing her a pencil but no paper. "Keep yourself busy for a few minutes or no ice cream."

Manya slid her tiny fingers under the puzzle, trying hard to keep it from falling apart. She flipped it like a pancake and lost a few of the pieces, but quickly put them back where they fit. She looked at her mother with her hair cut short. It was hard to make the pencil work because of the cracks, but Manya pressed into the blank pieces to make lines for bangs. She drew the heavy legs folded, and the body bent forward. She was meticulous about the folds of skin and wrinkles in the dress. She shaded in the face and big arms using the side of the pencil; etching in strong, dark eyes. When it was done, she took it apart and handed the pieces to her mother.

"Guess who it is," she asked. "Guess who I drew on the back of the puzzle?"

Marina put the paper she was grading under her leg. She turned to Manya and smiled, flipped her briefcase over to make a table to build the puzzle on. She put together the big hands in the woman's lap and the folds of her grey dress. She snapped the dark eyes into place and the pale ears and nose, and cried when she got to the woman's thick arms and legs. She looked at her daughter and then back at the puzzle.

"My God," she said. "It's perfect."

"It's you," said Manya. "Look. I drew you with your papers."

"Yes," said Marina, looking down at the large, round hands.

Marina reflected on her decision not to go into the arts. Unlike her mother's chaotic life as an actress, she wanted her own life to be calm and predictable. Her grades were good, and she graduated young. She never left her first teaching job at NYU. Aside from the weight, and the occasional challenge from Manya, her life, for the most part, was unruffled.

"There's no stopping you," she said, wiping back a tear and pulling her daughter close to her. "Art is in your blood. And yes," Marina added, kissing the top of Manya's head. "The puzzle *is* boring, but don't be so darn precocious."

They sat like that for a while in the sun. Marina ignored the stack of student papers and Manya did her best not to fidget when she was told to stop kicking the bench.

"Where does he live?" Manya asked.

"Somewhere out west," her mother said.

"California?"

"Oregon," Marina said. "His name is Ben," she added, but wouldn't answer when Manya asked if he lived in Portland.

"Can I do my circles?" asked Manya. They had an agreement. Manya was allowed to run, but only within sight of her mother. Circles around the fountain are okay. Or she can run up to the Washington Square Arch and back.

"Touch the brick!" Marina said, excitement in her voice.

"Okay," said Manya, bending on one knee, pretending to be at the starting line of a race. "You say when!"

23
RAT RACE

Marco could hardly contain himself. They'd agreed to *just look* at the Trump Tower.

"It's five minutes from your office," Marco explained to Andreas.

"You realize that you'll never have a cent to your name if we live there," said Andreas.

"No matter how well we may do on the sale of the house, that movie that's buzzing around in your head will never see the light of day; you'll be so busy at MBTV earning money for condo fees."

It was Sunday morning. They were in the kitchen on Victor Avenue finishing their coffees. Marco had the newspaper in his hand and was looking at a full-page ad for the Trump condo. Andreas was going to work in the garden, but he had agreed to meet Marco at the sales centre at noon. Marco kissed Andreas, hard, on the mouth.

Andreas looked at him. "It makes sense," he said. "You never know. The tumor might just come back. We don't want to be dealing with this falling down house if you get sick."

Andreas was referring to the ongoing problems with the fence along the laneway and the roof that had been repaired twice in as many years and the headaches that kept coming back and sometimes wouldn't leave for days.

"But we're just looking," he added. "We're not doing anything stupid. There are plenty of condos for sale if we decide to sell the house."

"But this is the tallest residential building in the country," Marco says.

"Marco!" growled Andreas. "Nothing impulsive. Promise?"

I'm not going to work, he'd announced over breakfast a few weeks back. *As a matter of fact,* he'd said, *I'm not setting foot in the MBTV studio again.*

Fortunately, by the end of the day, he came to his senses and called MBTV's producer, Helena Stephanopoules. *It'll pass,* he said into the telephone. *I'll be there tomorrow.*

***

Each treatment was only two or three minutes, but by the end of the twenty days Marco had had enough of radiation.

"I'll be a glow-in-the-dark cameraman," he told Andreas.

"I'm just glad that they caught this now," Andreas said. "Just think, the surgery will be over in no time and you can go back to work."

"Oh," said Marco. "Like that's a big incentive."

"I'm sure you can think of others if you try," Andreas said, handing Marco a glass of water and a Gravol as he lay in bed.

"I have plenty of incentive to get better," Marco answered, and he meant it. "I've learned to appreciate everything I've got."

He swallowed the pill and pulled back the blankets. "Get in here," he said.

***

Marco stood under the arched entrance of the Canada Permanent, a gorgeous art deco building across the street from the Trump. The surgery was a success, the headaches were gone and his hair had grown back. He had every intention to make the best of the day. It was Sunday, and Bay Street was unusually quiet. There was no traffic at all and it was a perfect summer day. The sun shone down across the high-rises along Bay Street; there was a beauty and calmness that can only be found in the heart of a city. The Trump was going up fast. Two floors a week. They were past the hotel section and into the residential part of the tower; the green granite curtain walls had just gone up. He sat on the sidewalk, imagining what it would be like to live in the core of the city—the King subway around the corner; Ben McNally books on Adelaide; restaurants, clubs and shopping everywhere. *It's all right here!* Marco was conscious of the fact that he sounded like a real estate ad. He would be high in the sky facing the lake. He would be inspired and, regardless of what Andreas said, he'd make his movie. The movie will be about perspective—how people see things. Clouds and stars. The peaks of mountains and the tops of buildings.

His thoughts were interrupted by the arrival of a man and a woman with big grey ears and wire moustaches walking down the street, hand and hand. The couple was followed by a giant chunk of cheese on wheels. There were rat children and rats in wheelchairs. There was a *Bay Street for Homeless Women* float and corporate rat teams from each of the downtown offices. *Rat Race for Inner City Kids,* said the placard one woman carried. She shook a small red bucket at him; Marco dug into his pocket for change.

"I have a loonie," said Andreas, dropping the coin into the woman's bucket.

"Thank God you're here," said Marco. "This Rat Race fundraising stuff is all too surreal for me."

"You think this is surreal," Andreas said, nodding across the street to the Trump building. "Wait until we step into that sales office."

***

Marco had the nightmare at least once a month—he was in a dark room. It might be the basement of the house in Ville-Émard. The walls were crashing and so was the ceiling. The heat was so intense it melted everything. The clock. The pictures. His skin and his brain.

He woke covered in sweat. The headache was unbearable. They were at their house on Victor Avenue, two days before the trip.

"It has nothing to do with 9/11," said Andreas, as they sat in bed discussing the dream. "You've had that dream ever since the radiation."

"You're wrong," said Marco. "It's the twin towers. I see the airplanes crashing over and over again."

"That's television's fault," said Andreas. "The whole world saw those planes flying into the buildings a hundred times. You need to go back to sleep. Do you want Joni?"

Marco nodded, Andreas got out of bed to fetch the iPod. Listening to *Clouds* was the only thing that helped him sleep some nights. *Bows and flows of angel hair...*

***

The sales office was surprisingly low key. When they walked in, a down-to-earth looking woman dressed in an unpretentious grey suit with black high heels approached with a clipboard in hand. She offered them coffee and asked them to fill out a questionnaire. Andreas gave Marco a skeptical smile, and passed him the questionnaire.

"What price range?" Marco asked Andreas, holding has pen above the various options to be circled.

"We are just looking," said Andreas. "Remember?"

"We still have to fill out the questionnaire," Marco said. "What price do you think?"

"That depends," said Andreas. "What do you think we could get for the house?"

By the time the agent got back to them, Andreas had become a little more engaged.

"The building looks pretty amazing," he said.

Marco nodded in agreement, but he was feeling a little guilty about dragging Andreas into looking.

"But probably out of our price range," he'd said.

The agent looked at the two men and smiled. "This will be painless," she'd said, leading them to the model of the needle pointed tower. "We'll find something that works for the two of you, I'm sure."

24
KITTEN

The cat was white, but dirty, probably from living under the house. He saw her crawling out through a crack between the concrete and the wood slats. At first he thought she was a rat, it was dark and her belly was low to the ground. She stopped when she saw him, that's how he knew she was sick. No wild cat would stop in place when it saw a human with a stick. He set his Molson down on the step and walked slowly toward her. She flinched when he touched her with his foot, but that was it, no big reaction. She was hardly breathing but he could see her swollen belly moving slowly up, then slowly down. She was about to give birth. Only she was dying. He used his boot to crush her head. It may sound cruel, but he didn't want her to feel what was coming. He flicked his cigarette against the side of the house, saw it spark red when it hit. He dug deep into his coat pocket for his Swiss Army knife. He cut along her belly, only it wasn't a belly—it's called a litter sac when it's full of kittens.

***

The cigarette must have rolled through the hole in the house she crawled out of. The fire department said the cat had built a nest of dried leaves and papers. The English guy called his father a *careless wop*; the French fireman, who the other guy called Luc, took pictures of the fire and told Franco to be *appy for the kid's nose to smell the smoke.*

"Get back to bed," his father told Marco. "Take the rest of them with ya."

"'E cannot go there, monsieur," the French guy, Luc, did his best to speak English.

"Wop?" Franco said, looking back and forth between the two firemen. "Giovanni Caboto, an Italian, found this country for the love of England."

"Qui?"

"John Cabot," said the English guy.

"Ah. Jean Cabot!"

"Giovanni Caboto in 1497," said his father. "I'm not as dumb as I look."

"But you *are* drunk, sir," said the English one.

"*Venez ici,*" said Luc, waving to Marco. "Come."

The house wouldn't be safe for a day or two, they told Franco. They all could come back in the morning to take a better look. For one night they could stay down at the station. *Toute la gang!* said Luc, putting his red fireman's hat on Marco's head.

The firemen helped his father into the front seat of the truck, his brothers and sisters piled into the back. Marco handed Luc his helmet back and he and his mother stood away from the truck.

"We'll stay a few minutes with the kitten," she said, pulling Marco closer. "Then walk, it's not far to the station."

She covered the dead cat with her apron. Marco picked up the squirmy grey kitten with the white face and two white paws.

The fire truck stopped a few doors down. Luc ran back to the house. He had his camera in his hand. "*Encore les photos*," he said to Marco, ruffling his hair.

The fireman walked over to the house and Marco followed. He looked at the small crack in the wood and the side of the house covered with black soot. He snapped his first picture as Marco put the kitten down on the apron.

"Ah," said the fireman. "*Un minou.*"

"The mother died," said Marco. "See."

Marco pulled back the apron before his mother could get the word *don't* out of her mouth. The fireman moved closer, bent down.

"*Merde*," he said. "*Qu'est-ce que c'est?*"

"She died," Marco said.

"Giving birth," his mother added.

"*Comme ca?*" said the fireman, as he brought the camera close to the dead cat.

"Come on Luc," shouted the other fireman from the truck. "Let's go!"

"You go," said the fireman, waving the driver off. "See you *dans quelques minutes.*"

Marco wanted to look through the camera to see what the fireman saw. The dead cat cut wide open; the pictures of the house with the burn marks up to the roof; the small hole in the side they made big with an axe. What did he see through the camera that he couldn't see with eyes? Marco wanted to look, more than anything he wanted to see through the lens of the camera.

"*Prenez une photo du petit minou,*" he said, handing Marco the camera, as if on cue.

"Don't drop it," said his mother, as Marco took the camera.

The fireman kneeled behind him and steadied his hands. Marco was shaking. The camera was bigger than any camera he had seen, and heavy. The fireman was gentle and his hand was warm over his. "Press."

Marco took the picture of the kitten. Then he sat on the grass with his back against the house. Something had happened.

"Give the nice fireman his camera back," his mother said.

But he didn't listen. Instead, he raised the camera to his eye. One more time. He wanted that feeling again. The world seemed different through the lens. Everything in a box, perfectly contained. He held the camera against his eye. It was difficult to get to his feet without losing his balance. He walked slowly across the damp grass, feeling his way to where the fireman stood next to his mother. Luc was short, almost the same height as her. He had his helmet off and his black hair was combed back and looked wet. His teeth were white and his whiskers dark. His coveralls were loose and he was wearing a blue shirt the same colour as his eyes. Marco had a funny feeling inside that he liked. His legs felt weak. He moved the camera over an inch or two to see more of his mother. Her hands were folded on her belly; she was wearing her pink bathrobe and nothing on her feet. Her bare feet were next to the fireman's black boots. Marco tilted the camera up and caught the two faces—his mother and the fireman, the nice French guy who smiled for the picture; and his mother who smiled too, so brightly that he hardly recognized her.

"Hold the camera still," she said.

"*Les yeux*," said the fireman smiling at his mother. "*Les yeux sont créés pour voir les femmes extraordinaires*."

"The eyes were made for seeing," translated his mother, looking down at Marco, her face as pink as her robe that was undone by the fireman's fingers. Right there in the yard.

25
ANDREAS

Andreas has become comfortable talking with Manya. Beyond her youth and intense beauty, she is a wise and joyful person. They are walking along the beach near the hotel in Hydra looking for a good spot to swim. Andreas had asked her if she felt unsafe traveling in Greece by herself.

"I'm used to being alone," she says. "I am an only child."

"I'm an only child too," Andreas says.

"And you avoided my question," Manya says, "about why you're leaving the Greek area in Toronto where you live."

"The ad is in the paper. The sign is on the front lawn. Marco wants to live in a high-rise."

"You don't have a say?" she asks.

"Sure I do," says Andreas. "To be honest, although I initially resisted, the idea of a maintenance-free condo over a squirrels-in-the-attic-and-eaves-troughs-overflowing house has a certain appeal."

"You seem so laid back. Do you *ever* get mad, Andreas?" she asks. "Really, really, really, really pissed?"

"Not really," he laughs, kicking the sand. Then, after a brief pause, he raises his finger in the air. "There was one time," he says. "I was working at the Toronto General on

New Year's Eve, and there was one case after another of really dumb situations and I wanted to get home to Marco."

"What happened?" Manya asks, excitedly. "Tell me, were you a complete jerk?"

"Well," he said. "I started the day in surgery. I was working on a little kid, a seven-year-old with *strabismus*."

"*Strabismus*?"

"Oh," he says. "Cross-eyes. The little guy was cross-eyed and at seven he had already endured his fair share of teasing."

"You can fix that?" says Manya.

"Sure," says Andreas. "I do something called the short adjustable suture. Kind of a bow tie slip knot technique."

"Oh," says Manya, spreading her beach towel in the sand. "Your story is full of anger and fury!" she teases.

"This isn't it," says Andreas, putting his towel next to hers. "The evening got busier and busier. There were two separate cases of men with severe trauma from corks popping in their eye."

"That's bizarre," says Manya, "and kind of funny. But you still don't sound pissed."

"Well," says Andreas. "I had just performed a surgery around the orbital bone after a woman had been in a car accident … I was exhausted, just getting ready to go home, when I received a call from Emerg."

"Okay," says Manya. "Now you're sounding ticked."

"It was about two little girls," Andreas says, sighing. "One was five and the other was nine. The parents, after guzzling too much champagne, bundled their kids up in hats and mittens and sent them out to play with kites in the dark."

"This isn't sounding good," says Manya. "Were you mad because the parents sent them out in the dark?"

"That's part of it," says Andreas. "I was furious because they gave the kids kites with strings made of copper wire."

"Oh-oh," says Manya. "I see where this is going."

"Yes. In their drunken wisdom, the parents decided that the kites would stay in the air if the string was supported with stiff wire."

"And?"

"The little one's kite got tangled in hydro lines in the laneway where they were playing."

"That is *dumb*," says Manya. "And completely irresponsible."

"She lost her eyesight. Completely blind at five. There was nothing I could do to save her tiny little eyes."

"That's sad," says Manya.

"I *was* sad," said Andreas.

"But you still don't sound furious?"

"Well," says Andreas. "The worst part of the entire eighteen-hour day was when I finally made it home. Marco was off at some party with his friends. He'd left me a note saying he was tired of waiting. He came home the next morning, drunk."

"Not good," says Manya.

"Not good!" says Andreas, bending down to pick up a

stone. "I was so angry I was shaking," he adds, throwing the stone in the water.

"You should have gone out and tied one on yourself."

"And I didn't," says Andreas. "My dad used to say that an eye-for-an-eye leads only to more blindness."

"That's gorgeous," says Manya.

"It is," says Andreas. "My dad was a pretty smart man."

He pauses a moment. Manya touches his shoulder.

"Besides," says Andreas, sensing her discomfort. "Marco is adorable. And lovely. And creative. And hot. And he has his kind moments."

"Really?" says Manya.

"Really," says Andreas, looking down.

***

Manya and Marco sip iced coffee at the hotel bar while Andreas showers before dinner.

"Andreas has an obsession with cleanliness," says Marco.

"How's that?" asks Manya.

"Ten minutes washing and rewashing his hands, an hour washing his face and shaving in the morning, then twenty minutes in the shower."

"That's hardly an obsession."

"Two to three hours sitting in the bathtub on Sunday afternoons, for crying-out-loud!"

"Perhaps his obsession isn't with cleanliness?" says Manya, "Maybe his interest is with water?"

"Ah," says Marco, suddenly feeling very sad. Looking

away from her, he adds, "Well, he'd better let go of his parents. It's killing him. It's killing us."

***

Water, Andreas, his mother had yelled. *Water*. But he froze. Andreas stood there. His father's head was on fire and Andreas stood there like stone. He stood there until there was only smoke and his father rocking from side-to-side on the floor. Andreas stood there while the waiter ushered customers out of the restaurant. He watched as his mother put the *Closed* sign on the door. Andreas stood there when the ambulance came and he stood there in the dark when they turned the lights out.

"Come, Andreas," his mother said.

He was stiff as a statue when she bent to pick him up. She carried him, in the dark, through the swinging doors to the kitchen.

"Help me find Papa's apron," she'd said. She wasn't crying, but something like it; she could hardly talk and she moved very slowly as she walked around the kitchen. By the light coming through the windows, Andreas could see broken glasses and plates, the pots and pans thrown about. There was black over everything. His head against his mother's skin, he could feel the words in her chest as she spoke. "Mama's going to be spending a lot of time in this kitchen now."

She put Andreas down, and sat next to him on the floor. He stood there looking at the back of her head and her legs sticking out like a giant doll's. She was leaning forward and her back was moving up and down. After a while, she stopped and lifted her head. She had a burnt cloth clenched in her hand. Wiping her tears with it and leaving a streak of black across her eyes, "I guess I won't be wearing this thing," she'd said, holding up what was left of the apron.

26
ANDREAS

"Happiness is more than brain cells and neurons, Marco. It consists of all kinds of intangible things that science has never been able to find."

"For a doctor," says Marco, "you're being very non-clinical."

Just before sunset, they sit on a sofa in the Kastro Bar looking out at the sea. Every time he thinks that he has arrived in the most spectacular setting in the world, they arrive at the next town and Marco is completely blown away again. This bar in Mykonos on the water's edge is all windows, jazz music, and suntanned tourists.

"How many ways can there be to describe 'blue'?" Andreas says, looking into Marco's eyes. Andreas gets very mushy when he has been drinking wine, and he's on his third glass of white. Marco sips his beer, looks away.

The bar is small and crowded. Renowned for its sunsets, tourists are crowding in for the view. Two women sit on the sofa next to them. The single chairs, all oriented toward the window, are also occupied, mostly by guys checking each other out.

Marco knows what to expect next from Andreas—a rapid decline into alcohol-induced sentimentality and then the inevitable sadness. He wants to pick up the conversation before the tears start, but he's not fast enough, he can feel Andreas sobbing.

"What's wrong?" he asks, knowing the answer before Andreas speaks.

"I wish they were here," he says. "My parents spent most of their lives missing Greece. They would have loved this place."

"Perhaps they are," says Marco, not sure if he really believes what he's about to say. "Maybe they're looking down on us from above."

"Thanks," says Andreas, trying to smile. "That was a good effort."

The view is breathtaking. Gold and pink light, waves rolling over the rocks, crashing against the old stone houses converted to bars and restaurants along the water's edge.

"They look so in love," Andreas says, nodding in the direction of a middle-aged man and woman wrapped in each other's arms.

"She looks like she's had about sixteen glasses of wine," Marco says. "Maybe that's happiness?"

The waiter has just brought Andreas his fourth glass of wine. Slurring, he says: "That's not a penis, it's oblif … oblivion."

"I love it," Marco laughs. "Hap penis. A penis."

But Andreas is not listening to Marco play with words, he is bent over, with his face in his hands.

***

Marco and Andreas take a side-trip to Naxos. They've hugged and said their farewells, agreed to meet Manya at a Koufonissi B&B two days later. Naxos is like Mykonos, only without the glitziness and hoards of people getting off tour boats to take over the town. It's a different kind of beauty—hills and sea, serenity.

Marco feels like his formula is working. By telling himself that he is happy several times a day, whether he is or not, his brain is getting the message. He has re-patterned his brain with joy. He feels different. Grateful for the good things they have every day—decent coffee, delicious food and Andreas. He sleeps better and is more optimistic. There is an aura of lightness colouring everything. *I am Happy*, he tells himself. Over lunch in a small waterside café, he shares the good news with Andreas.

"It's called 'vacation', Marco. You're happy because you're away from that job you hate so much and are hanging out in one of the most beautiful places on the planet. Why don't you just drop the *I am happy* nonsense?"

Marco had put the job out of his mind. But that was a secret that would have to come out down the road. He still hadn't found the right moment to tell Andreas that he'd been fired.

"Thanks for the vote of confidence," Marco says. Surprised by how over-the-top angry he feels, he pushes his chair back and stands over Andreas.

"You?" says Marco, "the 'pill popper', asking me to drop *my* happy nonsense!"

Marco is aware of people at the tables around them, but he doesn't stop.

"Well, Andreas, I thought I'd try to make myself happy because at any given moment there are dozens of religious wars taking place and somewhere in the world right now someone is being put in prison in the name of God for being gay, or a woman is being stoned to death for adultery, because President Obama is likely to be assassinated and Stephen Harper is likely to live a long dull life. And I've had a brain tumor that may or may not come back, and because I can't figure out how to make a movie or find it within myself to stop worrying about you every time you step foot into a swimming pool, lake, or this crazy blue water that's everywhere in this one-island-after-another-island country."

Andreas pushes his chair back and stands. "Come here," he says, opening his arms to Marco. "I'm not going anywhere."

***

It was three months after the car accident that killed Andreas' parents. He and Marco had gone to Provincetown. *The water will do you good*, Marco had said. *Remember how much your dad loved the water?* The waves were high and the current strong. Two swimmers dove under orange buoys. The lifeguard had blown his whistle, and the swimmers came back. Andreas dove under the buoys, too. There may have been a whistle but he didn't hear it, he swam fast and had covered ten yards in a few seconds. He did not open his eyes, but he knew he was much farther out because of the cold. *Six thousand steamboats*. Another stroke down, he knew there was no going back. *Seven thousand steamboats.* Soon his body would panic. Soon it would crave oxygen and light. *Eight thousand. Nine thousand steamboats.*

Another draw forward and another and another. At first there were two hands on his ankles and then there were four, and finally, six hands dragging him back to the shore.

***

Athena's gift to Greece: the olive tree with its green-brown fruit—compressed, delicious, alchemic. Oil to eat. Oil for skin and oil for lamps. Marco and Andreas are on the bus to Apiranthos and then the hike to Halki. The winding road above the valley seems too narrow for the bus, but somehow fits an oncoming truck. Cluster after cluster of olive trees, no air-conditioning on the bus. The heat making Marco sleepy. The pounding in his forehead has moved behind his eyes.

They walk above the cypresses, above the road and the valley, onto a winding footpath. Goats graze on the edge of a cliff. There's a small white church at the peak of a hill. An old man on a donkey rides up the dusty path, a sack of onions on one side, a sack of potatoes on the other, bent over and kicking, he must be ninety. Each step seems to take them closer to the sun.

"Up. Lots of hills in Greece," Andreas says.

Marco sips from his water bottle. Walking over the mountain is the only way to the town below. There's no special reason for having chosen Halki, other than to get away from touristy areas and explore the Greek countryside. Marco thinks about how he has never walked the stone path at the edge of a cliff, descended into sage-scented wind. The heat is intense and his baseball cap seems useless against the midday sun.

"I feel dizzy," he says to Andreas, who tags along behind him.

"Psychogenic vertigo," Andreas says. "But you're a Capricorn. You can do this."

They debate which path to take—one goes over another cliff and appears to turn back, while the other heads down to the town. They turn down a steep path, past more goats, through purple-flower thistle and over black goat droppings.

"It smells like feta down here," Marco says to Andreas.

"Yes," says Andreas. "The goats have a very distinct smell."

"Did you hear about the guy who murdered his lover and ate his body parts?" Marco asks Andreas, not sure why this has popped into his brain, seemingly out of nowhere.

"No," says Andreas, sounding annoyed.

"Well," says Marco, "according to the article I read in the *Herald*, after he drugged him, the guy cut off his lover's penis and ate that first. Fried with a little olive oil and garlic."

"Nice," says Andreas tripping over some loose stones.

"Then he put individual body parts in baggies and froze them for later."

"Nonsense," says Andreas. "Tabloid sensationalism."

"It's true," says Marco. "He had finger fillets and skull-bone soup. And when they asked him in prison why he did it, the guy said that it made him happy to consume the one he loved."

"That's disgusting," Andreas laughs. "Enough already, you're freaking me out."

As the path curves downward, the goats increase in number. The larger males at the front of the herd seem incensed, but move aside as Marco and Andreas cut along the path. Suddenly they are in the middle of a major herd of panic-stricken animals. One bleat echoes another off the cliff-side rocks. At the path's end, they hear a dog barking. As they get closer, they can see that it's large and vicious. Not your fairy-tale sheep dog.

"This doesn't look like Halki," Marco calls out to Andreas, who's already scrambling back up the hill. "I think we're lost."

They walk back to Apiranthos. The town consists of narrow stone passageways hardly wide enough for two people. They are in search of a place for dinner. The left lane looks the same as the right. It's dark now and the low ceilings cover the light from the moon and stars. Around one bend they find a coffee shop, around another, two drunken men with Australian accents begrudgingly move to let them pass. Marco is hungry and fed up. Sunburned and tired, they find a place called S'Agapo, which means *I Love You*. Set in a rose garden on the side of a cliff, the view of hills and pastures is spectacular. The waitress places a paper table-cloth over the soiled linen. On it is a map of Greece. For the first time since their arrival, Marco gets excited about climbing Olympus.

That night he dreams that he's trying to fit a sheet over the entire island. The cameras are rolling and he's directing some sci-fi movie about aliens' brains. He is a giant; the island is a flat, grey rock with blood-red etchings. The elastic breaks and he wakes with his arms caught in the bed sheets, Andreas snoring beside him.

27
MANYA

Manya walks away from the Hotel Poseidon. There is no wind, and the forty–degree heat makes her feel lazy. A solitary fishing boat in the port, two stray cats, the hills in the distance sloping and grey, she walks along the rocky shoreline in search of a place to sit. Andreas and Marco will be joining her at the hotel for breakfast. How wonderful that she managed to synchronize her travel plans with her new friends, she thinks. The guys are smart and good-hearted, and somehow she feels safer knowing they are near. But first, she wants to spend a few minutes sketching in her notebook. Koufonissi is one of the most serene places on the planet—very few tourists, purple wild flowers, and that green-blue water. In the shade of a dusty cliff, she relaxes into the morning. The feel of her pencil, fingers pressing against the paper, waiting for inspiration. She waits, but nothing comes.

She sets her sketchbook in the sand, walks over to a tree at the edge of the shore. Barkless and dead, it's anchored by stones. She wonders if it was brought here as an art piece. Or maybe it has sentimental value for someone. It doesn't offer shelter from the sun. There are no olives or figs on its branches, no leaves on its gnarled limbs. But the tears! Manya sits under the tree and sobs. She bends her ankles, rocking from side to side. Not self-pity or even grief. Rather, it's the unexpected arrival of two harsh facts—that George used her and that she let it happen. And, there was a third fact, the most difficult, it had to do with Marina … her mother had counted on her and she let her down.

***

After breakfast the three of them walk, Manya and Marco leading the way. They pass a nude man sitting in the sand at one end of the beach. He is handsome but dirty, with long, knotted hair. His genitals rest on the ground, sand-speckled and tanned like the rest of his body.

"He looks so content," says Manya.

"Yes," says Andreas, from behind them. "The Sandman at play."

They keep walking along the shore until they reach a place on the map known as the Devil's Eye. In contrast with the calm, clear water of the beach, here the lake looks dark and deep.

"Why do you think it's called that?" Marco asks.

"Well," says Manya. "If you step back for a look, it's shaped like an eye, and the deep part in the center looks like a pupil."

"But why the Devil?" asks Marco.

Manya jumps in.

"Greek people respect the unknown," says Andreas. "Be careful!" he yells.

"It's wonderful!" Manya says, treading water. "Come on in."

"No way am I jumping into something called the Devil's Eye," says Marco.

"Me either," say Andreas.

"Cowards!" Manya calls teasingly. "You don't know what you're missing."

It's an almond-shaped *eyeland* of rock with sea in its middle, Manya thinks. She floats, face up, in the midday sun. A mere speck in the pupil, she waits as gravity slowly turns her on the surface of the water. Later, they have lunch at a restaurant overlooking Pori Bay. Manya has risotto. How is it possible that this Italian dish has found its way to this tiny Greek island? Sunburned and relaxed, she sips a glass of white wine, closes her eyes. Perfect. The morning has a perfect ending. Her earlier cry over George has refreshed her. She feels closer to Marco and Andreas, perhaps because of it. In any case, they're good company. Fun and considerate.

"What are you grinning about?" asks Marco.

"Oh," she says. "I was thinking what a lucky coincidence that I bumped into you guys. Twice."

"I don't think it's an accident," says Marco. "There's no such thing as an accident."

"I don't know," says Andreas. "You meet someone at an airport. You have a good chat. You like her. You meet her again. You're on a similar travel route. Nothing overly esoteric about that."

"Oh," says Manya. "You are being boring. And wrong. We were meant for each other," she adds, poking him in the ribs. "People develop friendships because they see something in one another."

"What do you see in me?" asks Marco.

"Dear God, Marco," Manya says. "It's not that simple."

"Good grief," says Andreas looking up at the sky. "Maybe we should just finish eating and leave fate to the gods?"

Manya sips the last of her wine, tells them that she wants to walk back to the hotel alone. She stops at a pristine beach. Clear water over gold sand—rhythmic, sparkling, honeycombs of light. She watches an old couple nude on the beach. The man, in his eighties, stands with his arms in the air, stretching in the sun. She is much younger, probably mid-fifties. Naked, sitting spread-eagle, the woman claws a trench in the sand. Twin boys, probably her grandchildren, wearing Mickey Mouse arm flotation bands, run up to her with overflowing buckets, pour plastic pails of water between her legs. How gorgeous. What a stunningly perfect moment. Manya pulls out her notebook and pencil. Completely inspired, she draws.

They have dinner at *Melissa's*. The owner, a woman in her mid thirties, runs around and waits on tables. She tells them that Melissa means *Little Bee*.

"I know," says Manya, looking sad.

"Something wrong?" asks Marco. "Not really," says Manya. "Just remembering."

The restaurant is full of tourists. All three of them order *moussaka* with Greek salad. The lights flicker. There's darkness, then a stutter followed by light. Then after a few seconds, darkness again. The restaurant stays black. Voices in the dark are clear, calm and crisp. Andreas asks for the bill: *To logariesmo*, he says.

Slowly, through the dark, they wind their way down the hill to the path that goes along the waterfront to Hotel Poseidon. Candles are lit at the tables of outdoor *tavernas*, the one or two stores with emergency power shed dim light onto the street. As they move away from the town, it becomes increasingly darker.

"The stars," says Andreas. "Look how many stars."

The three of them stand arm-in-arm on the shore looking up. Like a million tiny candles, the stars flicker above the darkened town.

***

Happiness is a tiny glass jar. Gold with warm honey. This is how he sees it, the place in his brain reserved for joy. *I am happy*, Marco says. *I am happy*. He imagines the tip of his tongue licking the warm, sticky jar.

***

In bed, Andreas and Marco agree that without air conditioning it's best to leave the windows open. Soon Marco begins to feel the bites. There are no screens, and the room is quickly infested with mosquitoes. Andreas seems distant and sad. Marco wants to reach out, but doesn't. He wants to ask if Andreas has taken his medication, but can't bring himself to speak. He has never been supportive of the antidepressant cause and now's not the time to be pushing pills, so close to climbing the mountain. Andreas is awake. Marco can feel him thinking.

"I've stopped taking the Effexor," he says. "It was killing my libido."

"Bullshit," says Marco. "You have a perfectly normal sex drive."

"I thought you didn't like my taking medication."

"I don't," he says. "But I respect that you need it."

"They're gone," Andreas says. "I just have to face it. Mom and Dad are gone. I should never have insisted they come to our place that night."

"Let it go, Andreas," Marco says. "It's not your fault."

Andreas sits up in the dark. Marco knows something is coming, he can feel Andreas tense, he can't see him, but can see the shadow of his folded arms across his chest. "Are you fooling around on me?" he asks.

Marco has promised himself never to lie. He thinks it's a sin to make someone you love second-guess his or her intuition.

"Of course not," he says, knowing he is no longer seeing Bernd.

"Look me in the eye and say that," says Andreas.

Marco reaches over in the dark, puts his hand on Andreas' face.

"I'll never fool around on you, Andreas."

***

It was high school graduation. Andreas stood at the door in a suit that didn't fit him, the shoulders tight and the pant legs too short.

"Look how handsome our son is in your suit," Anastasia said to his father.

Andreas' father walked slowly across the room.

"Watch it, Dad," Andreas said. "I'll do my Helen Keller joke if you get too sentimental."

"It takes more than rearranging furniture to trick your old dad," his father said. "Now let me see that face."

Andreas stood still while his father moved his hands over his eyes and down his cheeks, along the nose, slowly down to the jaw.

"You shave every day now," he said. "You're probably making it with the girls?"

Andreas felt the heat in his face. Felt himself turning red.

"You're embarrassing him, Andreas," his mother said. "He's blushing."

"Proof. The blushing is proof, Anastasia. Our boy is a man now."

His father hugged him. "I'm proud of you son," he whispered.

He's determined he will be anything but queer. Andreas had asked Jessica to the graduation and she'd said yes. He sat with his parents, in the living room, waited for her to be dropped off by her brother.

"She looks like a young Nana Mouskouri," his mother said.

"Without the ugly glasses, I hope," his father said.

"No glasses, papa," Andreas said. "She has beautiful eyes," he added, trying to seem grown up.

When his mother left the room, his father patted the sofa beside him. "Come sit," he said. His tone had shifted. Even before he said a single word, Andreas knew what the conversation would be about.

"It will pass. This infatuation with boys," his father said. "It has been this way through all of history."

Andreas is shocked. They have never talked about sex before; he had no idea that his father had given any thought to his sexuality. "I don't …"

"Shhh," says his father. "Ask any Greek man if he would fight to death for his fellow soldier and he will say yes."

"You've never been in a war, papa," Andreas said.

"Not a war per se," he says. "Then I met your mother. Became a man."

***

Marco kicks off the blankets, lies in the sweltering dark—he can feel Andreas sobbing, the bed gently shaking. Andreas is clutching something in his hand, holding it to his throat. It's hard to tell in the dark—a piece of paper? What could possibly be making Andreas so upset? For some reason Bernd comes to mind. Could Andreas have found out somehow? Could he have found the *post-it* with Bernd's e-mail address and the invitation for a "hot time"? Marco never looked for it after using it once; it was pretty easy to remember: *Bernd@burn.com*. Maybe it's the job—

maybe Andreas found out that he's been fired? He knows he shouldn't have secrets from Andreas; he'll find the right moment to tell him about getting fired, it's just not now. It must be something else—probably being in Greece is making him think of his parents.

He doesn't encourage Andreas to talk, hates himself for not reaching out. The mosquitoes are biting his feet and ankles, so he turns on his side. His back against Andreas', Marco faces the wall, stares at the dirty grey stucco.

I am happy. They say you have to change the thought patterns. The brain is malleable, like vinyl, and you can change the thought grooves. *I am happy. I am happy. I am happy*. Damn mosquitoes. Stupid blackout.

***

Thursday, they're in Heraklion; Crete's capital smells like an ashtray. Marco wakes to an extraordinary sun shining through the orange curtains of the Kronos Hotel.

"It's going to be another scorcher," he says to Andreas. "And this room smells like cigarette smoke. But look at this," he says, standing at the window. "Just look at this view."

The sun rises over a castle, waves in the harbor. Andreas ignores him, pulls the covers over his head.

"Come look," he says jumping on Andreas. "Get up and look at the view from here," he says. He pins Andreas to the mattress, kisses him as the room fills with orange light.

"We have to catch the bus to Elafonissi," Andreas says, but doesn't resist the kisses.

***

Marco walks alone at Elafonissi. Andreas has asked for the evening to himself *to think*. It's impossible to nail down the precise blue of the water. Sky-blue? Teal-blue? Navy blue? Turquoise? None of these comes close. Probably because the colour is all of these in one. He watches as people gather tiny pink pebbles along the shore. A woman fills two beer cans; a child fills a plastic sand pail until it overflows. Fine as paprika, the colour of peppercorns, fleshy pink sand—the wet, bleeding shore.

He eats dinner by himself on a stone patio. It's dusk. Sparrows dart for mosquitoes. The moon sliced perfectly in half. *I am happy.*

He waits for the tug and pull in his head, but it doesn't come; instead, he worries about Andreas being alone.

28
KITTEN

It was for her own good; the cat was bleeding, but still alive. He approached her carefully, because you never know. She was pregnant with kittens and a mother will do anything when she is hurt. She couldn't have felt the rock, wouldn't have known what hit her. He didn't have time to be sentimental.

Franco told the story again of how he rescued Kitten, while they sat at the kitchen table. Marco had been sent home from school for fighting. He had a black eye and bloody nose, and his shirt was torn. His father had taken off his belt and it was coiled on the table between them.

"There were two of them," Marco said. "I fought back."

"Damn bullies," he said. "I should march down to that school right now. Who started it?"

"They did," Marco said, sobbing. "They called me a girl and Ricky threw the dodge ball right in my face."

"Why would they call you that?" his father asked. "Stand up and stop that damn sniveling," he said.

His father stood as well. He walked across the kitchen and put his empty beer bottle in the box by the stove.

"I don't know," Marco said. "They say things like that to people."

"Why a girl?" his father asked. "What were you doing?"

"Nothing," Marco said. "I was only …"

"Only what?" said his father.

"I was just talking," Marco said, lowering his head. "And skipping with a girl."

"You're a stupid boy," his father said. "A stupid, stupid, stupid boy."

The belt stung the back of his legs. *Fly high. Up to the ceiling above the bed. Through the roof and over the house. Montreal in the dark. Peaceful and sleeping.*

Then it was morning. His mother told him to roll onto his stomach. The bedroom was dark and the beds had been made.

"Your father is out looking for a job," she said.

She had a face cloth in her hand, and when she pressed it against his legs he felt the ice cubes. She held the cloth against the back of his legs with one hand, rubbed between his shoulders with the other.

"Your father loves you."

"Funny way of showing it," Marco said.

"You have to understand that where he's from boys don't play skipping with girls."

His hands were folded against his chest. The ice on his legs was making them numb.

"Turn onto your back," she said.

He didn't move. Marco pressed his fingers into his chest and pushed his face deep into the pillow. He knew she was being kind, but he didn't care. He would not move. He would never talk to either of his parents again.

She continued to rub between his shoulders. "When someone cares for you," she said. "Sometimes they do things we don't understand."

29
TUNNEL VISION

Three weeks before they left for Istanbul, Andreas said he was going to ignore the *Danger: Do Not Enter* signs, venture off the subway platforms, walk along the tracks into the underworld of the greatest cities. His plan was to start in Toronto, then move on to Montreal and Athens. He'd talked about the Brooklyn Transit museum, the massive subways of Paris, Bangkok and London. He went on about a ghost station in Berlin. He was determined to do this while he was still young.

"That's insane," Marco had said.

"I think it would be fascinating. Did you know that someone made a movie in the abandoned Bay station and renamed it *Charon*?" Andreas asked, but didn't wait for an answer. "Besides. I have been the 'good' son my entire life. Now I get to do something bad without worrying my parents to death," he said. Then, hanging his head, he added, "It's too late for that."

"Oh?" said Marco. "And do you get to be *bad* all by yourself?"

Andreas pulled Marco closer in the bed. "I've never done a single outrageous thing in my life. I need to do this alone."

"What do you mean by 'outrageous'?" asked Marco as he sat up in bed, stuffed a pillow between his back and the headboard.

"I mean," said Andreas. "You had plenty of boyfriends before we met. You partied. That's all you 'art' types at Ryerson did."

"Bullshit," said Marco. "I worked my ass off in school."

"Sorry," said Andreas. "I know that. I guess I feel sometimes that I have never done anything truly risqué. And I want to. That's all. Besides," he said. "You and I get to be Bad Boys together all the time."

"Your idea is weird, Andreas," said Marco. "I'm not trying to make you feel guilty," he'd said, "but it's dangerous."

"I'll be careful," said Andreas. "And I'll do it while you are off making movies. It won't eat up your time and I will get to live my fantasy."

"And when," said Marco, "did you become such a danger junkie?"

Andreas was quiet for a long time. The bedroom was dark, but Marco knew that Andreas had his eyes closed and was thinking.

"When I was in med school."

"Med school?"

"Yup," said Andreas. "In third year, I was staring into some British guy's eyes as he chatted away about the London Tube."

"And?"

"And he told me he got the sliver of glass I was trying to remove from under his eyelid running from the cops."

"And you found that exciting?"

"Not particularly," said Andreas. "But the notion of an underworld is. That these stations are invisible, like myth …."

"And you're just telling me this now?" said Marco. "I think you're losing it, Andreas."

Later, when they made love, Marco felt Andreas' passion. Unrestrained, forcefully alive.

"Phew," Marco said. "We better get you to the underworld. Fast!"

"You still care?" asked Andreas.

"Where did that come from?" asked Marco, not really wanting to know.

Aside from being great in bed and really attractive, Andreas was a good catch and Marco knew it. Unlike many of the guys he'd been with, Andreas was smart and kind and would never fool around on him and would stay with him until the day he died. He reached over in the dark and touched his shoulder: *I love you*, he whispered, as Andreas breathed deeply, turned in his sleep.

As luck would have it, Andreas' first opportunity to explore the seedy side of the underground came as a pleasant, low-risk surprise a week later.

"Guess what they are doing as part of Nuit Blanche this year?" Marco asked, too excited to wait for Andreas to answer. "They're giving tours of that abandoned Bay Street subway station."

"Really?"

"Yes," said Marco. "They're calling it the *Ghost Station Tour*."

"Let's do it," said Andreas. "Only let's not do it as part of the tour."

"You're kidding," said Marco.

"No, I'm not. If you prefer, I can go alone," said Andreas. "Let me know by Friday night if you're in. Subways are the heart and soul of a city. I'm so happy this is happening before we leave for vacation!"

"I don't think I agree," said Marco, hearing Andreas' excitement. "High-rises are the vantage points, the jewels and stars of a city."

***

Suddenly there was daylight. They were in a dark tunnel, the train rocking from side-to-side as they shot out onto a bridge. The sun against the window hurt his eyes. Andreas looked down, jumped up, pointing. "Look, Mom!" he said. "We're on top of a highway."

"And the river too," said Anastasia. "The Don River."

Then it was dark again. The train stopped. Doors opened. People got off and others got on. The subway train jolted as they pulled out of the station.

"Sit down," Anastasia warned. "Be careful."

Andreas remembers the crowds, the thousands of people pushing through the station and into the underground stores. Anastasia bought slippers for Andreas Sr. at The Bay then they went back down into the subway. They took another and, after a couple of stops, they walked up the stairs into daylight. They stood in front of the hospital on University Avenue. Anastasia took his hand.

"Your father's eyes will be covered," she said. "But he will know who you are."

How's that possible, Andreas wondered. *How can you see without eyes?*

"Can he see *you?*" he asked his mother.

Anastasia paused. She turned to him and squeezed his hand.

"They don't know if he'll see again," she said, "but your father loves you more than anything in the whole world."

30
BURN

Marco didn't tell Andreas that he'd lost his job. He didn't want to ruin their trip and he didn't want him to change his mind about the Trump Tower. He had enough savings to last through the summer; he'd worry about finding work after they came home from Greece. He woke in the dark every morning and walked through the quiet Riverdale streets, then across the ravine toward the city.

Walking west, the morning sun was at his back. Marco saw it reflected in the cars along the Don Valley and, once he crossed the footbridge over the expressway, he saw it in the windows of the houses of Cabbagetown. If it was rainy or too hot, he ducked into a coffee shop with his book: *Brain maps are continually changing*, Lowell wrote. *Each day is an opportunity to create a new one.*

Marco walked along Parliament Street to the Distillery District and waited for Soma Chocolate to open. The best chocolate on the planet—Kallari 70% cacao, organic, was his favourite. Through the open door, he saw enormous silver vats, inhaled the smell of cocoa, cinnamon and ginger. He found a place to sit with a coffee, scribbling down various movie plots and scenes in his journal.

Sometimes he walked with his camera. He tried to imagine the lives of the people in the tree-lined houses of

Cabbagetown with their lush gardens overflowing with zinnias, daisies, ferns and sunflowers. Early one Friday morning as he walked down Rose Avenue feeling rested and at peace with things—not worrying what to tell Andreas or where to start looking for another job—his thoughts were interrupted by the slamming of a door. A woman stepped onto the porch with a cigarette and a glass of wine. Dressed only in a short skirt and her bra, she was young, thirty at most. She had olive skin and long, dark hair—if it were the 1950s, she'd be Sophia Loren. Clearly, she hadn't expected to see anyone on her street at five in the morning, but she didn't flinch when she saw Marco and his camera. She took a long drag of her cigarette and a slow sip of wine before saying a few words to the well-built guy standing naked on the other side of the screen door. When she turned and went inside, the man cracked the door open a few inches, enough for Marco to see that he had an erection and deliciously thick thighs.

Marco kept walking up the street, but he couldn't get the image of the man out of his mind. He and Andreas were monogamous, but things hadn't been going so well in the bedroom since Andreas' parents died. After a few minutes, he heard someone behind him; it was the woman from the porch. She rushed past him wearing a black power suit and heels, holding her purse and briefcase in one hand and her laptop under her arm as she managed to carry a mug of coffee with her free hand. She looked back over her shoulder at Marco, but kept moving toward Parliament Street. Marco circled around the block. *One more peek at that hunk. Maybe he'll still be there?*

He had been waiting, his big foot holding open the door, just enough for Marco to know he was welcome.

Marco slowed his pace. At first, he pretended not to notice then he stopped and looked across the lawn to the man, still naked, behind the screen.

"You like coffee?" the man asked, holding up a mug identical to the one Marco had seen the woman carrying.

"Sure," Marco said, his body shaking. "A coffee would be good."

He walked up the steps and crossed the porch. Marco looked back over his shoulder to the street. Who did he think was watching? Who could possibly care?

His name, he said, was Bernd.

"Vern?" Marco asked.

"No," said the man as Marco kicked off his shoes in the hallway. "It's German: Bernd, sounds like burn."

A few weeks later, they met in an apartment at the Winchester Hotel, a gorgeous historical building two blocks away from the house on Rose Avenue.

"I rent this apartment so I can have a place to think," said Bernd. He sat naked in the bay window, looking out at the rain.

Marco joined him.

"You mean to get away from your wife?"

"I like my wife," said Bernd. "No. I meant what I said: I need a place to think."

Marco thought he'd died and gone to heaven. He'd met someone who knew the difference between love and possession. They sat for a few minutes, naked at the window, before Bernd stuck his head out in the rain—they had just had sex and he was covered in sweat. Marco did the same, like two gargoyles on the top floor of the old building, they laughed and howled out into the rain. When they pulled their soaking wet heads back in and rolled onto the mattress, it was Bernd who spoke first.

"You love him?" he'd asked, and Marco nodded, *yes.*

They were quiet for a few minutes then began to discuss movies. Hours passed and they fell asleep with the rain blowing through the open window over their naked bodies.

When Marco left, Bernd handed him a green post-it with his e-mail address: bernd.burn@hotmail.ca *'Any time for a hot time,'* he wrote.

"Call me," he smiled. "We can still talk movies, no?"

Marco stuck the post-it in his back pocket. He made a note to himself to remove it before laundry day.

Bernd Luft was a producer. Everyone knew his movies *Midnight Honesty, Oasis, Union Station* and *Good Life Bad.* He had brains, money and really, really good looks. His wife was "an accessory," he'd said.

"In this day-and-age, why would you need to pretend?" Marco had asked.

"You're joking," laughed Bernd, giving him one final kiss on the lips at the doorway. "You want to make a movie and you don't understand what props are for?"

"What's in it for her?" Marco asked.

"Sex, security, the same things we all want."

One day, rather than crossing the footbridge between Riverdale and Cabbagetown, Marco took the path down to the park at the bottom of the hill. He walked out to the baseball field and sat on the first base. Each workday morning for four years, he'd taken the all night Queen streetcar west to the MBTV station to be there on time for the morning showing; now, he sat alone in the dark. Absolute five a.m. silence. He had been awake before the birds and even had to strain to hear the rumble of traffic building on the parkway. No people or streetcars. Not even an early morning mosquito to disturb him. He took his notebook and a large thermos of coffee from his backpack. It wasn't a lie that he'd been telling Andreas; he was just delaying the truth. Writing was work, he rationalized—this is how a movie-maker creates; besides, why make Andreas sadder than he already was? And then it hit him: this is what solitude feels like. Alone in the dark, sitting on a baseball diamond in the belly of a dusty park— no boss, no *Maniac* theme song repeating in his head. Marco lay back in the gravel and looked up. He thought about the night sky—so much distance between us and them—the spinning, shocking, falling stars. *I am happy.*

The brain, David Lowell wrote, *is like everything in the universe—expanding, shrinking...it's up to us to direct how the change goes.*

Marco made a decision not to waste his time on the past. No more memories of dead kittens. No dark house of Ville-Émard or basement of Saint Bruno. He sat up, lifted his camera from his backpack and directed it at the sky. *It's all good here,* he'd told himself. The shimmering stars are half-hidden in the dark, but they exist. He was ready to be there one-hundred-percent for Andreas, give himself the full intensity of his love. When they first met on Euclid Avenue, it wasn't just the great sex; Marco loved

Andreas for the respect he had for his parents. *I respect them because they respect each other*, he would say. He loved Andreas for his calm, steady approach to problems; his sincerity and unbridled emotions—when he was hurt, the tears would flow and he would sob until the grief was out of his system; when he was happy, his laughing would make Marco smile for hours. In those early days, before his parents' deaths, Andreas saw the world as a gentle place; he was optimistic, ecstatic and careless ... except for in his work. *When I look into someone's eyes*, he would say, *I see what makes them live.*

Marco packed up the notepad and thermos, took his time walking across the park. He got soaked as the rain came down hard. Still, there was no hurry as he crossed the footbridge. Traffic was building, horns and headlights. He watched the rain retreat as light seeped through the parting clouds—the day was unfolding—hope lay in its mysterious grey-mauve creases. *I am happy*, Marco thought, as he crossed the sun-splashed bridge.

***

It's raining the morning they leave for their vacation. Andreas is outside loading the suitcases in the car. Marco can't believe how lucky he is. Andreas is smart and handsome and crazy in love with him, and they are on their way to a spectacular vacation. But there's a problem: no matter how hard he tries, Marco can't get his brain to believe his good fortune. In his mind, he runs his tongue over Andreas' entire body; he feels the strong back, kisses the warm, sexy lips. *I am happy*, he tells himself again. But the heat and flame of the thought fizzle as he bends to hide the key to the house under the flowerpot by the back door. *I want to be alone*, is what he really thinks.

31
NIGHTHAWKS

Manya keeps herself amused by creating hair bands that cost more to make than she sells them for. At least she's creating. At least she's having fun. The tourists love her Greek series; the Arched Victory hair band made of gold leaf laurel branches; her Greek lovers, a curved row of naked men performing various sex acts. She displays them prominently on a bright orange silk scarf. She asked the owner at the Poseidon for permission to sell her work there.

"No problem," he said with a smile. "I'll take one of these." And bought one of the Greek lovers.

***

The marathon is a week away. Mind over body, Manya trains along the pebbled roads. Except for minor pain in her hips, her body is strong. As she runs, she practices her mantra: *Eat dust, George. Eat dust.*

***

"Why would you want to do that?" George had asked. "Run a marathon."

"Why not?"

"Because you'll ruin these," he said, putting his hand on her leg.

They were at the Wyndham. The room was dark, but she could tell it was morning by the light coming through the cracks in the curtain.

"My legs will not get ruined," she'd said. "That's kind of dumb."

The truth was he'd started to be possessive of her. She shouldn't be walking through the campus at night, he'd say. Or, she shouldn't take the CTA trains and buses alone.

"Who's the guy who dropped you off in the lobby?" he'd asked when she arrived.

"He's in my Life Drawing class," she'd replied.

"Yeah, I bet," George said. "Is he the model?"

"No. He isn't the model. And so what if he was? Don't you think the fact that you're married makes this argument a little one-sided?"

"Maybe," he'd said, sliding his hand between her legs. "But I'm not sleeping with her right now."

"And I'm not sleeping with Ryan either."

Manya knew she should get out of bed and get dressed. She should pull on her jeans and shoes and walk out the door. She should walk down the hallway with its bright lights and tacky carpet and press the button for the elevator. If he followed her, she would run. She was fast. She could easily outrun him. Instead, she turned and kissed him, full on the lips.

"He's a friend for crying out loud!"

"Promise?" he'd said.

"Promise."

Eat dust George. Eat dust, is what she should have said.

***

Manya listened when George said that he had *tried*, but would *never* be understood by his wife. Weekends in the hotel consisted mostly of rented movies, take-out food, and sex. He kissed her neck; he kissed her breasts and her navel.

George wanted to see her school.

"Why don't we go there for breakfast?" he asked.

He wanted to see what student life is like. He wanted to relive his college days.

"The food is pretty bad," she'd said.

"But you'll be there," he told her, kissing her breast. "And you're delicious."

"And you are disgusting," she said. "Enough sex. I'm famished."

They lined up for lumps of steamy scrambled eggs, strips of greasy bacon and home fries. It was strange for her to be away from the hotel room with him. He was handsome and confident and wore tight jeans to show off his ass. They lined up to pay a cashier with big boobs and no bra.

"I'll pay," he insisted, winking at the cashier.

"I have money, George," she said. "Remember. I have an inheritance."

"So do I," he said, kissing her on the top of the head.

"She's about sixteen years old, George," Manya said, as they walked away from the cashier. "I saw you wink at her."

"It was a joke," he said. "Look, the poor kid's blushing."

No sooner had they found a table and sat down when George stood up and announced that he had forgotten his cutlery. Manya could have given him a minute or two and then walked back and caught him hitting on the cashier. She might have even caught him handing her his telephone number on the back of a napkin. But she didn't move from the table. She looked down at her eggs, stirred them with her fork. They were runny and getting cold, but she would wait. She wouldn't cause a scene at her school. *He can't help himself*, she told herself. *Men are different; they're impulsive and driven.*

"Sorry about that," he said, rushing back to the table. "They ran out of plastic forks and we had to go looking for more."

"We?" she'd asked.

"Don't tell me you're jealous," he said, tapping her head with the plastic fork.

32
KOUFONISSI

They sit on a rock watching Andreas swim. He takes a long time to surface from his underwater dives.

"Andreas has this thing where he counts ten 'steamboats' each time he dives," says Marco. "It's something his father taught him when he was young. Apparently, it's good lung conditioning in case he's drowning some day."

"I think Andreas misses his dad and mom," Manya says.

"Andreas is one of the strongest and smartest men that I've ever met," says Marco. "He'll figure it out."

"Wisdom has nothing to do with this, Marco," she says. "It's his heart that's breaking, not his head."

"I appreciate that, Manya," he says. "But I'm trying to make a movie *and* I don't have a paying job anymore *and* I haven't told Andreas *and* ... oops."

"You haven't told him that you got fired?"

"I couldn't," he says. "There were times last year when Andreas seemed as dead as his mom and dad. It wasn't easy, you know. Not everyone has the strength to run through trouble."

"Is that why you think I run?" she asks. "I run through trouble?"

"Let's face it," he says. "You don't sit still for too long."

"Running is good for the brain. It needs oxygen," Manya says. "Besides, running inspires me. I have my most creative moments when I'm near exhaustion."

"That makes sense," says Marco. "The brain is like a muscle, but I don't quite buy your excuse."

"Andreas needs you. You have to try harder for him."

"And what makes you such an expert on us, already?"

"I'm not saying I'm an expert on you and Andreas," she says. "I'm just telling you what I see. Besides," she pauses, "I've had lots of experience with gay couples."

"Oh?" says Marco. "Do tell."

"Well," says Manya. "It's kind of a long story … they own a grow-op called Organically Oregon … it's part of the reason I went to Chicago to study art."

33
GORGE

She sees by shadow and light, by shape and contrast, by the tightness in her shoulders when she's far above the tree line; looking down, Manya is on the bus to the Samariá Gorge. She sketches in her journal; one row behind, Marco and Andreas look at pictures from their trip to Naxos.

Along with twenty or so other tourists, the three of them get off the bus and stand at the entrance to the park. The walls of the gorge go straight up. A sign on a post reads: EXTREME DANGER FALLING ROCK MOVE FAST.

"That sign is hilarious!" says Manya. "What are we standing here for?"

The crowd moves forward into the canyon; the three of them hang back.

There are hundreds, possibly thousands of *inukshuk* in the Gorge. They are piled along tree branches, on boulders, along cliffs, and at the bottom of the dried up riverbed.

"This is sick," Manya says. "Looks like every person who has ever come through here has built one of these things."

"Sick?"

"Sick means good," Marco tells Andreas.

Manya bends to gather stones, telling Marco and Andreas to walk ahead so she can build her own tiny *inukshuk*.

She stands still, senses the sacredness of the place—the underside of cliffs layered with rocks, the hawk with wings like enormous black fingers circling the sky. Next to her, the roots of an old cedar wrap around a giant boulder like a claw or hand; a yellow butterfly flutters slowly past. The stones feel warm with spirit. She places the base of her *inukshuk* on the belly of a large, grey boulder, and then a smaller stone on each end. She thinks about each stone as she places it. When it's complete, she stands back to admire—suddenly, cicadas, full volume; and then silence, pervasive and disturbing. She catches up with Andreas and Marco. The three of them sit under a fig tree, sipping from water bottles, eating apples while fallen figs near their feet attract bees.

Marco stands to shake off his apple, but a persistent bee won't let go.

"Why they want my lousy bruised apple when there are all those sweet, delicious figs all over the ground, I don't know," he says.

Manya points to a group of tourists walking toward them.

"It's a herd of smokers!" says Andreas. "Every single one of them has lit up."

"Let's get out of here," says Marco, dropping his apple on the ground for the bees.

"Run!" says Andreas, laughing at the over-the-top reaction to the smokers. "Let's get to the safety of the falling-rocks gorge."

"Well, I'm going to say something," says Manya, pulling out a stack of *Ashes to Ashes* brochures.

34
BLUE STAR FERRY

Marco has learned to go with the flow. He's beginning to understand that Greeks are masters of moving people across water. He doesn't panic because the inbound ferry is late; he won't worry because a ridiculous number of people are waiting to board the ferry by the time it arrives. And even though no one says a word, they know when it's time to leave—pushing, waving, shuffling—the crowd surges forward along with a few dozen trucks.

It's almost over, the swimming and the walking, the quiet and the sun. They will take the overnight ferry to Athens, and from there they'll take the train to Litochoro and Mount Olympus for the climb and Manya's marathon. Marco looks back at Andreas, who has been shoved into the crowds. He appears calm. Weighed down by his backpack and duffle bag, tanned and gorgeous, he smiles at Marco. It all seems crazy and chaotic, but it feels right. Within minutes they have boarded and are undressing in their tiny cabin. Although there is hardly room to turn around, Marco is thrilled to discover there's a miniature shower. With his clothes off and the hot water running, he feels the tip and tug of the ferry pushing away from the dock. He is pleasantly surprised when Andreas joins him in the shower. There isn't much room to maneuver, but they manage. Skin burnt from the sun, salty from swimming, sex is fast and passionate. Afterwards, weak and wet, they sleep under the thin, clean sheets.

Occasionally, Marco wakes because of the surreal rocking of the ferry chugging through the dark; feeling as though he is going to fall off the edge of the bed. Next to him, Andreas seems to be dreaming, his legs kicking through some imaginary sea, as though he's swimming for his life.

35
LITOCHORO

Four or five *tavernas* edge onto the town square. All with giant television screens. All filled with men watching the World Cup soccer championship game. They smoke. Drink coffee or beer. Whenever Greece scores or makes a great save there is a collective roar. Boos and jeers when the other team does something right. No women. It frightens Marco. All-male mobs are trouble. He knows the collective energy and mindset, even at an innocent gathering, can turn on a dime. These men are full of the spirit of the sport. They are happy and united. But there are rules for being in the arena. He must not be reflective or shy. Must not cheer for the other team or be attracted to the guy with big arms. Marco looks away, but not in time. The guy taps his buddy on the arm and they both nod to where he and Andreas are sitting. They're only there because they were trying to get a cheap meal, build up carbs and protein for the climb up the mountain. Soon all of the men in the *taverna* are looking at them.

"What did you do?" asks Andreas.

"Nothing," Marco answers, remembering his father's long-ago question about the boy at school. "Let's go."

Luckily, Greece scores a tie-breaking goal; Marco and Andreas escape with only the humiliation of whistles and catcalls.

Marco likes the bed and breakfast. It's small and clean, and the old woman, Iphigenia, who looks after it, is genuinely pleasant. They have a great balcony that looks out at Olympus—a cap of snow on top, a wreath of clouds at its base. The river running alongside the B&B makes a soothing sound and the pine trees and sparrows remind him of Canada. On the rooftop patio, where they've come for breakfast, the old woman sits knitting, a television tuned on to the news. The chief of police has been shot. She shakes her knitting needles at the screen, stands as they sit at their table.

Manya joins them looking refreshed and fit. "It's almost the big day," Andreas says. "You look great."

"Yes," adds Marco. "All these Greek guys will be chasing you up the mountain!"

As always in Greece, breakfast consists of chunks of white bread, cheese-spread—*La vache qui rit*—honey, homemade jelly and *Nescafé*. The old woman moves slowly, bringing them water and more bread.

"You climb?" she asks, nodding toward the mountain. "Eat," she says, walking away.

"I can start carbing up now," says Manya, spreading cheese onto a slice of bread. "You two should be doing the same. "It's a long hike up that mountain."

"But fairly easy," says Andreas.

"Easy as ten thousand feet can be," laughs Marco.

From where they sit, they can also see down onto the fountain in the town square. Still bothered by what happened in the *taverna* the night before, Marco attempts to change his mood: *I am happy.*

"You know, Marco," says Manya, noticing his eyes are closed and that he appears to be in one of his *happy* trances. "There are other ways of helping your brain along."

"Such as?"

"I think you should create an image," says Manya. "You could, for instance, focus on the sunlight in the streams of water in the fountain. Imagine things that make you happy while you are repeating your mantra."

"He'll figure it out," says Andreas, touching Marco's hand.

Marco can hear them, but he's deep into his imagination—*I am happy*, he imagines, splashing into the sun-lit fountain.

36
ART

Manya makes people smile; wherever she goes they stop and look at her.

"It's that long, black shiny hair," says Andreas.

"No, it's not," says Marco. "Look at her body; and that smile—who has teeth that straight and white? She's too perfect to be real."

"Okay guys," Manya says. "I'm standing right here."

They are searching for a backpack in Litochoro. There's a dollar store and a Mountain Gear store on the main street. The dollar store is filled to the rafters with dusty tents, suitcases and backpacks—none of them look as though they would last five minutes in the real world. They decide to walk up the street to the pricier Mountain Gear store.

Manya is preoccupied with an e-mail she received from Joanna, a promising fourteen-year-old in her grade nine drawing class. Normally, Manya doesn't encourage her students to stay in touch; and usually, after graduation, they aren't interested in her either. But Joanna is gifted and it seems that there is no one in her home life to encourage her.

Miss Antoniades, Joanna wrote. *What do you think of my waves?*

Joanna attached a photograph of her charcoal drawing of waves. It was extraordinary. Beautiful and moving. Manya had sent Joanna immediate feedback. She explained that *how you see it* isn't like taking a photograph. *How you see it* in art has to do with trusting where the first line takes you, then the dance of waves, abandonment and the emotional content of light. This kind of lecture is too intense for most of her students, but Joanna seems to have understood.

Bravo, Joanna, she wrote back, *your waves are spectacular.* But Manya has not received a reply. Joanna's mother must have intercepted the correspondence. Joanna's mother thinks art is for heathens.

"There it is," Manya says, pointing to the store across the street. "Mountain Gear."

"And what have you been thinking about, Gorgeous?" asks Marco. "Your head seems to be somewhere else."

"Sorry," says Manya, pushing open the door. "I've been thinking about a student. Her mother wants to keep her away from the evils of art."

37
HOTEL ENIPEAS

"I have movie," says Iphigenia. "English movie."

Marco looks at the others. The room is quiet, except for the wind and the rain beating against the window. Manya looks down, picks up a ceramic statue of the Virgin; Andreas pretends to be reading a magazine.

Hotel Enipeas isn't really a hotel, it's a B&B filled with religious artifacts—a crucifix above the television, an oil painting of Jesus with a lamb above the dining room table. The guest rooms are orderly and spotless, and although Iphigenia has not said anything about Marco and Andreas, she makes a point of placing a Bible on each of their pillows and separating the two single beds they push together at bed-time each night.

"No, thank you," Marco says, certain her selection will not go beyond *The Sound of Music, The Ten Commandments* or *Sister Act.*

"You look," she says, handing Marco a stack of DVDs.

He shuffles through *The Pianist, Babette's Feast* and *Shrek.* He stops at *Moulin Rouge.* "This could be fun," he says to the others.

It's the night before the climb and they've made a pact to go to bed early. They've all agreed that they will need their wits about them because the rocks will be very slippery from the rain.

"Sure," says Manya. "I've seen it before. It's a fun movie."

"Me, too," says Andreas. "Worth seeing again."

Iphigenia takes the DVD from Marco and puts it in the player. She hands Manya the remote and sits in a chair, covering her legs with a pink and green quilt. She takes out a ball of orange wool and her knitting needles from a basket on the floor beside her.

There's a moment of awkwardness when no one moves. Then Marco sits on one end of the sofa.

"This baby's mine," says Manya, patting the chair next to Iphigenia.

Andreas sits on the other end of the sofa.

"There's plenty of room up here," Marco says, patting the space between him and Andreas.

"No. No," Manya says. "You love-birds sit closer."

Andreas smiles and looks at Marco. Iphigenia drops a knitting needle on the floor. Marco looks out the window; his headaches are back, but he won't tell the others. He loves movies and knows this one's a masterpiece. It will be a distraction and a source of inspiration. In his fantasy, he's going to run off to some far corner of the world and create a movie as complex and entertaining as *Moulin Rouge*. All he needs is a decent chunk of time alone to think it out. He'll make his father proud, put Ville-Émard on the map.

He waits as Manya sets up the movie; *I am happy*—he sends the message to his brain. Marco inhales as the thought works its way through the haze inside his head. But nothing. No subtle movement or pleasant sensation to carry him into the movie. The doctor in Istanbul was worried because he had passed out. Andreas had to keep him awake for twenty-four hours. There was an egg-sized lump and blurred vision, but no broken bones. He required a few stitches, nothing too serious, but the doctor was adamant that he should cancel the climb. For Marco, not doing the climb isn't an option. In the beginning, Marco had to convince Andreas to go up the mountain, but now Andreas has done a complete about-face and is obsessed with going to the top and Marco can't disappoint him. Besides, exercise stimulates the sensory cortices. The exercise will bring blood and oxygen to the vulnerable areas of the brain. And, there are others to consider—Manya will be joining them for the first part of the climb; she sees it as part of her training for the marathon. The three of them will set out together in the morning. They've asked Iphigenia for a 5:00 wake-up.

"I don't know," says Andreas, looking outside at the rain. "Maybe the gods are trying to tell us something about the climb."

"Relax," says Manya. "Rain never stays around for long in Greece."

I am happy, Marco tries again, as the movie begins and the camera zooms into Paris's red light district. Nothing. No subtle sensation from under his skull, only a slight itch in the back of his head where the stitches went in. He closes his eyes, takes a deep breath. He feels a shift on the sofa as Andreas moves closer—*I am happy*, he tries again. Finally, it arrives, the tingle and flow across his brain.

There is a close-up of Christian, the tortured writer—handsome and lovely, with *a story of love and tragedy* to tell. The courtesan, Satine, spits up red on her white handkerchief. She is pale and thin and the sight of the blood makes Marco dizzy, brings him back to the mugging. His head throbs and he feels sick. The others can't know. A good night's sleep will take care of the nausea.

"This is a digital masterpiece," he says. "Look at the colours. The sets are brilliant."

"And hilarious," says Manya. "I love the Long Suffering Penniless Poet."

Andreas whispers to Marco: "Are you all right?"

"Shhhh…" he says. "The good part is coming. The scene where Satine uses her acting skills to convince Christian that she doesn't love him."

"That's terrible," says Andreas. "Why would you like that scene? My favourite part is when Christian sings *It's a Little Bit Funny* to her."

"Christian is gorgeous," whispers Marco. "His eyes sparkle like little emeralds through his entire song."

"His eyes are blue," says Andreas.

"Green."

"Blue."

"*Shhhh…*" says Iphigenia, shaking her knitting needles at them.

The scene where Bollywood meets Hollywood is manic and beautiful—an extraordinary outbreak of people, sounds and colours. The cameras are everywhere at once. The audience at the Moulin Rouge seems to merge with the audience watching—when the Evil Duke gets hold of the gun, Marco feels as if he can run right over and tackle him.

The final scene when Satine is dying on stage in front of a gasping audience is gut-wrenching. Christian's pleading and tears are arresting. Limp and pale in his arms, Satine is tragically gorgeous—it's the perfect ending to a tragic love story. Marco can hear the others sniffling. He rests his head on Andreas' shoulder.

Iphigenia passes Manya a box of tissues. "How beautiful," Manya says. "What a rollercoaster ride."

"Did you know that Orpheus brought Eurydice back from death?" Andreas says, after Iphigenia switches on the lamp by her chair. "He did it with music so beautiful it made the plants and rocks weep."

"Those myths are very powerful," Manya says.

"Don't say myth," says Marco. "Andreas thinks they're true. Get him to tell you about Icarus falling into the sea or Persephone banished to the underworld and he'll start sobbing."

"That's not very nice, Marco," says Manya. "Who are we to say what happened in the past? Maybe there were half-human, half-animal gods roaming the planet?"

"A girl after my own heart," says Andreas. "I think that I will take the non-believer to bed now."

"Goodnight," Marco says. "Tomorrow's the big adventure!"

"Goodnight my handsome co-climbers," Manya says, kissing Andreas on the cheek and Marco on the forehead. "Conserve your strength for the big day."

Iphigenia has already left the room. The quilt is folded neatly on the chair, her knitting needles forming a cross over the ball of wool.

***

In their room, Marco and Andreas move the beds closer. Transforming two single beds into one king-sized mattress is an art. First, they have to move the two frames closer then push the mattresses together until they touch. The single sheets are covered by the bedspread, which acts as a unifying undercover, then the blankets. Marco's headache is gone and he feels sexy.

"We should save our strength," Andreas says. "Big day tomorrow."

Marco tries to act grown up. "Sure," he says, but Andreas picks up the anger in his tone.

"This is not rejection," he says, pulling Marco closer. "You know sex is something I never turn down."

It's true. Andreas, before his parents' deaths, had always been big on passion. But Marco can't help himself. "Let's push the beds apart then," he says. "Why risk the temptation?"

Marco gets out of bed and pulls the headboard away from the wall.

"You're being ridiculous," Andreas said. "And don't talk to me about temptation…"

"What are you getting at?" asks Marco, certain now that Andreas has found out about Bernd.

"Never mind," he says. "Just stop being ridiculous."

Marco walks to the foot of his bed and pulls it away. He goes to the top and does the same at that end. Inch by inch - top of the bed and then the bottom, top of the bed then the bottom - he separates the two.

"Great," says Andreas. "What's bothering you?"

"Everything," says Marco. "The weather. These stupid little beds. Manya and her perky little Ashes to Ashes campaign. We should never have invited her along."

"But you *loved* her a few days ago."

"Well, I've changed my mind," Marco says. "She's a sell-out. She could have been a great artist and she sold out."

"She's twenty-five years old, Marco. She has plenty of time to be 'great'."

"This stupid anti-smoking campaign and all her girly-girl pink everything. I mean, seriously, have you ever seen her in any other colour? And her running," he says. "It's a blatant metaphor for avoidance. Think about it, Andreas. Have you ever had an in-depth conversation with her about anything?"

"She teaches art, Marco. She's not stupid."

"Don't kid yourself. She was given a break that some people would kill for and she's throwing it away."

"Come here," says Andreas, patting the mattress. "What break?"

"She told me. Her grandmother was famous and left everything to her. She's got a fortune. She doesn't have to work. She doesn't have to make those stupid hair bands.

169

She's doing this cigarette thing out of guilt because her grandmother died of cancer."

"You need to leave your job, Marco. Take a risk. Get out of that television studio. There's nothing wrong with Manya. From what I can see, she's perfectly happy."

"Well," says Marco. "For an ophthalmologist, you're blind as a bat."

"And what are you getting at?" asks Andreas.

"Never mind," says Marco. "It's about work. But I don't want to get into it now."

"Fine," Andreas says, turning off the bedside lamp. "Go to sleep. We can talk tomorrow."

"Sleep?" says Marco. "I'm going for a walk."

"Look who's running now," Andreas mutters.

***

Manya stretches in bed, a good stretch the way her cat does, not the painful stretch she endures before and after each run. She falls asleep quickly. In her dreams, she is running through Manhattan. The cars pull aside for her. Pedestrians move off the sidewalk. Times Square is a mountain—covered with sheep, goats, trees, cars and neon. An installation. Surreal and glorious. She wakes with the wind and rain against the window. She gets up and looks down at the street below. The little fountain has been shut off. The *taverna* is closed and the square is empty.

38
KITTEN

The cat is white and dirty, probably because someone kicked her on to the street. She is hissing and growling, miserable and in pain. He will put her out of her misery by dropping a stone on her head. He steps on the stone with his work boots, being careful not to get blood on them—he'd spent thirty bucks on them just two days earlier. He is on his way home from work. He isn't disturbed by the sound of the cracking skull or the way the bottom teeth sticks out. He has to move fast. One of the kittens has already been born. He slices along the litter sac, and the other kittens came out, thick and limp like turds. They all died inside her, except the strongest. *Do you like her, son?* he asks. *She's a fighter.*

This is the version of the story Marco always hears when his father has been drinking.

"Nature has its way," Franco says. "The right way and the wrong way. If you know what I'm saying."

Marco knows where the conversation is heading.

"Where'd you get the new shirt, Dad?" he asks.

But his father can't be diverted. "When you get to Toronto, stay away from the queers," he says.

"Sure, Dad," Marco says. "We should probably take the boots off."

"Do you have a roommate there?" his father slurs.

"I have three roommates," says Marco. "It's expensive in that city."

"Oh, son," his father says. "There will be orgies in that house. Four young guys with normal sex drive … it will be one girl after the other."

"We'll be studying, Dad," says Marco. "Film school is hard."

"Film School? Oh, yeah," his father says. "Don't know if there's a living in that."

***

The streets of Litochoro are quiet and dark. Except for the occasional stray cat, nothing is moving. There isn't a sound, only the rain and his feet splashing through puddles. Marco mulls over what Andreas said. Of course, he's right. Andreas is always right, damn it. The realization that he is jealous of Manya hits him like a hard fact. An image of Bernd standing naked in the window of the Winchester racks him with shame. He crouches against a wall. At first the sadness is slow, nothing more than tightness in his chest and throat, but when he gets to his feet tears flow, and the crying is deep. Why be so nasty to Andreas? Why the guilt? After all, he only saw Bernd for two weeks.

***

Manya feels like a warm-up run. She looks out the window. It's still raining; streetlamps light up the cobblestones. She finds her shorts and her sweatshirt. She slides a hair band on, bends to pick up her shoes. She finds her way through the dark and cracks open the door.

***

Marco will make it up to Andreas on the climb. He'll carry the heavy backpack; rub his stiff shoulders and aching feet. *I am happy.* He lifts his head, looks down the cobblestone street. Pink shorts and sweatshirt, a flash of pink in the rain, it's Manya running toward him.

She stops and stands next to him. "Are you all right?" she asks.

Marco feels raw, but the darkness seems to have lifted.

"I'm fine," he says, looking up at her.

"Fucked up, Insecure, Neurotic and Enjoying it," she says. "F.I.N.E."

Marco laughs. "No, really," he says. "I'm okay."

"You know," she says, kneeling beside him. "Your secrets will kill you."

Marco thinks for a moment. She's right. He has to talk to someone or he'll burst.

"Andreas would die if he knew," says Marco. "Can you keep a secret?"

"He already knows," says Manya.

"Knows what?"

"Your secret," she says, standing and stretching one leg and then the other. "The one being cheated on always knows. I have no idea if he knows for a *fact*," she says. "But he adores you, and he's no fool."

173

Marco feels defensive, but before he can say anything, she is off again—a flash of pink in the rain.

39
ASCENT

"Part of going up is coming down," Andreas says. "Some say coming down is harder."

"I'll worry about that on the way down," says Marco looking over to the mountain. "Let's get up there first."

They are walking the trail between Litochoro and Mount Olympus. They have decided to walk the eleven kilometres and meet Manya at the log cabin restaurant at the base of the mountain in Prionia. The rivers, cliffs, rock formations and trees are extraordinary. Up a steep hill and then down again to link up with the next path, the next hill. Marco has always had flying dreams. When he was eighteen, he and three friends drove from Montreal to Manhattan just to see the Empire State building. He has always loved tall buildings, has always dreamt of heights. Over treetops and cities. Over valleys and along rivers. In one dream, he was a flying Rabbi from a Chagall painting.

Marco has pain in his right knee, but otherwise this part of the journey is uneventful. He can't believe he is going to climb a mountain. He looks up and sees Olympus in the distance. He gets his first pang of fear. *I am going to climb a mountain.* The drops are shear, several thousand feet. People have died on the mountain. They don't have ropes or climbing boots. They are both fit, but not athletes. Andreas hangs back, waiting for him to catch up.

"It's probably not such a good idea for us to be too close," he says.

"Why not?" asks Marco.

"What if the one in front slips or something?"

Marco gives him a look.

"Ever hear of the domino effect? If the guy in front falls, he takes the other one with him."

"Fine," says Marco. "I'll hang back."

After about a kilometre, they come to a rest area that surprises them because it has a river. They are both overheated and thirsty.

"Go for it," says Andreas when he sees Marco eyeing the river. "It's as pure as you'll ever get."

The water is cold and wonderful. It's odd to be drinking water that doesn't taste of chlorine or plastic.

"It tastes like nothing," says Marco. "Delicious."

40
EURIPIDES

"The guy with the donkeys is called Euripides."

"For real?" Marco asks, thinking back to the pet names that Andreas has for everyone at the Tim Hortons at home: Hermes, Kronos...

"For real," says Andreas. "I heard the tour guide at the rest area tell them."

"You know that there are a lot of upset priests in Greece because of the trend for young couples to name their kids after the ancient heroes and gods."

"Well, it could be awkward baptizing an Electra, Apollo, Athena or Pericles," says Andreas. "But what an honour to be named after Zeus or Poseidon."

"They weren't real people," says Marco. "You're supposed to name your kid after someone real."

"Who says they weren't real," says Andreas. "What do people know these days beyond CTV and CNN? The older generations respected these stories. If my mom and dad were here right now they'd been ecstatic to be so close to the gods."

41
MARCO

The mid-mountain refuge is adequate. There is food and cold water for showers and drinking. There are bunk beds, four to a room. Marco on the top, Andreas on the bottom. Lights out by ten. The two Swedish guys in the other two bunks snore. The moon lights up the room.

Marco decides to risk a kiss and slides down to Andreas. A kiss leads to another and then they whisper. "A two-minute cuddle," says Andreas.

"Sure," says Marco, his hands beginning to roam.

Morning comes and he feels rested. It's the tall Swedish guy who wakes him as he shuffles across the floor in the dark; Marco moves closer to Andreas, pulls the blankets over his head.

After dry cereal and yogurt, they make peanut butter sandwiches and take them outside with cups of steaming coffee.

Church bells, goat bells, bells on the necks of the donkeys arriving with food for the refuge.

"Those dogs are happy," says Andreas.

"What makes you say that?" says Marco.

"Look at them running across the snow down there. Through the woods, up through the trails. Just the two of them roaming and running. Living 100% by instinct—that's freedom. That's joy."

"But they're starving to death," says Marco. "I wouldn't turn your back on that sandwich."

***

The trees are gone and the birds; only the sound of the wind pushing over the rocks and light over the tree tops and the lesser mountain; they are about eight thousand feet up. Marco is acutely aware that it's a long way down. It feels different from New York's high-rises or the way he imagines the Trump will be. He tries to lean into the climb; Andreas is about ten feet ahead, but he is having difficulty breathing. The rocks are smaller and looser up here closer to the peak. Andreas slips back a little. Marco is gasping for oxygen.

Manya has come as far as Skala. "Are you okay?" she asks Marco.

"I'm good," he says, not too sure if he really is.

Manya has been encouraging. She'll continue the climb to Skolio, the two-thousand-nine-hundred-and-twelve metre peak—then turn back to Litochoro. Andreas and Marco will go from Skala to Mytikas—only six hundred metres more, but it will involve a thirty-minute rock scramble.

"There's a big difference between being a tourist and a mountain climber," Manya told them. "You guys be careful."

"Do you really have to go?" asks Marco.

"Come on," shouts Andreas, a few feet ahead. "You'll see Manya again when you get back."

42
UNDERWORLD

The large black dog on the rain-beaten path ahead is a frightening vision; a soaking-wet, large black dog that isn't wagging its tail, barking or growling, makes Marco stop dead in his tracks.

"It came from over there," he says, pointing to a cave not too far from where they are standing.

"Ah," says Andreas. "Skylos. Hellhound."

"It's a stray dog."

"A dog eight thousand feet up, coming out of a cave, is something to notice."

"How the hell did you ever get to be a doctor?" asks Marco. "I've never met anyone as superstitious as you."

Then it disappears. They turn away for a second, and the dog vanishes. Marco walks through the rain to where it came from, looks down into a dark cave.

"It's gone," he says.

"That's my point," says Andreas. "You probably shouldn't get too close to that cave. The underworld is no place for an unbelieving tourist-turned-mountain climber."

"You freak me out when you talk about hellhounds and spirits."

"We *are* on Mount Olympus," he says. "Do you think these myths just came out of nowhere?"

"Yes," says Marco. "All stories come out of thin air."

"Thin air and *experience*."

"What kind of experience?" Marco asks, inching across the wet stone. "It's not like anyone has ever seen the *Underworld* for real."

"I'm saying don't dismiss the fact that a big, ugly dog just appeared eight thousand feet in the air and then, just as quickly, vanished."

Marco feels as though he is being watched. He looks back at the cave. "Did you see that?" he asks Andreas.

"See what?"

"Something with big teeth and big eyes looking out of the cave."

"Start whistling," says Andreas. "Walk fast and don't look back."

Marco crosses a patch of wet, sharp stone and begins to feel dizzy. His eyesight is blurred and the ground beneath him feels like it's about to crack open. *Great*, he thinks to himself as he slides back. *I survive brain surgery and being mugged only to fall off some stupid-ass mountain in a country far from home.*

"Get both feet on the ground," Andreas shouts. "Straighten up!"

But he can't. Marco can't stand straight or stop his body from sliding toward the cauldron. It has begun to rain and the stone is becoming harder to grip. He looks down and feels sick.

"Marco! Drop your backpack!"

"I can't let go of the rock," he shouts back. "I feel dizzy."

"Unclip, now! You'll stop sliding if you're lighter."

Marco hears the urgency in Andreas' voice. He hears him getting farther and farther away. His fingers are raw from trying to grip the sharp rocks. The thought of dying paralyzes him. He's almost too frightened to breathe. He focuses on the backpack, slowly moves one hand toward the clip. The jolt of the release almost sends him flying back—he can't look, but he hears the backpack sliding across the scree, followed by silence as it falls over the edge into the cauldron.

"Are you all right?" Andreas shouts. "Look up, not down."

"I'm scared stiff," Marco answers, but he takes a small step forward. Inches his way up to Andreas, whose back is pressed against the rocks, rain streaming down his worried face.

Marco inhales, struggles to get oxygen. The cool air from the rain helps with his breathing, but every inch up the mountain seems like a mile. He inhales again. Each step is calculated and careful, a suitable measure of reach and defiance. He looks up toward the peak of the mountain; they've covered a lot of ground and he feels more solid on his feet without the backpack. *I am happy. I am happy. I am happy.*

Andreas is behind him now. "Take your time, Sweetheart," he says. "I've got you if you start sliding back again."

43
GRAFFITI

"We did it!" Marco yells. "The top of Olympus, Mytikas!"

"The Throne of Zeus," Andreas says, looking out over the mountain range. "Greece is my kingdom!" he jokes, pink-faced and smiling.

Marco takes Andreas' hand. "Let's savor the moment."

They stand side by side. The air is cool and the sun feels warm on his face. "I understand Joni's song now," Marco says.

"Which one?"

"The one about clouds. You know, *I looked at clouds from both sides now…*"

"I don't think she meant the lyrics to be taken so literally," Andreas says, looking down at the layer of mist covering the deep cauldron.

"I know that," says Marco. "I get the metaphor. I'm just saying that I understand the melancholy tone, the joy of experiencing something incredible and then the sad reality of time passing, the inevitable letting go."

"Look who's the Greek philosopher now," says Andreas, giving Marco a hug.

"Turn around," Marco says.

When Andreas turns, Marco lifts the pack off his back.

"A pillow," Marco says, pointing to the backpack. "Get down here," he adds, patting the ground next to him.

He unzips Andreas' jacket and slides his hand under his sweater. He feels Andreas' warm skin and his heart pounding as he draws him close. He kisses him on the lips. They are free, above the world. No doors to shut or blinds to draw. Marco holds Andreas tight. They make love on a small patch of rock—uninhibited, no thought to what could happen if they get too near the edge.

"Wow," says Andreas. "That was amazing. You were totally out of control!"

"What's that supposed to mean?" Marco asks.

"Abandoned. Over-the-top sexy," Andreas answers. "Don't be so defensive."

"You make it sound like I'm usually uptight." Marco can see Andreas feels bad, but he keeps going. "You're the one who has been down this whole trip."

"Your choice of the word *down* doesn't escape me, Marco. I told you. I stopped taking the medication. As you just witnessed, the plumbing is working just fine."

"Now don't *you* go getting defensive," says Marco. "I'm not talking about sex. Your comment about *out of control* hurt. That's all."

"I was talking about your job, Marco. It's always on your mind. The brain tumour is on your mind. Living at the top of some big city high-rise is always on your mind. Never content," he takes Marco's hand. "You're like Henderson: *I want. I want. I want.*"

"Nice holding back," says Marco, aware of the sarcasm. "Who the heck is Henderson?"

"Saul Bellow's Rain King, the guy in the book that inspired the Joni song."

"No way?" says Marco. "Joni Mitchell read Saul Bellow."

"Yes way," says Andreas, tickling Marco in the ribs. "That book inspired the lyrics, "…say I love you right out loud!"

"I get it," says Marco, pushing Andreas away and standing up. "I'm not very forthcoming in the *out loud* area. And I'm a little discontented sometimes."

But that is all Marco is prepared to give him. No apology. No confession or make up kiss. "Hey, there's graffiti up here," he says. "Who the hell would deface the top of a mountain?"

"Marco?" Andreas says. "We can talk if you want."

Feeling somewhat nauseous, Marco ignores him, and when Andreas bends to pick up a stone, he turns away.

"People have been writing their names on mountain tops and caves for a long time," Andreas says, looking at the graffiti. "This is a big moment, Marco. Look what we did together!" he says, motioning out over the hills. "Look where we are. Two feet away from a ten thousand foot drop!"

Then, letter-by-letter, rock-against-rock, Andreas begins to etch into the mountain:

MARCO@MYTIKAS

Andreas stands back, surveying his work. "Here you are, Marco. On top of the world!"

Marco is pleased, but the words that come out of his mouth don't convey gratitude.

"Happy, Andreas?" he says. "Now you too have defaced Olympus. If I see a cigarette butt up here I'm going to throw myself over the edge."

"Don't look on the ground between your feet then," says Andreas, throwing the stone over the cliff.

Going back down is easy. Marco maneuvers over a pile of rocks, lowers himself down a small ridge. Sure-footed and full of energy, his confidence soars. He's forgotten about the fight, moves at a steady pace over the loose stones.

Andreas is a few yards behind him. "Be careful," he shouts. "The rocks are still wet."

Marco can hear fear in his voice. "Don't worry," he answers, without looking back to check on Andreas.

44
MANYA

The morning of the marathon Manya wakes before the alarm. Her legs feel heavy but strong; she rubs her calves. She clenches her thighs, releases and stretches her muscles before swinging her legs over the side of the bed. She looks down at the black box near her feet. *This is it, Marina*, she thinks. *Home at last with grandmother Meltiades ashes.*

Andreas and Marco are probably home now, ecstatic after mastering the mountain. Manya walks to the bathroom in her bare feet. The floor is cool and it feels good. She stands in front of the sink brushing her teeth, can't believe how dark her skin has become since the start of training for the marathon. New York, Boston, Athens … it's been a long haul. Her hair has grown long, and her eyes stand out against her tan. She feels ready. Manya walks through the hall without turning on the light. She sees the glow of the screen saver in the front room. She sits at the computer and types out her note:

Dear Gary and Ben,

Your website looks good, I see that you've arrived in the twenty-first century. But that's not why I'm writing—to give you a backhanded compliment—I'm writing to say I'm sorry. You have no reason to forgive me, but I want you both to know

*that I think about you and our tiny house on Cannon Beach.
I'm in Greece now. I have a teaching job and I'm running the
Olympus marathon—inspired by Grandmother Meltiades-
Marina would have been happy. I'm about to put on my shoes
and head for the start line, but I couldn't do that until I sent
you this note. Thanks for involving me in your chaos. I'm a
better person for having endured your weird parenting. I miss
and love you both.*

xoxo Blind Girl Running Through the House.

Manya presses *Send*. "That feels good," she sighs.

She tiptoes in the dark, back to her room. She puts on
her *Ashes to Ashes* tank top, pulls it over her bra; then her
shorts, socks and shoes. She bends to pick up the black
box, and someone knocks on the door. She knows what
the news is. She has had a sinking feeling all night. When
she opens the door she sees Iphigenia, her hands together
as if she were praying and her head bowed.

"They no come back," she says.

Manya knows the answers to her own question, but
feels she should ask: "Did you go into their room?"

"Yes," Iphigenia says, wringing her hands, looking
around Manya's room.

"They are not in here," says Manya.

"Bed stay same in room," says Iphigenia.

"Come in," whispers Manya.

They sit on the edge of the bed. Manya feels a little
self-conscious—clothing in piles on the chairs, dirty and
clean; dishes on the bedside table; candy wrappers and

empty pop bottles on the floor next to the box with the ashes.

"I'm usually not so messy," she says, nodding at the wrappers and empty bottles.

Iphigenia doesn't say anything. Sighing, slowly walking to the door, she turns to Manya, says, "You find."

Manya closes the door behind Iphigenia. She pulls sweatpants over her shorts and her pink nylon jacket over her tank top. She fills her backpack with Power Bars, oranges and apples, a clean, dry shirt and socks. She walks back along the dark hallway and through the kitchen to the balcony. She cuts the clothesline with her Swiss Army knife. *Be prepared*, as they taught her in Girl Scouts: a rope may come in handy. In the kitchen, she fills her water bottle. As the water runs, she thinks about Andreas, his attachment to his mom and dad.

Back in her room, she puts the rope into the backpack and uses a bungee cord to secure the black box to the outside. She turns out the light and pulls the door shut behind her. She tiptoes through the hallway and finds Iphigenia sitting in the dark.

"Take this," she says to Manya, handing her a baggie with two boiled eggs.

"Thank you," Manya whispers.

"And this," Iphigenia says, handing her a blue and white cameo.

"What?" asks Manya.

"Maria," Iphigenia says, pressing the cameo into Manya's hand. "Maria Meltiades, brave woman for all of Greece."

Manya bends down and hugs Iphigenia. "Thank you," she says, kissing her on the cheek.

She takes a taxi from the Litochoro Taverna to Prionia at the foot of the mountain. The fifteen-minute ride seems to take hours. She hands the driver forty euros and walks into the dark with a flashlight. One step and then the next. She jogs over a small footbridge, up a pathway with a marker pointing up to the summit. One step and then the next, she picks up her pace as the sun begins to bring light to the dark path. She resists her desire to sprint, knows that she'll need her strength. She has no idea what she will find, if anything, but there's no time for doubt. One step and then the next.

45
MARINA

One July morning in Washington Square Park, Marina is silent for a long time. She wears an oxygen mask and rests on their favourite bench. Manya is ten; she sits close to her mother and draws in her scrapbook. Although it's only nine in the morning, it's already very warm. Manya looks over at Marina, who has her eyes closed, a Kleenex in one hand and the tubing for the oxygen in the other; she stares down at her drawing, but can't concentrate on the picture; she turns to her mother again: "Would you like some Coke?" she asks.

"That would be nice," Marina says, nodding her head, the plastic tube bouncing on her chin.

Manya takes the drink from her school bag, and twists off the lid. The soda is warm; it fizzes and spills. Marina smiles, reaches over and pats Manya's leg dry with the soggy tissue she has been holding in her hand.

"Thank you," Manya says.

"Thank you," Marina says back.

Others arrive in the park—the usual dog walkers, a man with the *Times,* a woman with two small boys.

"Your father lives in Cannon Beach, Oregon," Marina says, without turning to Manya. "You should go see him."

"Go see him?" says Manya. "I don't even know him."

"Pass me my purse," says Marina. "I have a picture of Ben for you."

Manya reaches into the front part of the walker and pulls out her mother's purse. She sets it on her lap. Marina digs around for her wallet.

"He's gay," she says, handing Manya a crumpled photograph.

"Bengay?" says Manya, laughing, but stops when she sees the expression on Marina's face.

"He used to get in trouble when he was young. But, hey," Marina adds, trying to sit straight. "That's all out of his system now and he wants you to visit. And," she continues, faking excitement, "he has a really nice friend named Gary. You could have two dads."

"That's gross," says Manya, hanging her head. She's on to her mother. She will not go to Cannon Beach. She looks at the photograph.

"He looks weird," Manya says. "Yuck, he has long hair and a beard."

"They grow things," says Marina.

"Like what?"

"Herbs."

"Whatever," says Manya, dropping her scrapbook on the ground.

"Manya?" says Marina. "You'll have to go, sweetheart."

"Why?" asks Manya.

"My health is getting worse."

"I won't go," she says.

"You can run and swim," says Marina. "They live near the ocean."

Manya climbs up on the park bench, puts her head on her mother's lap. The oxygen machine makes gurgling noises. She closes her eyes.

Marina places her hand on Manya's head, gently strokes her hair. "Melissa," she says. "My little bee."

***

Ben and Gary come to Marina's funeral. They dress in black suits that look too small for them and they smell like lavender and sage. Manya sits between them kicking the underside of the pew with the backs of her heels.

"Shhh," says Ben, gently touching her arm.

But she doesn't stop. Her legs keep moving—tap, tap, tap, tap, tap, tap. In her mind, her mother is not that still, dead woman in the box with white skin and red lips. Her real mother sits on the bench in Washington Square Park marking students' papers, watching closely as Manya runs circles around the fountain. *Run*, Marina says, cheering her on. *Run, Manya. Run.*

They are younger than she thought they would be. Ben tells her his "Big Three-O" is coming up, and Gary says he's not far behind.

"We were really young, Manya," Ben tries to explain, about his relationship with Marina. "First year at NYU. I was nineteen."

They sit on the steps outside the church. The others have all gone, mostly people from their apartment building and Marina's students. They look at her with sad faces; two teenage girls bring her flowers and tell Manya that her mom was *the best prof ever*.

"There are beaches with giant boulders in the water," says Gary.

"Yes," says Ben, watching Manya kick her legs. "You can run as fast as your little heart desires all over Cannon Beach."

They'd driven all night. Manya was in the back seat with boxes and bags; Ben and Gary were in the front listening to music. After about four hours of driving through the dark, Gary lit a joint.

"I'm not about to hide who I am," he said when Ben gave him a dirty look.

"Mom smoked it for pain," said Manya, speaking for the first time since they got in the car.

"What!" said Ben, almost swerving off the highway, "Miss Goody Two Shoes?"

It was Gary's turn to give the dirty look to Ben.

"I mean," said Ben, struggling for words. "Your mom had certain rules."

By the time they stopped at The Lazy Susan Café in Portland, Manya had decided that she would live with these guys, at least until she was big enough to run away. They played the radio really loud and they sang together. When Gary sang the words *like a virgin*, he'd clutch his chest, pretend to be Madonna. They seemed gentle, and she'd already figured out that, unlike her mother, they would be easy to outsmart. They told her they go back to New York, at least once a year, to deliver their *product*.

"What's product?" Manya asked as Ben steered the car along the interstate.

Both men were silent for a moment, then, Ben told her that *product* is what they grow.

"Like what?" she asked.

"Oh," said Gary, struggling for words. "Just things that we have lots of room to grow in the hothouses."

"Oh," said Manya. "You mean weed."

The men didn't answer. Neither of them said a word. *This is going to be fun*, Manya thought to herself.

The restaurant is a big farmhouse with two tables set up in the front room. The dining room smells like coffee, bacon and burnt toast.

"What would you like for breakfast, Little One?" Ben asks her, lowering the menu from his face.

Manya thinks back to the routine. Every morning Marina would make her way to the kitchen. She would plug in the kettle for tea, and put the frying pan on the stove for eggs. Two fried eggs, and toast with peanut butter. One slice each. A small glass of orange juice and a low-fat yogurt.

"I'll have eggs and toast and yogurt," says Manya to the waitress.

"How would you like your eggs, darling?" she asks.

"Like the start of a good morning—bright and sunny side up."

The grownups laugh, but to Manya her comment is not a joke; she'd heard that phrase from her mother almost every morning of her life. At first when she starts to cry, they try to console her, especially the waitress who sits next to her.

"What's wrong, sweetheart?" she asks.

"Her mother just died," said Ben, looking at the waitress for help.

Manya could feel the waitress's warm hand on her back. She could tell that Ben was worried. She cried harder and harder, and after a few minutes of trying to shush her, she heard the waitress say, "Let her go.. This little girl needs to fall apart."

***

"You're too young to be off on your own," Ben had said. "Chicago is no place for a sixteen-year-old girl to be hanging out."

"Yes," Gary piped in. "They'll eat you alive and spit your bones to the ground."

"Have another joint, Gary," she'd said.

"Watch your tone, missy," Ben said. "He's making a good point."

"I can't believe this conversation is happening," she said. "The two of you, making a living from selling pot, having me lie for you and pretend I'm blind, *and* ..." she emphasized her next statement by pointing directly at Ben, "Not to mention, dumping me as a kid."

"Whoa, whoa, whoa!" said Ben. "Your mother did the dumping. It was her decision to protect you against my *lifestyle.*

"Marina was not against you for being gay," she'd said.

"She was a smart, open-minded person. That much I remember."

"I'm not talking about being gay," said Ben, looking down at the dining room table covered with marijuana, baggies and a scale. "She hated pot, had a fit every time I lit up a joint. That is, until she needed some."

"That's mean," said Manya. "She was sick and you guys have been stoned since the day I came here. A joint for breakfast. A joint for lunch. A joint to get you through the stress of meeting my teachers on the first day of grade six."

"We were not high on your first day of school, Manya," Ben says.

"Oh, yes you were!" Manya said, looking at Gary.

"You smoked up on her first day of school?"

Gary took his time answering Ben. Manya had caught him standing at the side of the school. She was only ten, but bright.

"Two puffs," he said. "Two little puffs."

"Excuse us," said Ben. "We need to talk."

She knew what their talks were like. They'd go into the bedroom and close the door. They'd yell and they'd cry. It would go on for hours, and sometimes a glass, a shoe, or a picture would get thrown against the wall—whatever Gary could get his hands on. She knew she had plenty of time to finish packing and sneak out the back door. She left the car with the note at the train station in Portland. The keys were in the ignition. She'd weighed it out—there was a fifty-fifty chance they'd find the van. A fifty-fifty chance that someone would find the note on the dash: *This van belongs to Ben Carnival of Organically Oregon.*

***

The people in town loved Ben and Gary. They would drop by to see the operation—*Organically Oregon*—how nice, they'd say, buying basil, mint, or a couple of tomatoes. The customers who wanted *product* disturbed her, Ben knew this and would do his best to make sure Manya was away from the farm if one of those customers came by. She wanted a normal family, a mom and a dad, not a dad and another pothead dad. At school she'd talk endlessly about Marina. *She's a teacher*, she'd tell her friends. *And a runner, like me*, she'd lie. *She can write and draw and plenty of guys want to marry her, but she can't be bothered. Men*, she'd say, feigning indifference. And when they asked her about Ben and Gary, she'd say, *Oh, those guys. It's just the place I stay.*

46
FIRED

"The person we're interviewing today is remarkable,…" said Helena Stephanopoulos, MBTV's sex-kitten host-producer extraordinaire, "…try to keep your camera steady."

Whatever, Marco thought to himself. "Will do," he said to Helena.

"He has an enormous brain," she said. "He's perfect for the big anniversary event."

Creative, conniving, eye-catching—Helena Stephanopoulos, the face that launched a thousand shows. Doctor Lowell didn't look particularly imposing, and his head wasn't unusually bulbous. Marco focused his lens on this week's *Author of Merit*.

"The brain…" David Lowell, began, "…is capable of changing. Evolving. Yielding. Growing. Responding to whatever we ask of it."

Marco began to shake. Just a little, but the tremor was constant and noticeable. Helena gave him a look and he tried to steady the camera.

Doctor Lowell held up the book and pointed to the cover.

"For example," he said, "I designed my book. As a lifelong scientist, I told myself that I didn't have an artistic bone in my body. Then one day, I had an inspiration. What would happen if I gave up that limited idea of myself and started telling my brain I was a painter? Every day for six months, I told myself I was Monet or Picasso. I didn't doubt myself, and I refused to give my brain any message other than the memo that I am a brilliant painter. Then," Lowell said, "I picked up a brush and imagined this cover. Not bad. If I say so myself."

The cover was of a human skull, a profile of a dissected brain. The painting was well crafted, with swirls and explosions of red, orange and gold. The brain looked three-dimensional.

"It is pretty interesting," said Helena. "I can see how it would fly off the shelves of the stores. Number one on the *New York Times* bestseller list for nine months is a major accomplishment. But artistic cover aside…" Helena added, "…let's go back to the content. *I Thought I'd be Happy* has an intriguing subtitle: *Wired and fired, plugging your brain into bliss.*"

The shaking increased, Marco couldn't contain himself. It had been a long time since he'd felt truly content. Yes, there was Andreas, but beneath the stamina of love's unfolding, there was something ugly he couldn't see, like a tapeworm or prion, eating up the happy side of his brain.

"Yes," said Lowell. "Survey after survey shows that the number one need for people right now is the desire to reconnect to feelings of happiness. Consumerism isn't doing the trick any more; and many in the Western World have lost faith in God, so they are searching for practical ways to get back those feelings of ecstasy that flew out the door with their Bibles and rampant consumerism."

Marco had a hard time concentrating. He couldn't hold the camera steady and he kept thinking back to a comment from Andreas over dinner a few weeks earlier.

"You're sort of cranky," he'd said, placing his hand on Marco's shoulder. "Loveable, but not such a happy guy."

"What's that supposed to mean?" Marco had said defensively. But he knew Andreas was right and that he had to do something about his state of mind. Only, until now, he hadn't had a clue where to begin.

"It's a wrap," said Helena Stephanopoulos, but Marco wasn't there to hear her. He'd passed his camera off to the camera assistant and was crossing the street against traffic and horns—on his way to McNally's to buy the book.

***

It was five in the morning, and the sun hadn't come up yet. Marco was searching for the light switch in the studio.

"You're fired," said Helena Stephanopoulos, stepping into the room as if through a hole in the dark. "Of all the dumb-ass lame things you've done to date, this has to be *the* most ridiculous," she added, flicking on the lights.

Marco had been up all night reading the Lowell book. He was in a sleep-deprived haze that, to some extent, worked as a shield against her rage.

"Our thousandth anniversary show! Why?" she'd asked, but didn't wait for an answer. "Doctor David Lowell, for crying out loud!"

47
KITTEN

He had to be steady and watch the pressure. Then they came out in a lump, the brown-red mass of six. Only the grey kitten with two white paws, one in the front and the other in back, was still alive—all the others were dead.

"That's the way it is in nature," his father said. "One lives and that's better than none. Do you like her son? She's soft as a little cloud. I've named her Kitten."

***

"That's *her* name,…" his mother said, nodding in the direction of the living room where his father was watching television. "Your father's girlfriend, Kitten. The one from Strip Club a GO-GO on Crescent Street."

Marco looked at his mother. Kitten was in a box; he'd been teasing her with a ball of wool. He was puzzled and didn't know what to say.

"Never mind," she said. "You're too little to understand the mess we're in."

***

"I have two brothers and three sisters," he told Andreas.

"That's one big Italian family!" said Andreas.

"And a cat," he said. "I had a cat named Kitten, but she died."

It was the day they'd met and the two of them were on the hardwood floor of Andreas' apartment. He passed Marco the joint; a piece of ash fell on his leg.

"Ouch!" he said. "Don't forget we're naked!"

"How could I," Andreas said, moving closer. "What happened to the cat?"

"She died in a fire," said Marco, touching Andreas on the leg.

"Sorry," he said. "What kind of fire?"

"A fire at our house when I was nine," Marco told him. "My mother and I were at the dentist when it happened."

"That's sad," said Andreas.

"Please…" said Marco, leaning over Andreas, pressing against him with kisses, "…it was a long time ago. Let's not ruin this."

***

"I'm taking Marco to the dentist," Antonietta told his father.

They were standing in the doorway of the house in Ville-Émard. He could see the black silhouette of his father in front of the television, the red glow of his cigarette in one hand and a beer in the other. His two older brothers were on the sofa with him, one on each side. His sisters, the triplets, sat in a row on the other sofa, each in an identical nightdress; each with the colouring book and box of crayons his mother had set in their laps.

"At seven o'clock at night in a blizzard?" his father said, coughing. "Wearing a new purple sweater that I've never seen before?"

"I got it at a yard sale," she said. "I'm taking him to the hospital. It's an abscess or something."

"Come here," his father yelled. But Marco couldn't move.

"Come here," his father yelled louder. "Let's see that tooth."

Marco began to cry. He stood at the door and did not move.

"Come here right now!" his father yelled. "Don't be a goddamn sissy."

"We'll be back in an hour," his mother said, rushing into the living room. Standing next to his chair with two cold beers and nodding at the television she said, "We'll be back before the news is over," she continued. "The snow has almost stopped, and these should keep you good until we get home," she said kissing him on the mouth and placing one bottle in each hand.

Then they left. She held Marco's hand as they walked up the sidewalk through the blowing snow. She walked fast and he began to cry. "My face is frozen," he'd said.

"Don't start," she said. "Or no fire truck for you, young man. And remember," she added, "it may be a while before we see them again."

"Who?" asked Marco.

"Your brothers and sisters," she'd said.

When they got around the corner, she cut through the laneway. They walked through the snow in the dark until they reached the back of their house. They crept alongside the house to the pile of snow where she'd buried the suitcases. "Help me," she whispered. Marco could see her breath in the cold. "Brush them off," she said.

As Marco bent over to help, something in the window caught his eye. He wasn't sure if the curtain moved or if there was a person there, but one thing he saw for sure was the glow of a cigarette. He did not tell his mother. He did not move. And then it went away, the red speck backed into the room where they'd left his father sitting in front of the flickering television.

"*Station de Pompiers*," she said to the driver as he placed the suitcases in the trunk. "*Station de Pompiers Ville-Émard.*"

The fire station seemed empty. There were two red trucks and three firemen. The French guy, Luc, stayed, but the others disappeared up a ladder to the top of the station. There was also a dog. A spotted black-and-white dog, just like on television.

"Can I pat him?" Marco asked.

"*Oui*," said Luc, standing with his hands behind his back. "But," he added, playfully rocking from side to side on his heels. "I abb some ting helse."

Luc handed Marco his camera. Marco could hardly hold it in his hands, he was so excited.

"Be careful," his mother said. "That's an expensive camera."

"Take pictures," said Luc, sliding his arms around Marco's mother's waist. "Six *petites* and still *magnifique*," he said, kissing her neck.

Marco looked at the fireman and his mother and set down the camera. He sat on the concrete and let the dog lick his face.

"It's okay," said his mother, removing the fireman's arm from her waist. "He is just going to show me the station's new truck."

"*Oui. Oui,*" said Luc, pointing to the shining red truck.

His mother bent down and placed the camera in Marco's lap. "Go ahead," she said. "Take a picture of the dog."

Marco picked up the camera and looked through the lens. He snapped a picture of the red truck. He turned his head and snapped again—giant rolls of grey hoses, a pile of oxygen bottles, an axe and the dog. The dog licked the camera and he snapped a picture of the teeth and eyes. He laughed and took another shot. The dog running after a ball that Luc threw. The dog rolling over and sitting up with his tail thumping the floor.

"Now you keep yourself busy for a few minutes," his mother told him as she walked to the truck with Luc. "I won't be too far."

The camera held to his eye, he snapped the picture— Luc's hand on her rear, helping to push her up the big step into the back of the truck. Marco wanted to break the camera and hit the dog. He wanted to pull the alarm and break the windows of the truck with the axe. But then something happened. It was fast and terrifying. The alarm sounded. The floor and walls vibrated with the ringing. Within seconds, the other three firemen slid down the silver pole and his mother jumped out of the truck, pulling on her mauve sweater.

"Move," shouted one of the firemen. "Two-eleven avenue Beaulieu!"

"Oh my god!" shouted his mother. "That's us!"

By the time they got back, the street had been fenced off. Fire trucks, sawhorses and yellow tape blocked the way. Police officers wouldn't let the taxi pass, no matter how much his mother pleaded. Marco and his mother ran through the snow. Marco fell and she yanked him up by the hood of his coat. His fingers were frozen and there was snow in his boots. The street was sheer ice—the next-door neighbours stood watching. Water rushed from the hose as they sprayed the outside of the house.

"Looks like it started here," said one of the policemen, pointing to the side of the house. "A cigarette."

Luc saw them and came down off the roof. He shook his head as he walked toward them. He directed them to the back of the Emergency van, but she would not get in. Marco watched his mother standing in the drifting snow and mist from the hoses.

"No," she said. "This can't be happening."

She would not move. She dug her hands deep in her coat pockets. The buttons were undone and the purple sweater was covered with a thin glaze of ice. Her hair was blown back with streaks of white, frozen stiff.

"We're taking the little one," a woman in a black coat said, taking his hand. Marco could feel her stiff leather gloves fold over his frozen fingers. "We're all right here," she added, pointing to the back of an ambulance.

When the double doors opened, the woman in the black coat lifted Marco up. Inside, his father sat with his older brothers, one on either side of him. His sisters were there, squeezed in on the other side of the van. They looked the same as when he last saw them, only now they were covered in blankets, crowded and shivering in the back of the ambulance.

"Close the door," his father said. "You're letting in the cold."

***

"So how was the dentist?" his father asked, a few days later.

They were in Saint Bruno, at Uncle Renzo and Aunt Rosa's. They were staying in their basement until the house got fixed. Sometimes policemen or detectives came to the house. Marco didn't understand the difference. There was an investigation. *Two fires in a row is no accident,* said the guy in the black coat who squeezed in between him and his father in the back of the ambulance the night of the fire. *Guess I'm just stupid,* his father replied.

Marco hated the basement. It was dark and cold, and the floor smelled like pee. *The dog lived down here when she was a pup for a while ...* Uncle Renzo told them as he helped his father set up cots. *I killed the smell though, with ammonia,* he'd said.

His mother had taken his brothers and sisters to the attic to get blankets and pillows. His father said he needed Marco to stay and help him finish setting up the beds.

Marco couldn't talk, didn't know what to say in answer to his father's question about the dentist.

"What's the matter, son," he asked. "Cat got your tongue?"

"I can't remember."

"Well, maybe I can help," his father said. "Open your mouth."

When his mother came down to the basement with his brothers and sisters, Marco was spitting pieces of soap. She dropped her armful of blankets onto a cot.

"What's going on?" she asked, looking at Marco.

"Not much…" said his father, "…just teaching the boy what happens to liars."

Then Marco coughed and a tooth shot out, bloody and gleaming, onto the smelly floor.

***

When the family returned to the house in Ville-Émard, the six children in one bedroom and his parents in the other, things were pretty much the same as before, only now none of them talked too much. His father would smoke and watch television, and his mother would sit next to him in the dark. The day Marco came back with Luc's camera, they didn't seem to notice. *A friend gave it to me*, he lied. And, for a split second, as he held up the camera to show them, he saw through the smoke and the flickering light of the television, what looked like hope or love in his mother's blue-grey eyes.

He took the camera to the room that he shared with his brothers and sisters. He placed it under his pillow and crawled in bed. He counted the minutes until morning, and when the sun came up, before the others were awake, he tiptoed into the kitchen where his mother was making coffee and snapped a picture of her.

Keep it, Luc had told him. *Prends les photos de la plus belle femme du monde entier.*

"I look horrible," his mother told him, putting her arm around his shoulder and planting a kiss on his cheek. "Don't you dare show that picture to anyone."

48
MARCO

A few weeks later during a thaw, Marco walked along the side of the house. There were new sideboards and a new roof and, except for the occasional smell of smoke in the wind, you'd never know there had been a fire. Marco dug his heels into the mud and kicked at a chunk of ice in the ground. It wouldn't budge. He kicked it again—grey and dirty, but still it wouldn't move. He dug with his heel and then, with the end of a hockey stick, dug some more until he got it unstuck. When Kitten flipped out of the ground, Marco saw the red Swiss Army knife stuck in her side. He began to run. He ran through the yard and down the icy lane that he'd snuck through that night with his mother. He ran down the street trying to breathe through his nose. When he opened his mouth in the cold, his teeth hurt, especially the ones near where the tooth got knocked out. He kept running, one street and then another and another and another until finally, out of breath, he reached the fire station. The garage was empty, all the trucks were gone and no one had ploughed the snow in the driveway. Then Luc shouted, slid down the pole.

"*Bonjour, monsieur*," he said.

"My kitten died," Marco said.

"Not good," said Luc. "Your toot is gone?"

"It's your fault," Marco said, shaking.

"*Non*," said Luc. "It was cigarette."

"My brothers and sisters could have died."

"*Oui*," said the Luc.

"My father's not dumb," said Marco. "He killed the cat and started the fire because of you."

He did not say a word when his mother picked the tooth off the floor and wrapped it in Kleenex. He did not cry or spit out more soap. He swallowed the blood and he swallowed the foam. He looked up at his mother, and then his father. *Who would believe this?* he'd asked himself—four cots on one side of the dark basement for the girls and his mother; four cots on the other side, for father and sons.

***

Why me? Marco wondered. *Why only two suitcases? Why not one of his brothers or sisters?* But he'd never asked. Then one day, out of the blue, while he sat at the kitchen table with his mother, he asked the question. She put down her cup of coffee and looked over at him. He was fourteen years old, the others had all moved out of the house in Ville-Émard. A wiry boy with the feathery start of a moustache, and acne brought on by teenage anxiety, he was beginning to take on his father's long-gone good looks. Franco had become obese and hardly ever moved too far from the sofa where he always seemed to be sleeping. Antonietta was still beautiful. "It's simple," she answered. "Of all my children, you were the one I wanted to take."

Marco didn't know what to say. He knew that he should have said, *Thank you,* or some other words of gratitude, but he didn't. The words that came out of his mouth surprised him. He had heard other kids at school use them, but bad language didn't come natural for him: "Screw you," he said, nodding in the direction of the living room. "Do you think it's been fun being the one he hates?"

49
FLAME

When the telephone rang at four in the morning, Marco knew it couldn't be good news. It was his sister, Aurora.

"She would have wanted you to go, Marco," she said. "Don't let this ruin your vacation."

"I'm Italian," he said, after he hung up the phone. "I can't *not* go to my own mother's funeral."

"It's a memorial service," said Andreas. "We've known this for months. We had all agreed,..." he said, turning on the bedroom light, "...if your mom died before we left, the service would take place when we got back."

She had been specific. No fancy funeral. Not a cent on flowers.

After he lost his job, Marco spent two weeks wandering around during the day and sitting at his mother's bedside each night. Her lung cancer was a surprise to everyone. She had never touched a cigarette in her life. *Second-hand smoke*, the oncologist said. She came in and out of consciousness; the doctors assured him that she wasn't in pain. One night, after a week of silent bedside visits, she reached out and took his hand. "Marco," she whispered. "I wasn't wrong."

"Of course not," he whispered back. "Of course not, Mama," he added, kissing the back of her hand.

"I was in love," she'd said. "That love was a blessing."

Marco knew she wasn't referring to his father.

***

Two years earlier, his father had died of a heart attack in the living room while watching *Deal or No Deal.*

"Hi, Ladies," Howie Mandel said, as Marco walked into the room.

"Hi Howie," said the twenty-six women, each carrying a numbered briefcase.

It was a two-hour episode of *Deal or No Deal.* Staring at the high-heeled women, his father asked, "Is Kitten still alive?"

His mother had gone shopping and there was no one else in the house. When Marco started to answer the question about the grey-and-white kitten his father cut in.

"Did I ever tell you how I got her, son?" he'd asked, turning the volume up. *Deal or no deal? Four-hundred thousand dollars is a lot of tacos to turn down,* said Howie. Marco listened as suitcase number fourteen was selected, and the audience screamed. *No deal! No deal!*

"I was driving home from work one night," his father said. "Straight down Saint Catherine, and at Crescent I saw a sign: Club A Go-Go. Come in, it seemed to say, just one drink. And that's all it took was one beer and a twenty-dollar bill…" he'd said. "…In my little Kitten's red bra."

Then he took a deep breath and put his hand to his chest. His face turned red and Marco knew, even as he dialed 911, that this was very bad news. When his father slumped in his chair, the operator told Marco to get him to the floor and start mouth-to-mouth. Marco tilted the head and pinched the nose. He could smell cigarettes and beer as he'd inhaled, blew into his father's mouth. "He's turning blue," he cried into the phone.

"They're almost there," the man's calm voice reassured through the receiver. "They're almost there," he repeated.

***

A few weeks earlier, there had been the *Deal or No Deal* Los Angeles firefighters special. Instead of twenty-six women in identical shoes, dresses and jewellery, twenty-six buff firefighters marched on stage in identical coveralls, helmets and boots, carrying twenty-six numbered briefcases.

"The people who make these specials must all be fruitcakes," his father had said, looking at Marco and then his mother—who remained silent, mesmerized by the shirtless men and their numbered briefcases.

50
FLYING

How far would Andreas and Marco have gone? Maybe they have made it to the top and arrived safely back at Hotel Enipeas by now. *Iphigenia is probably serving them boiled eggs and coffee at this very moment,* Manya thinks. She crosses a foot-bridge over a shallow river. She will not abandon them. She will find them, whatever it takes. Running into them at the airport was a coincidence; meeting them again in Greece was fate.

***

Andreas flew off the mountain like Icarus. Only there was no melting, waxed wings or sun-fired plunge into a green-blue sea. It was terrible and fast. He rolled past Marco like a stunt man in a B movie. He bounced, hit one rock, and then another and another. Marco froze. Like a fossil, but breathing, he pressed his temple against the slate, and the rest of his body into the creases of sharp grey rock.

Hang on. Hang on. You can do this. Marco waited for the shift and drop in his head. But nothing moved, inside or out. He was frozen to the side of the mountain, too frightened to breathe.

51
SKYLOS

After the river, there's a steep incline and then a small plateau and the entrance to a cave. Manya rubs her eyes; she is sweating and the salt makes them sting. In the cave there are eyes, disgusting eyes that hold her. *Do not move,* she tells herself. *Not an inch.* The eyes come forward along with the slick black coat, ears and legs. It's only a dog. A large, black dog. A stray: *Way up here?* It doesn't wag its tail, bark or growl. Her eyes are stinging and she's terrified; Manya goes over her self-defense. *Pick up a rock. Bend slowly and pick up a rock.* The dog will be all over her in three seconds. *The backpack?* She could slide it off and swing it at the dog, and run like the wind? Her Swiss Army knife, she could reach slowly into her pocket and get it. Then she stops. No need for further plans, the dog is gone; it has disappeared into the back of the cave. Manya can't help but wonder what kind of cruel sign his arrival is meant to be.

***

Ben and Gary came to Chicago for her nineteenth birthday. They pleaded with her to come home, back to Oregon. They had changed. They were happier, but more serious; neither of them seemed stoned.

"So this is what you're like when you're straight?" Manya said.

They were at a restaurant close to the School of the Art Institute of Chicago.

"We haven't had a joint in three months," Gary said.

"You were the best thing in our life," Ben said, "and we chased you away."

"You didn't chase me away," Manya said.

"Oh, yes, we did," said Gary. "We knew that the kids at school were teasing you about us and we didn't talk. We knew it was wrong to have you play Blind Girl and help us distract the IRS guy but we did it anyway. We knew it was wrong to be stoned in the morning and at lunch and at bedtime. We never tucked you in. We never kissed you good night."

"I'm not going back," she said, pushing her plate of cold pasta across the table.

"Do you want something else to eat?" Ben asked.

"I want you guys to leave," she said. "I have an inheritance."

"What?" Ben asked.

"Yes," she said. "While you guys were busy getting stoned, I got rich."

"When did this happen?"

"When I was born," she said. "I just had to wait until I turned sixteen. And don't tell me the two of you didn't know about it."

"Of course we knew about your inheritance, Manya," Gary lied, "We're your guardians." And sitting straight, raising his arms in the air, he added: "That's fucking fabulous, darlin'!"

"Well, you're not getting any," she said. "Not a cent for weed."

"We don't want your money Manya," Ben said, looking sad. "Our produce is actually doing well now that we remember to water it."

Manya was aware of the good-looking guy at the next table flirting with her.

"He's trouble," Gary said, catching the man winking at her.

"It's a little late for you to play the overprotective parent," she said. "Just leave."

She turned her shoulder when Ben put his hand on her back. She stood and walked away when Gary said, *please?*

George stood up, followed her down the hall as she walked toward the washroom.

***

In the morning, after Manya leaves for school, Marina pushes her walker to the bedroom. More and more, she feels the pain in her chest but ignores it. It's too late for her, but not too late for Manya to have a happy, healthy life. She opens the bedside drawer and pulls out a bag of licorice and a bag of cookies. She sets the TV converter on the pillow and cracks open a can of Coke; she places it on the floor where she can reach it. She maneuvers the walker so that her backside is at the edge of the bed. She pulls back the blankets then falls onto the mattress and catches her breath. After a few seconds, when she is able, she lifts one leg and then the next onto the bed. She rolls to one side and inches over, pulls herself up against the pillow. She inches over a little more, pulls the walker close to the bed. She reaches for her Coke and sips. She flicks on *Oprah* and sets the alarm for three o'clock. It's important to be out of bed before Manya gets home. It's important to hide the chip bags and the cookies and to brush her hair. *Help me make the bed, Manya,* she'd told her before sending her off to school. *I have lots to do today,* she said, reaching for her dusty briefcase.

***

The routine went like this: the minute the guy from the IRS knocked on the door, Manya would put on the Stevie Wonder hair band that Gary helped her make. She would grab her white cane and turn off all the lights. Ben and Gary would have set up the dining room table with *Organically Oregon* labels and brown paper bags. They'd spread piles of dried oregano, thyme and sage around the table. When Ben gave her the thumbs-up, Manya would open the door. She would stand and stare, wait for the inspector to speak. When he would pull out his identification badge and hold it out to her, with the skill of a pro, she would pretend not to see it. She would turn and run through the house, pretending to bump into furniture and break a glass that would have been strategically placed at the edge of the table.

"Oh, excuse me," the inspector would usually say, putting the badge back in his inside coat pocket. "Is this a bad time?"

"Hi, there," Manya would have said, huffing and puffing, stopping directly in front of him and staring straight ahead.

Before the IRS guy could speak, Ben would shout from across the room. "That's my daughter," he would say. "I have my hands full around here," he would add, pointing to a pretend mail-order project they had set up on the table.

"You're a born actress, girl," Gary would say, after the inspector had left.

52
ROSES

Ben and Gary wait for Manya at the finish line in Litochoro. They have flowers, a dozen red roses each that are
beginning to wilt in the midday sun. The first marathoner
comes in waving his arms in the air. After a few minutes,
more runners cross the finish line. Some of them do a
victory dance, while others bend over and cry. Marco had
told them Manya would be among the first. As time passes, however, they get more and more disheartened. Those
clocking in at four-and-a-half hours look exhausted—sun
scorched and drenched in sweat, they've pushed themselves to death's door.

"Good candidates for a heart attack," Gary says.

"She'll be here," says Ben. "She's one determined girl."

For as long as Ben can remember, Manya had loved to
run. Even those first few months at Cannon Beach, when
she was angry every minute of the day, she'd put on her
shoes and slam out the screen door. Gary would look up
through the haze of his high, and watch her sprint across
the stone-clustered beach. She could easily have run this
race at the front of the pack. Then again, this is Mount
Olympus—altitude and steep hills would be new to her.

From where Gary and Ben stand, there seems to be
many Manyas approaching the finish line.

"There she is," Gary shouts, jumping up and down, waving his bouquet of roses. But when the person gets closer, it's not her.

"Maybe she decided not to run?" says Ben.

"Manya change her mind about something? I don't think so," said Gary.

It was Marco who sent the e-mail after she and Manya had discussed Ben and Gary on the beach in Koufonissi.

"You should invite them!" Marco had said.

"I think this place would be a little out of their comfort zone," Manya said.

"Why's that?" Marco had asked.

"I'd rather not get into it with you, Marco," Manya said. "Let's just say they're a little too self-involved to go all the way to Greece just to see me finish a race."

Let's surprise her, Marco wrote. *We'll be at Hotel Enipeas in Litochoro.*

He sent the message through their website. He didn't tell Manya. After Ben's e-mail response to him: *This time we'll be there for her*, Marco had no doubt they'd show.

***

Gary and Ben sit on a patio eating calamari and *tzatziki*. Or rather, not eating, as neither of them has touched their food. They'd waited until every runner crossed the finish line. They're almost too disappointed to talk now, but Gary talks about little Manya, to keep Ben distracted.

When the waiter brings two glasses of water, Gary blurts out: "We've been clean and sober for two years."

"The whole world doesn't need to know, Gary," Ben says, turning red.

Then the ambulance comes. It passes so close that they can almost touch it from their chairs.

"Yikes," says Gary. "Something terrible has happened to some poor soul. Ambulances always make me feel nauseous."

Then, it's as if a bomb has been dropped in the middle of the table. The two of them jump up at the same moment.

"Where would that ambulance be going?" Ben asks the waiter, almost knocking the tray out of his hand.

"Katerini," says the waiter, setting the drinks on the table. "Big hospital."

Ben is the first out of the taxi. Katerini General is like any modern hospital. It's bright and clean. There are nurses walking around in pink, white or blue uniforms. There's a woman with a bloody nose fishing around in her purse for a Kleenex, and a man vomiting into a plastic bag. There are nurses with clipboards, stretchers and IV poles. Everyone seems too busy to help.

"Please," says Ben, pushing his way to the front of the line. "We are looking for an American woman."

"Wait with the others," the receptionist says in flat, perfect English, pointing to a crowded waiting area.

"Has an ambulance been here from Litochoro?" asks Gary.

"Yes," says, the receptionist. "Please wait."

Then, like a vision, Manya walks down the corridor. Ben is the first to see her—a little disheveled, worn down, but utterly Manya.

Ben is first to reach her, and Gary right behind him.

"Oh, my God. Oh, my God. Oh, my God, she's alive!" Gary yells, jumping up and down, the roses, drooping and broken, flopping up and down in his arms.

"What?" says Manya. "How—?"

Gary and Ben surround her with flowers and hugs.

"Your friend Marco e-mailed us," says Ben. "Hope you don't mind."

"I don't mind," Manya says, hugging her father. "I can't believe you guys are really here," she says.

"Of course we're here, Manya," says Ben. "But what happened? Why are you here at the hospital?"

"It's my friend Andreas," Manya says, taking her father's hand. "I'll tell you all about it."

***

Manya ties a rope around his waist. "Look in my eyes, Marco" she says.

Step by step, she talks him down the side of the mountain.

"Look. In my eyes," she says. "You're safe."

But it isn't her steely blue eyes that stop him from falling. The rope and sips of water are only part of what urges him slowly down the mountain.

Marco had turned slowly and, as he turned, his camera slipped from his hand and tumbled down the rocks. He'd forgotten that it was there, the hand-held Canon. He was certain that he was going to die, but then he heard Andreas' voice like an echo bouncing up from the cauldron. *Be happy,* he was sure he heard from the depths. *I love my little sweetheart.*

There was a warm breeze from the Thermaic Gulf and the rolling sound of a few loose pebbles under his boots; then he felt the thought like a pinch—tightening then loosening, a steady pounding under his ribs, through his pounding heart: *I love you too, Andreas.*

"That's it," says Manya. "Step down. One small step. Now, the next."

***

There was no reason for the fall. The rain had stopped and the rocks had dried off. Andreas was following him with ease down the path. But Marco can't reconcile with the notion of suicide either. The nurse slides a needle into his arm: "This will make you comfortable," she says. There is an old woman across from him, and what appear to be three adult children sitting around her bed. They speak Greek, but Marco gets the essence of the scenario. *I love you*, the son seems to be saying as he strokes her grey hair. "I love you," the daughter says, as she kisses the back of her hand. "I love you," the other son cries, as a priest enters the room and pulls the green dividing curtain between them and him.

Andreas had seemed so happy at the top of Myti-kas. He did it for his parents, he said. But Marco knew that he made the climb for him as well. Yes, Andreas was depressed since his parents' death. Yes, they had a small fight. But it seems impossible for Marco to think that Andreas was capable of leaving him like that. *I love my little sweetheart*, he'd say at least once a day. How is it possible that he threw himself off a mountain? The sedative flows into his body along with fluids for re-hydration. There is weeping from the other side of the curtain.

53
LAUREL WREATH

"Put it under your pillow before you go to sleep," his mother said.

"I'm too old for the Tooth Fairy," said Marco. "I'm nine now."

"You're never too old," she said, handing him the tooth wrapped in Kleenex. "You never can tell what comes in your sleep."

***

Manya thinks hard about her project. She rolls up her sleeves and, one by one, slides the silver bangles off her wrists and sets them on the dining room table at the bed and breakfast. Iphigenia said she could have the table for one hour before she prepares lunch for the other guests. She pulls back her hair and puts on a puzzle band—she'll use her *Glorious Illuminator*, with its suns, moons, light bulbs and surging wires for inspiration. On a sheet of cardboard she draws several images—a tiny version of Mount Olympus, Andreas smiling, and Marco with a hand-held camera, a red heart and a grey brain surging with pink endorphins, a fluffy mauve cloud, a chunk of chocolate, the green-glass Toronto Trump Tower, and a silver-blue airplane. She applies a thin coat of varnish over them and, once they dry, she cuts out each small drawing as if it were a piece of a jigsaw. She draws two laurel wreaths in gold pencil and carefully pastes each image onto a band. She takes the drawing of Andreas. She kisses the face, young and handsome, with olive skin and brilliant green eyes, pressing it onto the wreath; then the red heart and the glowing brain, followed by the tower and a blank piece of puzzle; then the clouds, the mountain and airplane. When they're finished, she places the bands along with a box of chocolates into her bag.

Exhausted and achy, she walks back to the hospital. She takes her time, savoring the sun and warm air, smiling at an old woman with a cane who passes her on the street. This will be Manya's last full day in Greece. She savors each step—solitude and warmth, a breeze lightly scented with wild sage.

Marco is sitting up in his bed when she arrives. He looks more like his old self—sad, but blue-eyed and adorable. He gives her a tentative smile when she enters the room. Manya sits on the edge of his bed and takes his hand. She notices that the other bed is empty, and Marco catches her looking.

"The old lady died," he says. "It's been gloomy around here."

They both look at the bed, stripped of its blankets and sheets.

Manya brings them back to the moment.

"So … Marco," she says, digging into her purse for the box of chocolates.

He kisses her on the cheek. "Dark chocolate from Sokolate Kolonaki. Thank you very much," he says. "I'm impressed you remembered how much I like chocolate."

"There's something else," she says, reaching back into her bag. "You suggested when we met at the airport that I should make a pleasure band. Well, here it is," she says, trying not to cry, handing him the first laurel wreath. "You made it to the top. The two of you climbed Olympus together and this is your crown to take home."

At first, Marco can't speak. "Amazing," he says at last, running his index finger over the drawing of Andreas. "There's perfect detail in his face."

Manya reaches into her bag again.

"There's another. One for Andreas as well." She hands him the second wreath. "They're almost identical. Only instead of Andreas, I drew you."

Leaning over, Marco takes his time looking at each image. He runs his finger over the smooth, varnished surface. He can't look at Manya. He sits up straight, looks across the empty bed and the wall.

"They're beautiful," he says. He won't cry, not with Manya in the room. She probably thinks it's all his fault. "I have to have a shower now. The nurse is waiting."

Manya looks around the room for a nurse, but no one is there. "I'll come back," she says.

54
HEPHAESTUS

Andreas had explained about Hephaestus. He told Marco that he was a kind and loveable god, but very ugly. When his mother, Hera, saw him for the first time, she was so disappointed that she took her son and threw him from the top of Mount Olympus to the depths of the sea, causing the deformation of his leg. Hephaestus was rescued by two Nereids, Thetis and Eurymore, who raised him inside a cave.

"Are there no limits to these Greek tragedies?" Marco asked.

"Not really…" said Andreas, "…only as far as the mind can reach."

55
PUZZLE

"I'm no fool," Manya says, taking his hand. "I know I haven't caught everything. I know there's more to your life than meets the eye."

"Do you mind going now, Manya? I want to be alone."

"That's your big problem, Marco," she says. "Thank god Andreas tolerated this need of yours to push people away."

"No time for guilt…" says Marco, "…next time you visit, please leave it outside the door."

"Not guilt…" she says, turning to leave, "…this 'happiness' mantra is a decoy, a façade, a shield."

Once Manya is out of sight, Marco takes the pleasure bands and throws them on the floor. He gets off the bed and picks them up. He takes the one she'd made for him and breaks it in half, and then half again. He throws it toward the window and it lands on the empty bed, the image of the Trump Tower facing up and Andreas face down. He curls up in a ball on his bed and looks down at the band she'd made for Andreas. Finally, when he calms down, he places it under his pillow. *You never can tell what comes in your sleep*, his mother once said.

***

Manya said goodbye to Ben the night before he and Gary left Greece. They went for a walk by the Enipeas River behind the hotel.

"So," said Ben, sounding awkward and looking down at his feet. "I hope we get to see you more often."

"I hope so too," said Manya.

"What about your grandmother's ashes, Manya?" asked Ben.

"Yes," she answered. "I did manage to scatter her ashes on Olympus, across the Plateau of the Muses."

"Have a seat," said Ben, pointing to a log near the river's edge. "To be honest," he added, "you don't sound too thrilled."

Manya didn't reply. She thought back to when she was a little girl and how she would spend hours wandering through Washington Square Park. She would watch the joggers, the dog walkers, and teenage boys on their skateboards, read her book, and tried not to be bored.

She sighed, felt as though she would die from the weight of her thoughts.

"Is there something you want to tell me?" asked Ben.

"Well," said Manya, looking at him. "As you know, I was just little when Marina died, but I had a job to do. I was supposed to remind her to take her insulin every night at five."

"And…" asked Ben. "What happened?"

"As you know, we lived alone in that apartment near Washington Square."

"Yes," said Ben.

Ben watched as Manya's face changed from an extraordinarily beautiful young woman to an old, distressed crone. She sat holding his hand. She pressed his fingers to her cheek and rocked back and forth.

"We had a routine before I left for school. Marina would say, *Home from work at five, high five*, and I'd say the same thing back, as I raised my hand to clap hers. Even though I knew that she only pretended to go to work," said Manya.

"What do you mean?" said Ben.

"Even though she was diabetic, she would spend the day in front of the television eating junk food. I could tell by the chocolate bar wrappers and the chip bags I'd find in the garbage when I got home. Besides, I knew she never left the apartment because she could hardly walk from room to room she'd become so big. And then," added Manya, turning away from Ben. "I let her die."

"What?" said Ben, leaning in closer. "I can't hear you."

"*High five, see you at five,* she said one morning, raising her hand to slap mine. I shot her 'high five' back, and then I left our apartment. Only I didn't go to school," Manya explained.

"Manya," Ben said. "What happened?"

"I went to the park. The same park we always went to," said Manya, trying to sit straight. "I sat on our usual bench by the library, but after a while I got bored."

"How old were you?" asked Ben.

"Nine," said Manya. "I was nine going on thirty."

"This isn't sounding so good," said Ben. "I should have been there for you."

"Well, there were these two other kids in the park with their mothers and…" said Manya, searching, unsuccessfully, in her pocket, "…they were twins and it was their birthday, so they were allowed to stay home from school. They'd asked me if I wanted to put on a play with them, *Alice in Wonderland*. As you know, Marina was open-minded about most things, except theatre—she didn't want me to fall into the trap that her mother had fallen into."

"That's kind of extreme," said Ben.

"But I did this anyhow. The three of us invented a tall Alice and a short Alice, a March Hare and a Cheshire cat, and before I knew, it was time for supper."

"That's a fun thing for a kid to do," said Ben. "You shouldn't feel so bad."

"Well," said Manya, "in my head I could hear Marina, *Hi five, see you at five*, but I kept getting more and more involved with *Alice*, until eventually the mother drove me home. It was well after five, already dark."

"So you missed supper," said Ben. "And Marina was pissed."

"Marina was dead," said Manya.

"Christ," said Ben. "What an ordeal for a little kid to go through," he added.

"It was my job," said Manya, hanging her head. "To give her insulin at five o'clock each night."

"You were a child, Manya,…" said Ben, "…that's too much responsibility. Marina could have taken her insulin without you there."

Manya wiped her nose on her sleeve, "I think she was still in love with you."

***

Bats flitting along the branch tips of eucalyptus; sun inching over the river; a melancholy glow on Marco's face: "To see infinity in a grain …" he says, sifting sand through his fingers. "Andreas used to say that he could see infinity through his ophthalmoscope."

Manya and Marco sit on the steps of Hotel Enipeas waiting for the taxi to arrive. It's going to be a hot day, but right now the air is crisp. Marco has his strength back, and it's time to leave. They will take the early train from Litochoro to Athens. From Athens, Manya will fly to Istanbul and then on to New York. Marco will fly directly to Toronto, Andreas' ashes in the belly of the plane. It's hard for him to believe; the man with the booming voice and big passion, reduced to ashes. If only he had appreciated Andreas more, focused on Andreas' happiness and not just his own, none of this would have happened.

"Guilt is not going to help you," says Manya. "Get your head out of the clouds, Marco, go into the underground, travel the subways, weave together myth, desire and real-life drama; honour Andreas; don't wallow in self-pity."

"I'm not *wallowing*, Manya."

"What do you call this?" she says, holding up an envelope with Iphigenia scribbled across the front.

"Who gave you that?" Marco asks.

"You know Iphigenia doesn't speak English. She asked me to read it to her."

"I was having a bad moment when I wrote that."

"Your bad moment has been going on for decades, Marco. *Dear Iphigenia, This may be the last letter I ever write.* Cut the drama, Marco."

56
SWIMMING

On Toronto's Grenville Street, the morgue squeezed up against a low-income apartment, cold, grey concrete—appropriately ugly, more so than any building he could have imagined. Someone met them at reception. They brought them each a glass of cold water and then to the bodies. They handed Andreas Anastasia's note scribbled in eyeliner on the back of an envelope.

Pedhi Mou, his mother had written.

Your father is gone. Quiet and still…

"I shouldn't have insisted," Andreas told Marco. "I should never have pushed them to drive in the snow storm."

…the angel is coming now, I feel her wings…

***

His father did not teach Andreas how to swim above the water. The other fathers would hold their sons or daughters by the hips, or dangle them by their swim suit, just above the surface; arms flapping, legs kicking, the child shrieking with delight or terror, the parent shouting words of encouragement. Not Andreas Sr.

"Three stacking breaths," he said. "That's it *Pedhi Mou*, now dive."

His father was smarter than the other fathers.

"Anyone can stay on top," he said. "But a wise man knows what to do when he's sinking."

His mother started to speak, but his father had placed his finger against her lips:

Shhhh…!

The lake was clear and Andreas watched for small fish. He was fascinated with patterns in the sand.

"It's ripples," he'd said to his father, gasping for air, pointing down into the water. "Waves right inside the sand."

"Close your eyes when you are underwater," his father said. "The eyes are sensitive. Concentrate. One steamboat. Two steamboats… You'll know you're strong enough when you can make it to ten."

Andreas had not asked his father what happens when you can't make it to ten; he had seen the terror in his mother's eyes before he dove into the water.

***

One steamboat. Two steamboats…

Marco was ahead of him, climbing down the mountain with speed and confidence. *He'll make it*, Andreas thought. *Marco will be happy.*

Andreas reached into the zipper pocket of his backpack and pulled out the folded envelope.

Pedhi Mou, Anastasia had written.

Your father is gone…

And attached to the envelope, was the little green post-it:

Bernd.burn@hotmail.ca

There was the initial shock of the tumble, and then his heart racing.

Three steamboats. Four…

Andreas flew past Marco, who was hanging on for life, out over the cauldron…

Five steamboats. Six steamboats. Seven…

That day, Andreas saw Marco in the streetcar window—sexy, projecting fierce attitude. *I want that guy*, is what he thought when the streetcar stopped at the light. He would have followed that car around the entire city if he had to. Well, he got him and his malleable brain. His distant, loveable self.

"So, Andreas," Marco had said, looking around the messy apartment, stopping at the laundry heaped in a chair. "If the eyes are the windows to the soul…you must see some pretty weird shit in your job?"

"I can see that we're going to be together a long time," Andreas said, pulling his naked body closer to Marco's.

"Maybe," Marco said. "My soul's like a white trash garage sale—a fireman's hat, a cat named Kitten, an autographed picture of Sophia Lauren."

"Oh," Andreas said, as Marco snuggled into his naked body. "Your soul contains much more than memorabilia from this lifetime."

Marco, with his head still in the clouds, clinging to a rock—*I love my little sweetheart*, Andreas shouted, one last time. And he responded. Hanging on for life, Marco shouted back, only Andreas was falling too fast to grab his reaching-out hand or hear his pleading words.

Eight steamboats ...Nine steamboats...

***

When she spotted someone clinging to the side of the mountain, Manya felt hopeful. She'd known something was wrong from the minute Iphigenia told her the boys had gone missing. As she got closer, she saw it was Marco. He looked terrified.

"Manya?" he'd whispered. "You're a vision for sore eyes."

"Are you okay?" she'd said. "Where's Andreas?"

Marco did not answer. He nodded his head in the direction of the cauldron then he began to shake.

She tied the clothesline rope from the hotel around Marco's waist. *One step and then the next.* She coaxed him down the mountain—through his outbursts, through his fear, guilt and grief.

57
STEAM

Marco stands in a window looking out over the city. This is how he always knew it would end—alone in his apartment at the recently completed Trump. With his new camera, he pans out over the roof of the Deloitte offices, down to the lake. How many years had he waited for this moment? How long had he fantasized about standing in solitude, savoring the city's skyscraper beauty, waiting for the inspiration that would rush at him with unimaginable force. Marco places the camera on the floor and stares out at the night sky. There's not much to see in the dark, except for the boxy shadows of the half-lit high-rises and the red lights of the island airport blinking across the lake. He looks for the northern star and thinks about what Manya told him the day they sat in the Athens airport waiting for their flight home. She said there was a place in the universe, a wrinkle in space where past, present and future intersect. She'd explained this special place wasn't heaven, but something like it. There's no guilt or shame, and you get to see that the people you once loved are safe. She talked to him about the importance of art in her life. There are moments in her painting, she explained, when she is utterly present with the paint and shadows of her canvas; the sound of water running through the old pipes in her apartment building; the deep, contented purr of her cat curled up on a newspaper by her feet. She told him all of this in the departure lounge at the Athens airport. She said that breathing is a gift that can be heartbreaking. She said that if she inhales deeply enough, she could feel the pulse and spirit of all the people she has loved in her life, including Marina. She told him to be open to that pulse and, even when it hurts, not to be afraid of grief. It's just the scab coming off, she said. There's a whole new you underneath. Then she hugged him tightly and walked into the line of people boarding the aircraft. She shouted back at him to promise to call her when he was ready to start shooting *Steam*.

Marco feels sad and worn down. It seems like a long time since the day he and Andreas flew out of the Toronto Island airport; eating chocolate, drinking red wine, clutching Lowell's book in his hand. And when they first met Manya at the Newark airport he knew in his gut that they would somehow meet again, even as they boarded their flight for Istanbul. He had no idea, however, how complicated and tragic the reunion would be; no idea she would be the one to save his life. Manya, head-to-toe in pink, stood beside him, offering him sips of water.

"Look at me," she'd said. "Don't look down. Look in my eyes."

Marco picks his camera off the floor and walks away from the window. He scans the floor-to-ceiling painting, *Boy With Wreath of Laurel* that Manya gave him when he saw her in Chicago to talk about *Steam*. "I'll do the movie," she said. "But find a decent producer!"

He puts the camera on the dining room table, crosses the room and sits in the wingback chair that was once

Andreas' favourite. He places his laptop on his knees and opens the cover, and searching through his memory bank for the e-mail address, he types: bernd.burn@hotmail.ca.

He thinks about how much he will miss Andreas and begins to sob. Not defeatist or even sadness, the tears have the essence of joy in them, a kind of respect or grace—*Steam* will be one-hundred percent for Andreas—not just the ophthalmologist or lover, the movie will be a tribute to his vision; his archetypes of the underworld, surfaced and screened.

Bernd, he types. *I need your help to make a movie.*

He sits tall and inhales, feels his heart thumping between his ribs, strong and steady. He counts backwards from ten, exhales and presses *Send.*

I am happy, he says, setting his laptop aside and walking back to the window. He waits for the tug and twinge under his skull—old brain shrinking under, new brain swelling up. *I am happy*, he insists, looking out at the buildings—floor over floor, boxes of light—wired and fired synapses of the city.

Acknowledgements

For Marnie Woodrow who coached, teased and prompted me as I embraced certain characters and asked others to leave the pages for good.

To Halli Villegas for her gentle spirit and powerful vision for Tightrope Books.

To Nathaniel G. Moore for all his hard work in getting this novel out to the world and Jeffrey Round for his careful edits and encouragement.

Gratitude and love to Laura Lush, Eddy Yanofsky, Suzanne Collins and Vivette Kady – the Phoebe-Walmer Collective. And to Heather Wood for always showing up and putting others first. For my family and friends – I couldn't ask for a more loving and accepting clan.

Thanks to Don for climbing the mountain with me and for sharing his love of Science and Gods.

***

"Both Sides Now" is Joni Mitchell's glorious song, written by Jesse Harms and Sammy Hagar: Sony/ATV Publishing LLC.

"Maniac" is from Michael Sembello and the movie Flashdance, 1983.

Henderson the Rain King is the title of Saul Bellow's 1959 novel: Viking Press.

Norman Doidge's book, The Brain That Changes Itself: Stories of Personal Triumph From The Frontiers of

The Brain, (Penguin Books, New York, 2007) was both a source of information and inspiration for the novel.

The line of poetry that introduces the book is from Jack Gilbert's poem, "Winter Happiness in Greece" in the collection: The Dance Most of All (pg. 16), Alfred A. Knopf, New York, 2010.

Cover Photograph by Herbert Tobias, 1957: Berlinische Galerie; copyright VG Bildkunst, Bonn

Jim Nason photograph by David Leyes, Toronto

DESPERATE TIMES CALL FOR DESPERATE ACTIONS!

Numbly, Bob followed his classmates into school. In a trance, he opened his locker and took out his books. Then he blindly stumbled down the hall toward his classroom.

I've got to come up with a plan right away, he thought frantically. *There's no way I'm going to learn ballroom dancing with that ... that vampire!*

I'll just have to get expelled by this afternoon!

Look for these other LUNCHROOM titles:

LUNCHROOM

2

FROG PUNCH

Ann Hodgman

Illustrated by Roger Leyonmark

SPLASH™

A BERKLEY / SPLASH BOOK

FROG PUNCH

Chapter One

Mr. Haypence on the Warpath

"Bob, what's this letter from Mr. Haypence?"

Bob Kelly's hand froze in midair on its way out of a deluxe bag of barbecued potato chips. He stared, openmouthed, at his mother, who was standing in the kitchen doorway and holding a crumpled piece of paper in her hand.

"It fell out of your jacket pocket," she told him. "Is it okay for me to read it? It says 'To all Hollis Parents.'"

At last Bob found his voice. "Mom! You shouldn't go poking around in my stuff!" he said accusingly. Then he realized he was still holding the potato chips, and hastily crammed them in his mouth.

"Well, you should hang your jacket up when

1

you get home from school," his mother answered.

Bob glared at her. *Crunch, crunch.*

"You *are* in sixth grade, after all," Mrs. Kelly went on. "If I hadn't had to hang it up for you, I wouldn't have seen this note. But since I have seen it"—she smoothed out the crumples—"and since it's addressed to me, I'm going to read it. I'm sure you don't mind."

Bob finished the potato chips at last. He did mind. He minded a lot! *Why did I leave that note in my pocket?* he thought furiously.

He glanced apprehensively at his mother. His mother was actually smiling as she read the letter. "Oh, how wonderful!" she exclaimed.

"After-school ballroom dancing for the sixth grade! What a nice idea!" And—not realizing that the letter's message was already burned indelibly into Bob's brain—she began to read aloud.

"'To all parents of Hollis Elementary School sixth-graders: Recently we have been undergoing an acute loss of manners and school spirit in the sixth grade. Despite Hollis Elementary's excellent facilities—including our unique new state-of-the-art lunchroom—our sixth-graders do not seem to have learned how to be considerate to their elders, or show proper respect for school property, especially their new lunchroom.

"'As principal, I am naturally very concerned

by this. I have concluded that the problem is that the youngsters are not being given enough opportunities to polish their social skills. Therefore, I am instituting a series of after-school ballroom-dancing classes for all sixth-graders. The classes will be held in our brand-new lunchroom, beginning next Monday after school, and will continue for two weeks. Special bus arrangements will be made, and attendance is mandatory. I believe parents will be truly impressed and delighted by the change I expect ballroom dancing will bring about in the demeanor and manners of the sixth-grade class. Yours sincerely, Wilfred Haypence, Principal.'"

Ignoring Bob's horrified expression, Mrs. Kelly put down the piece of paper and beamed. "Isn't Mr. Haypence wonderful?" she said. "That man's always trying to think up ways to keep you kids happy."

"Well, he sure didn't do it this time," Bob muttered.

"Why, Bob! You don't think ballroom dancing sounds like fun?"

"Mom, I think ballroom dancing sounds like the most terrible, awful, stupid, idiotic—"

"*Now, Bob!*" his mother interrupted warningly. "You can just stop right there."

"Stop right where?" came a piping voice. Bob's seven-year-old sister, Lynn, walked into the

3

kitchen. "What is Bob saying?" Lynn asked eagerly. "Is he saying bad words?"

"Lynn!" said Mrs. Kelly.

"Well, soldiers know bad words, don't they?" Lynn sniffed. "Don't you think I should learn just a *few*, Mom?"

Mrs. Kelly sighed. "There will be plenty of time for you to learn bad words when you're a soldier, Lynn. But as long as you're living in this house, you're going to have to do without them."

Bob glanced over at his little sister and shuddered. As usual, Lynn was dressed in camouflage fatigues, a toy machine gun was slung over her shoulder, and a toy grenade was sticking out of her pocket. She was also carrying a plastic bayonet. She looked pretty threatening for a seven-year-old. But then, Lynn wasn't like any other seven-year-olds. Bob knew she was . . . scary.

At the age of five, Lynn had decided she wanted to become a soldier. Now she always referred to that great moment as "the time I joined the army." She was never without her weapons, and she owned a miniature army of G. I. Joes. Bob was constantly stepping on them, sitting on them, tripping over them, and he had the scars to prove it.

I bet no one else in the sixth grade has to suffer the way I do, Bob thought. *I mean, who's ever*

4

heard of a second-grader asking Santa for a hand grenade?

Mrs. Kelly's voice broke into his thoughts. "Let's go back to this note a minute, Bob," she said. "What exactly does Mr. Haypence mean when he talks about 'an acute loss of school spirit' in the sixth grade? You kids aren't causing any trouble, are you?"

"That depends on what you call trouble," Bob said. Under his breath, he added, "And for Mr. Haypence, an acute loss of school spirit means not putting your lunch tray back when you're done with it."

The real problem was that Mr. Haypence was so proud of Hollis Elementary School's new lunchroom that he acted as though it were some kind of museum.

It *was* a great lunchroom, no doubt about that. And Mr. Haypence was probably right when he said there wasn't another cafeteria like it in all of Pasadena—perhaps even in all of California. Bob, for one, had never seen another lunchroom with ornamental waterfalls, walk-in microwaves, space-age vending machines, not to mention rest-your-neck torture chairs. But did that mean Mr. Haypence had to make such a fuss about it all the time?

The real trouble had started last month, right

5

after Bob's sixth-grade class had held a huge pizza party that they'd called Night of a Thousand Pizzas. There'd been a little problem about a few toppings—about five tons, to be exact—and Mr. Haypence hadn't been exactly thrilled when he had learned that the sixth-graders were planning another huge party to get rid of them.

"Our new lunchroom is not a nightclub!" Mr. Haypence thundered. "And I won't have you kids treating it like one." And he'd arranged to have all the leftovers hauled away to the city dump, ignoring a plea from Ms. Weinstock, the school dietician, that it was "a crime to waste ten thousand pounds of perfectly good food."

After that, things had gone from bad to worse. Mr. Haypence started hanging around the lunchroom all the time just to make sure the sixth-graders didn't come up with any more of what he called "criminal plans to ruin our lunchroom." Then he realized that the kids were committing major acts of vandalism every single day at lunch.

Crimes like throwing their balled-up napkins into the trash instead of walking over and dropping them in, or piling trays at the tray-return window instead of waiting for the cafeteria workers to take them away one by one, or drinking milk out of the carton without using a straw! The list went on and on. Jostling one another in the lunch line! Not having the exact change at the cash register!

"But, Mr. Haypence, why should the kids have to pay with the exact change?" Ms. Weinstock asked timidly one day in the lunchroom after Mr. Haypence had been ranting for even longer than usual.

It was her first year on the job, and she spent about eighty percent of her time in terror of being fired. (The remaining twenty percent was devoted to her search for even healthier lunch foods than the ones she was already forcing down kids' throats.) "Isn't that why we have a cash register? To give people change?"

Mr. Haypence's face turned purple. "The cash register makes no difference at all," he sputtered. "Not having the correct change is an *attitude* problem. It shows that our students don't properly appreciate our wonderful, brand-new lunchroom. It shows that they're sloppy!"

He made it sound like the worst insult in the world. "Rocky Latizano!" he bellowed suddenly. "Stop chewing and listen to me!"

Rocky Latizano, the sixth grade's human garbage pail, looked up—still chewing—at the principal, a pained expression on his face. "But I'm eating a cheeseburger!" he mumbled indignantly.

"I don't care *what* you're eating!" said Mr.

7

Haypence. "A lunchroom is not for . . ." He broke off suddenly.

"Eating?" Bob muttered to his best friend, Bonnie Kirk, who was sitting with him at the table next to Rocky's.

Bonnie giggled. "Not if he can help it," she whispered back.

Bob liked Bonnie a lot. She was the most sensible girl in the sixth grade, and the funniest. They'd known each other since kindergarten, when Bonnie's family had moved down the block from Bob's. Ever since then, they'd walked to school together every day.

"He'd rather have us starve to death than actually eat in here and maybe mess the place up or something. . . ."

"Don't talk so loudly!" hissed Tiffany Root, the biggest worrier in the sixth grade. "You'll get us all expelled!"

"A lunchroom *is* for eating, but you must do it with the right attitude," Mr. Haypence was saying. "And that, unfortunately, is just what is so sorely lacking among all you kids. Look at how you're treating your beautiful lunchroom! It looks like a dump! A sewer!"

"Is he talking about that straw on the floor?" Bonnie whispered. "Because, otherwise, the place looks okay to me."

"He's not really talking about anything," Jonathan Matterhorn muttered. Jonathan had two older sisters who'd already been through Hollis. "Mr. Haypence acts like this whenever the school gets anything new. My sisters said that when the new playground was built, he wouldn't let anyone run on it for the first *year*. They had to walk—slowly."

Junior Smith suddenly started waving his hand frantically in the air. Junior's goal in life was to become a millionaire by the time he was thirteen, and he was always trying to cut deals. Bob had once heard Junior bragging about how much he charged his own mother for doing household chores.

"Mr. Haypence!" Junior shouted excitedly. "I'll keep the lunchroom clean for you. Just pay me a small fee . . . oh, say, a couple thousand dollars a day . . . and I guarantee—"

"Junior, someone who really cared about this school would offer to clean up the lunchroom for *free*," Mr. Haypence proclaimed solemnly. "And I'm afraid that's the problem we have here. None of you has any real appreciation for this place! None of you has any respect for your teachers or your principal or this nice floor that you keep smearing your garbage around on!" Mr. Haypence was shouting now. "And I'm going to do something about that!" And ballroom dancing was that something.

9

* * *

"It sounds perfectly reasonable to me," Mrs. Kelly said, smiling. Clearly, she wasn't going to be any help, Bob thought.

"But Mom," he protested, "dance classes won't give us school spirit. They'll make us hate school even more!" Bob protested. "You should write Mr. Haypence and tell him so. You've got to get me out of this!"

"You have to take *dance classes*?" Lynn squealed before Mrs. Kelly could answer. "What a wussie!"

"That's enough, Lynn," Mrs. Kelly said sharply. "Bob, honey, don't take it so hard. Mr. Haypence is just trying to give all of you more of a . . . a sense of graciousness. An appreciation for the finer things in life."

"You mean for the lunchroom," Bob replied grumpily. "Is a lunchroom a finer thing in life?"

Mrs. Kelly paused. Then she did what she always did when she didn't know what to say. She changed the subject. "Well, it's really not a bad idea to learn a little formal dancing, anyway," she told Bob after a second. "Besides, it's mandatory, so you might as well just put up with it."

"But Mom, all the girls are taller than the boys!"

"You bet they are," Lynn said. "Boys are sissies!"

10

"Lynn, stay out of this!" Mrs. Kelly said crossly. "I'm sure the classes won't be nearly as bad as you expect, Bob. You might actually enjoy them!"

"Yeah, Bob," Lynn said, grabbing the last handful of potato chips out of the bag. "Plus, I bet you'll look *adorable* in a ball gown."

"I can't believe this whole thing," Bob grumbled to Bonnie Kirk next morning as they walked to school.

"Well, there's nothing we can do about them," Bonnie said. "It probably won't be *that* bad."

"Not that bad! Bonnie, what's the matter with you? Can you see *us* gliding around like a bunch of idiots from the Ice Capades?"

Bonnie shrugged, and Bob sighed. Was his best friend—the most sensible girl in the sixth grade—going to turn traitor? *What was it about girls and dancing?* Bob thought disgustedly.

They reached the front steps of the school. With a sinking heart, Bob noticed that Jennifer Stevens was only a few steps ahead of them. Jennifer was the prettiest girl in the sixth grade, but she was so stuck on herself and such an airhead that Bob couldn't stand being around her. Yet the past couple of weeks, whenever he turned around, there she was. It made him kind of nervous.

Don't say anything, he begged Bonnie silently. *Just don't make any noise, and maybe Jennifer won't see us!*

"You might actually get to like dancing, Bob," Bonnie suddenly announced in a nice loud voice. "Give it a chance..."

"Bob! Bonnie! Are you talking about the dance classes?"

"So much for silent prayers," Bob told himself.

"Won't it be fantastic?" Jennifer said, giving Bob a big, juicy smile—an unusual expression for Jennifer, who usually looked bored. She shook her hair back from her face. "I can't wait, can you?" she cooed. "I think it's going to be so much fun. Kind of, you know, romantic, don't you think?"

She stared straight into Bob's eyes.

Bob turned pale. He suddenly felt too sick to say a word.

Luckily, Bonnie spoke up. "We'd better get inside," she said coolly. "We'll be late if we keep standing out here blabbing."

Numbly, Bob followed Bonnie and Jennifer through the main entrance. In a trance, he opened his locker and took out his books. Then he blindly stumbled down the hall toward their classroom.

I've got to come up with a plan right away, he

thought frantically. *There's no way I'm going to learn ballroom dancing with that...that vampire!*

I'll just have to get expelled by this afternoon!

Chapter Two

No Way Out?

Unfortunately, Bob couldn't think of any sure-fire way to get expelled that wouldn't involve really big trouble—like the police or the fire department. And he didn't want to get expelled that badly. So, at the end of the school day, he was still sitting at his desk.

"I guess there's nothing to do but make a run for it when the bell rings," he decided. He glanced at the clock on the wall behind his teacher's head. Only five minutes to go.

Mrs. Doubleday was talking about the history of Central America. Bob hated history except for the time he got to study the Plains Indians— definitely cool in Bob's book. But today, it didn't bother him a bit. He'd never been more eager to

14

stay in class! And Mrs. Doubleday had never seemed more interesting—even if she was talking about the world's most boring topic.

"...so that's how the Panama Canal was built," Mrs. Doubleday finished. She rolled up the wall map and faced the class. "Tonight, I'd like each of you to write a short description of how *you* would have dealt with the hardships of building a canal in—"

Suddenly, the three-o'clock bell rang.

I'm out of here, Bob thought.

And so were a lot of other people. All at once, the boys in Mrs. Doubleday's sixth-grade class began to race wildly for the door.

"Freeze!" Mrs. Doubleday shouted.

The boys stopped in their tracks.

"What's the matter, Mrs. Doubleday?" Bob asked innocently.

"Nothing's the matter, Bob," his teacher answered. "But aren't you guys forgetting something?"

"Something?" repeated Jonathan Matterhorn, scratching his head. "No, I don't think so. What *kind* of something?"

"A mandatory-ballroom-dancing-in-the-lunchroom kind of something? Dance classes start this afternoon, remember?"

"Oh, yeah," said Diego Lopez with a weak

15

laugh. "I—I guess we forgot about them. Silly us."

"Silly you," echoed Mrs. Doubleday. "It's lucky everyone didn't forget."

"Oh, we wouldn't miss dance class for *anything*!" purred Jennifer Stevens. And she smiled at Bob right in front of everyone.

Bob wished he could just disappear into thin air. But no such luck.

"Okay class, let's get going," Mrs. Doubleday said briskly. "No running in the halls, please."

For once, there was no danger of that—not from the boys in the class, anyway. Never had any of them moved down the halls so slowly. "You could speed up a *little*," Mrs. Doubleday said. "You're not going before the firing squad, you know!"

"Now I know what it's like to be on a chain gang," Bob muttered to Rocky Latizano, who was behind him in line.

"Hey, it could be a lot worse," Rocky consoled him. "I mean, the classes *are* meeting in the lunchroom and not the gym. At least we can get something to eat while we're there."

"Besides," Junior Smith piped up from behind Rocky, "dances are a great way to network. Say you go to some dance at a country club and meet some big-business type of guy. He might offer you a job."

"Who'd want to be hired by someone who lets himself be seen at a dance?" Bob asked crossly.

"Well, you never know," said Junior. "There are lots of very important guys out there who like to tango or even—"

"Hurry up, boys!" Jennifer Stevens glanced back impatiently from her place at the head of the line. "You're making everyone late!"

Bob glared at her. "I can't believe some people are actually looking forward to this," he muttered to Diego Lopez, who was just ahead of him.

"Welcome, welcome!" Mr. Haypence boomed as the class filed into the lunchroom. "The young ladies will stand at that end of the lunchroom . . . excuse me, the ballroom." He pointed toward one end of the lunchroom, where Bob saw that a gleaming black grand piano had been set up. Sitting on the piano bench was Mrs. Moody, the school's music teacher.

"And the young gentlemen will stand at the other end of the ballroom. Line up neatly, please, ladies and gentlemen."

When everyone had lined up and the teachers had left, Mr. Haypence tilted his head at Mrs. Moody. She let loose with a crash of chords.

"Attention, please!" shouted Mr. Haypence. "Hollis Elementary's first dancing classes will now commence. Gentlemen, march forward!"

No one moved.

17

"March! Forward!" Mr. Haypence repeated impatiently.

A few of the boys shuffled forward an inch or two.

Mr. Haypence glared at the line. "A little more forward, please," he said coldly.

"How far?" hollered Rocky Latizano.

"Up to the young ladies, of course!" said Mr. Haypence. "Each gentleman will advance until he is facing a young lady on the opposite side of the room. Then he will give her a stiff West Point bow."

"A *what*?" someone hollered.

"A stiff West Point bow," said Mr. Haypence. "I shall demonstrate." Abruptly, he dipped forward and straightened up again, like a pigeon pecking at something. "Now, gentlemen, give it a try!"

There were a few scattered bows along the line. But for the most part, the boys—including Bob—stood mutinously still. Across the lunchroom, some of the girls giggled.

"Try again," said Mr. Haypence in an ominous tone. This time, every boy in the line managed at least an imitation of a bow.

"Well," said Mr. Haypence, "that's not very impressive. But I know you'll improve after a few more tries. Now, men, I want each of you to walk across the room and bow to the young lady

18

standing opposite you. She will be your partner for the first dance."

I can't do it! Bob thought. *I just can't.*

But Mrs. Moody began to play a stirring march—and somehow Bob found that his legs were carrying him, robotlike, across the room . . .

. . . and straight toward Jennifer Stevens.

She smiled when Bob reached her. "I knew I'd get you for the first dance," she said.

Bob learned many things over the course of the next hour as he danced with girl after girl. He learned that there's a dance called the cha-cha, during which it's possible to step on your partner's feet about twenty-five times a second. He learned that when you hold your hand on a girl's back during the fox-trot, you leave a big, wet, sweaty patch on her dress. And he learned that watching Mr. Haypence hop and swoop around the room to demonstrate the polka was dangerous to your health, because you almost choked to death trying to keep from laughing.

"Bob, stop it!" Tiffany Root implored as Mr. Haypence executed a sort of diving-board leap across the floor. "He'll hear you!"

But her warning came too late. Mr. Haypence had already noticed Bob's purple face and shaking shoulders.

"MISTER Kelly!" he shouted, coming to an

abrupt halt. Mrs. Moody looked up, startled, and the piano faltered to a stop.

"Are you sick, Mr. Kelly?" asked Mr. Haypence.

"N-no, sir," said Bob unsteadily.

"Then perhaps you would like to demonstrate these dance steps yourself?"

Bob sobered up immediately. "Oh, that's okay, Mr. Haypence," he said. "I—I think you're doing a great job."

"Well, *I* think we could all learn a great deal from watching you," Mr. Haypence said. "Please come out here to the center of the room."

Bob slowly obeyed. He thought he heard Jennifer Stevens and a couple of other girls snickering, but none of the boys laughed. They were probably all too grateful not to be in Bob's position.

"All right, Mr. Kelly," said Mr. Haypence. "Let's see *your* polka. Mrs. Moody, could you please?"

The notes of a cheerful little polka came bouncing through the air.

Then, as Bob continued to stand there, the notes trailed away to a tinkling halt.

"Weren't you paying attention to my demonstration?" asked Mr. Haypence. "The part I saw you watching certainly seemed to give you a great deal of pleasure."

"I...uh...I can't remember much of it, actually," Bob stammered.

"What you need is a partner!" Mr. Haypence said firmly.

"No..." Bob began.

"I'll be his partner!" It was Jennifer Stevens. A wave of giggles swept the lunchroom.

Bob's heart stopped, but not for long enough to be of any help to him.

"Splendid!" Mr. Haypence exclaimed. "I wish all the students had your enthusiasm, Jennifer."

Jennifer walked to the center of the room and faced Bob. Bob felt like screaming at her.

"All right, Bob, let's see your stiff West Point bow," Mr. Haypence said heartily.

Bob closed his eyes and dipped his head very, very slightly in Jennifer's direction. If you hadn't known it was a bow, you might have thought he was just blinking at her.

"And now," Mr. Haypence continued, "take her hand and—"

"Mr. Haypence? The bus drivers are getting kind of impatient out there."

With a gasp of relief, Bob turned and saw Mr. Skinner, Hollis's gym teacher, standing in the lunchroom door.

"The drivers say they're supposed to have the kids out of here by four-thirty," Mr. Skinner went on, "and now it's almost—"

"Yes, yes, I know what time it is!" Mr. Haypence snapped. He turned to Bob. "I'm afraid we'll have to reschedule this little demonstration, Mr. Kelly," he said. "And now, young ladies and gentlemen, please file quietly into the halls and out to the parking circle. I'll see you *all* tomorrow."

"Are you all right?" Diego Lopez asked Bob as they filed out. "That was a close call."

Bob shuddered. "Too close. I can't believe we have two whole weeks of this stuff. I'll never survive."

"Mr. Haypence, I've never had such a good time!" a voice rang out.

Bob and Diego quickly turned around. Jennifer was standing at the doorway staring up at the principal.

"It was just great," she said happily. "The best class I've ever had in this stupid school!"

A slight frown creased Mr. Haypence's forehead, but Jennifer went on before he could say anything. "Two weeks just isn't enough," she said. "Can't we have classes for two *months* instead?"

"Hey!" protested Bonnie, who was standing next to Jennifer. "Girls' basketball starts in—"

But Mr. Haypence didn't hear her. "Why, Jennifer, that's an excellent idea!" he exclaimed. "I'm glad to see that you've got so much school spirit. I'll check the schedule, but I'm sure two months of classes will work out just fine."

Bob gulped. Somehow he was sure, too. And he was also sure that eight weeks of dancing classes would definitely finish him off.

Chapter Three

Sabotage!—Or Maybe Not

But unfortunately for Jennifer Stevens and Mr. Haypence, eight weeks of dance classes turned out to be impossible. Bob and Diego heard Jennifer complaining about it on the playground a couple of days later.

"Mr. Haypence said he wished we could keep on with the dance classes, but the fourth-graders need the lunchroom next week to rehearse the play they're putting on," Jennifer said to a circle of girls gathered around her. Many of them looked far from unhappy to hear this news, Bob noticed. In fact, some of them—Bonnie included—looked positively joyful.

But Jennifer was too steamed up to pay attention to how her audience was reacting. "Can

25

you believe fourth-graders have so much power over what *sixth*-graders can do? It's like totally unfair!"

"But if the fourth-graders don't learn their lines, their play might be a flop! They'll be embarrassed in front of the whole school," Tiffany Root said. "And that would be *awful*!"

"Tiffany, nobody cares about that but you and the fourth-graders," Jennifer retorted. "What about *us*? Which is more important—our social life or some stupid version of *Mary Poppins* that everyone's seen a million times?"

"*Mary Poppins*!" Tiffany cried anxiously. "Oh, but they've *got* to rehearse for that! Because there is a flying scene, and someone could get badly—"

"Tiffany, will you quit worrying?" Jennifer interrupted crossly. "The point is that we've only got a week and a half more of dancing classes, and then—*bang!*—that's the end of our social life until we start junior high! What are we supposed to do till then?"

Diego and Bob looked at each other. "Do you believe what she's saying?" Diego practically yelled.

"I know," Bob said. "I don't trust Jennifer Stevens. Even if she suddenly gets amnesia about this stupid social-life business, we still have a week and a half of dance class left...."

But as the days dragged on, Jennifer didn't mention stretching out dance classes again, or any plans to improve the sixth-grade social life—or at least, not that Bob heard. Then again, he was doing his absolute best to keep any thoughts connected to ballroom dancing out of his brain, so maybe he didn't hear her.

To put it mildly, the dance classes never got any less horrible—at least as far as the sixth-grade boys were concerned.

For the sake of his future career, Junior Smith tried hard to like them. "Maybe if you just think of dancing as a way of making contacts, it won't be so bad," he suggested one afternoon as they walked into the lunchroom. "After all, you never know if one day . . . oh, Dawn Todd, say . . . might have a great stock-market tip for you."

Bob eyed Dawn Todd doubtfully. As far as he knew, Dawn was interested only in tropical fish. She kept sixteen tanks of them at home, and she was always bringing especially pretty ones to science class in little plastic bags.

"Dawn might have a tip about what to feed guppies," Bob said, "but I can't believe she'll help you with the stock market."

"Okay, maybe not Dawn," Junior agreed. "But I still think these classes will be useful in the long run."

Junior went on thinking that until he did an

27

especially deep West Point bow and ripped his pants in front of everyone. From then on, he hated ballroom dancing as much as everyone else.

They all kept trying to get out of dance class. But that turned out to be a lot harder than anyone had expected.

"Uh, Mr. Haypence," said Jonathan Matterhorn one afternoon as everyone was filing out of the lunchroom. "I won't be able to come to dance class tomorrow."

"Oh? And why is that?" asked the principal.

"Well, I . . . uh . . . I have to get a haircut."

"How . . . nice!" Mr. Haypence said. "We'll all look forward to seeing your new hairstyle . . . especially me."

"Oh, but I'm not—I'm not actually *having* my hair cut. The barber just wants to—to check out how it's growing," Jonathan stammered. He looked nervously around the room until he noticed Mrs. Moody's piano. "And, uhh, I also have a piano lesson right after. I'm practicing for my recital."

"And what pieces are you playing for the recital?" asked Mr. Haypence.

"Pieces? Oh. The Brahms . . . uh . . . Sonata. I mean Beethoven. Concerto in Middle C Major Minor. Also some scales. And some allegros. All kinds of stuff."

"I'm sure you need your practice," Mr. Haypence assured him.

Jonathan's face brightened.

"And on the day after tomorrow, I'm also sure your classmates would appreciate a demonstration of the music you'll be playing at the recital. Perhaps we could dance to it!"

Jonathan's face paled. "Oh, but..."

"Yes," Mr. Haypence continued grandly. "We'll all be looking forward to a mini-recital by our own Mr. Jonathan Matterhorn the day after tomorrow!"

"Help!" Jonathan yelped under his breath. But there was nothing anyone could do.

"Can't you play 'Three Blind Mice' or something?" Bob whispered as the sixth-graders filed into the lunchroom two days later.

"I can't play *anything*!" Jonathan hissed back.

Nevertheless, with Mr. Haypence at his side, Jonathan approached the piano. He sat down.

There was a very long pause. At last, Jonathan stretched out one tentative finger and struck a single key.

"Middle C," he announced. "I think."

The principal regarded him grimly. "Well... well... I *trust* we won't have any more defectors from dance classes," he said. "You have only a week left. It's so important that you learn as much as you can *while* you can."

Give me a break, Bob thought forlornly. *What I'm learning is how much I hate dancing.*

After that, no one tried to escape.

On top of everything else, Mr. Haypence was getting so suspicious that he gave the boys a hard time no matter what they did. When Bob accidentally fell into the lunchroom's ornamental waterfall one afternoon during dance class, for example, Mr. Haypence wouldn't even let him out of the lunchroom to dry himself off. It really had been an accident, too. Bob's partner, Mary Featherstone—the tallest girl in the sixth grade—had been so intent on counting the number of cha-cha steps they were supposed to be doing that she hadn't noticed she was marching Bob backward toward the waterfall until he fell into it headfirst with a big splash. For the rest of the class, poor Bob had to dance the tango, the polka, and the classic waltz while his shoes squelched. It wasn't a pleasant experience.

Meanwhile, on the home front, Bob's sister Lynn never let up on him. "Why, Bob," she exclaimed one morning at breakfast when she'd purposely jogged his arm and made him drop the sugar bowl, sending a sparkling cascade of sugar all over the floor. "I thought all that dancing was supposed to make you more graceful!"

"Lynn," Bob growled, "if you don't shut up, I'll stiff-West-Point-bow you right in the—"

"Just ignore her," his mother said wearily. But about a cup of sugar had gotten into the treads of Bob's sneakers, and it didn't work itself out for a week.

But something even worse than dance class, wet shoes, and a bratty sister was bugging Bob. Ever since dance class had started, Bob couldn't seem to go anywhere without running into Jennifer. She kept smiling at him and talking to him. Worst of all, she kept staring at him the way Bob imagined a *Tyrannosaurus rex* might look at a cheeseburger.

"I wish these classes would never end, don't you?" she whispered to Bob on the second to last day as he grimly whirled her around the room.

Bob wanted to scream. But all he said was, "Well, as a matter of fact, I'm kind of looking forward to them ending. I guess I'm just not the ballroom type."

"But you're such a good dancer," Jennifer insisted. For the third time in two minutes, Bob had managed to step on Jennifer's toes.

I've had it with this nonsense, Bob thought. "Well, if I never dance again, it will be too soon."

"Oh, but you will dance again, Bob," Jennifer said. "It's sooner than you think."

Bob halted abruptly. "What are you talking about?"

"Wait until tomorrow," Jennifer said. "You'll see."

Tomorrow came way too fast.

It was the last class. Everyone was smiling—especially the boys—and their smiles grew even wider when Mrs. Moody had played her final waltz. Then Mr. Haypence stepped forward and handed each member of the sixth grade a hokey-looking certificate that said: "You now are an expert in ballroom dancing." The certificate was decorated with big shiny gold stars and pictures of dancing feet. Bob and all the rest of the boys said in chorus: "Thank you very much, Mr. Haypence." Then they all stampeded into the bathroom to throw their certificates away, and after that they all burst into loud cries of "Hooray" and "Free at last!"

A few minutes later, with his stupid certificate safely flushed, Bob was heading for the door. On the way there, he passed Mr. Haypence's office. He couldn't help hearing Jennifer's voice inside, talking excitedly.

"...and I think I have the absolutely *perfect* ending for all these wonderful classes, Mr. Haypence," he heard her trill. "A formal dance for the sixth grade!"

Bob could feel the color draining out of his face. "No," he pleaded silently. "Say *no*!"

"Why, Jennifer, what an excellent idea!" gushed Mr. Haypence. "Then all you sixth-graders will get a chance to put everything you've learned into practice! A dance would be simply fabulous! And what an opportunity to polish social skills!"

"I thought you'd like the idea," Jennifer said with satisfaction. "We can decorate the lunchroom just the way high schoolers do, with lights and a mirror ball and crepe paper and stuff, and we can hire a deejay . . . "

Bob's legs were so weak with horror that he practically melted onto the floor.

"It's an excellent idea," said Mr. Haypence with decision. "In fact, I guarantee that I'll see to it that every single student in the sixth grade will be there!"

And that's exactly what he did in the letter he sent out two days later:

To all parents of Hollis Elementary School sixth-graders: I am delighted to announce a unique and ingenious method for putting our ballroom dance lessons to good use: a dance for the members of the sixth grade!

Our brand-new, beautiful lunchroom will be the site of this social event!

Attendance at this dance is mandatory. School spirit depends on participation from *everyone*, especially boys.

Sincerely, Wilfred Haypence.

Mr. Haypence wasn't taking any chances with this letter, either. He had it mailed to every sixth-grader's house without telling anyone.

When Bob got home from school on Monday, the letter was already lying, opened, on the piano. And from the look on his mother's face, Bob could tell she thought Mr. Haypence had just come up with another one of his wonderful ideas.

Chapter Four

Operation: Destroy

The Watson twins, Louie and Larry, were classmates of Bob's who were more commonly known as the Human Demolition Team. Accidents just seemed to happen when they were around. No one could figure out if it was because the twins loved wrecking things, or because they couldn't *help* wrecking things. But either way, they left a trail of ruin wherever they went. Fish tanks seemed to shatter if the twins even looked at them. Chairs holding Larry or Louie tipped over backward twice as often as twinless chairs. And as for baseballs and windows—well, it probably made more sense to break all the windows around *before* the twins stepped up to bat, just to get the suspense over with.

That was why Bob was feeling a little nervous as he led Larry and Louie up the front walk toward his house. "Now, remember, my mom won't be really happy if you, like, destroy the house, you know," he warned them. "So remember, *be careful*, okay?"

"Hey, no problem!" said Larry, stumbling slightly and bashing into the pot of chrysanthemums on the Kellys' front step. "We know how to act right!"

"Yeah," said his twin. "We're not animals!"

"Your best bet is to tie their hands together once they get inside," advised Diego Lopez, who was right behind the twins. Jonathan Matterhorn, Rocky Latizano, and Junior Smith, who were right behind him, all nodded in agreement. "And their feet!" Jonathan added. "No, never mind. They might trip. You'd better just tie them to the sofa or something."

"What's the matter with you guys?" Louie asked in a hurt voice. "We're not going to cause any trouble or anything. Agghh!" He went crashing through the screen door. His brother Larry followed him. And they both landed in a heap on the floor in front of Bob's mother.

"Oh. Sorry!" they chorused. "Hi, Mrs. Kelly!"

"Are you fellows going to study for a test or something?" Bob's mother asked as the rest of the boys filed up the front steps.

Bob winced. *Fellows!* he thought with a shudder. *Why do I have to have a mother who uses words like that?* "No, we're having a meeting," he said.

"Oh, that's nice. About what?"

"School stuff," Bob replied evasively.

"Great," said Mrs. Kelly, eyeing the Watson twins nervously. "Since it's such a nice day, why don't you have your meeting outside?" And she slammed the front door firmly in their faces.

Bob sighed. "Come on, guys," he said.

He led them all around to the patio. "Now," he said when everyone had settled down. "I think you can guess why I asked you over here today. You see, the time has come to—"

"Do we have to do all this talking on an empty stomach?" Rocky interrupted.

"Rocky, you had three Cokes and about a hundred cookies on the way home!" objected Bob.

Rocky looked hurt. "It's not polite to keep track of how much your guests eat," he said with dignity. "Anyway, I didn't have anywhere *near* a hundred. I just think we need a little snack to help us think better, that's all."

"Well, if you want to ask my mother for something, go ahead," said Bob.

Rocky paused. "It can wait," he finally said. "I've got some stuff in my pockets that I can eat first."

"Glad to hear it. Anyway, back to business," Bob went on. "We've got a job to do."

"You mean we've got a job to do, *fellows*," Diego broke in slyly.

"Oh, shut up," Bob said crossly. "I bet your mother sometimes uses dumb words like that, too. Anyway, does everyone agree with me that this dance really stinks and that we've got to get rid of it?"

His listeners all nodded in heartfelt agreement.

"Well, that's why you're all here," said Bob. "We've all got to come up with a plan to stop it."

"Why don't *you* think of one?" Rocky asked. He pulled a lint-covered licorice whip out of his pocket. Then he folded it in half and stuffed it into his mouth. "I mean, should *we* have to do all the work?" he mumbled thickly.

Bob sighed. "Because seven heads are better than one. I did find out one thing today," he continued. "The name of the place where the school's getting the deejay. Anyway, I had this idea that maybe we could somehow persuade them not to send a deejay to our party."

"How?" Diego asked.

"Hey, I know!" Larry Watson said excitedly. "We could blow up the guy's car! I saw a movie like that once. See, we plant the bomb in the car just before he leaves for the dance. He opens the front door, and—*kaboom!*—he's history. Boy, that'd teach him!"

"I think that murdering someone is maybe going a little too far," Bob said quietly. "Besides, we'd end up in jail...."

Larry's face fell. "Oh, yeah," he said. "So what are we going to do?"

"Well, maybe Larry's got part of a good idea," Diego said after a pause. "What about a bomb threat? We could call up the deejay place... what's it called?"

"Dancin' Deejays," said Bob.

"Yuck. Well, we could go over to Dancin' Deejays and tell them there'd been a lot of bomb threats at the school recently, and that it probably isn't the best time to send a deejay to the dance. We could just say we were, uh, friends of the school or something."

"No, we can say we're terrorists!" Jonathan Matterhorn said, his eyes shining. "I mean, *sons* of terrorists. We say we're the sons of terrorists, and we have it on excellent authority that a bomb will be planted somewhere in the lunchroom, and—"

"So, Jonathan," Bob said. "You'll put on this foreign accent and tell Dancin' Deejays you're the son of a terrorist, and—"

"Hey, what are you talking about?" Jonathan said quickly. "*I'm* not telling them!"

"Well, it was your idea," Bob pointed out. "Besides, you'd be the best at it."

"Yeah, it's the perfect part for you," Diego chimed in, and everyone on the patio—except Jonathan, of course—nodded energetically.

"No way!" Jonathan said frantically. "What if they arrest me?"

"Look, Jon," Bob said, "let me explain something. Everyone knows you're the best-looking guy in the sixth grade. Now, the girls are going to be asking the boys to this dance. That means that probably fifty percent of them will think of you first, and that means..."

"Okay! Okay!" Jonathan broke in. "But you're all coming with me. If I get arrested, I want you guys arrested, too!"

The idea of getting arrested turned out to be too much for Junior. "I'm afraid I can't afford a police record, guys," he explained when they all met in the playground the next morning. "It might wreck up my job prospects later on, and it will definitely ruin my chances of getting into an Ivy League school. I'll definitely be with you guys in spirit. Just don't mention my name, okay?"

So it was a slightly smaller group that walked over to the Dancin' Deejays' offices after school that day. "Wow!" Bob murmured to Diego when they walked through the door.

The Dancin' Deejays' offices suffered from a severe overdose of perkiness. Their walls were covered with brightly colored plaques bearing slogans like "Deejays Are Deelightful!" and "Have You Hugged a Dancin' Deejay Today?" The receptionist's desk was the color of bubble gum, and on it sat a stuffed panda holding a big red heart, a fluffy yellow stuffed duck, and a giant stuffed baby-blue hippo with a tag around its neck that said: "Hug me."

Smilin' Steve turned out to be the name of the deejay who'd been assigned to the sixth-grade dance. But he definitely wasn't smilin' as he stared at Bob and his friends. Instead, he looked more like he should have been called Stupefied Steve.

"You're *what*?" Smilin' Steve asked in amazement.

Jonathan cleared his throat. "Ve are ze sons of intairnassional terrorists," he repeated.

Ouch! Bob said to himself. So much for Jonathan's being a great actor! He sounded more like the bad guy in a really terrible old movie. "I unnairstant zat you are plannink to be ze Mastaire of Ceraymonies at ze Hollis Elementary School dance," Jonathan went on. "Ve are here on a mizzion to warn you zat zere is a vairy grave danjaire in store for you."

Smilin' Steve looked faintly alarmed. Not as though he was worried for his safety, more as though he was worried that Jonathan was crazy. "What *kind* of a danjaire—I mean danger?" he asked.

"Eet ees ze danjaire of a bomb threat to ze lunchroom."

"No, wait a minute!" Larry suddenly whispered loudly and spittily. "It's a bomb threat to the deejay. They said they were going to blow up the deejay!"

"Yeah!" Louie agreed in an equally wet whisper. "Tear him from limb to limb, they said!"

"So you guys don't want your school to have a dance, is that it?" Steve was definitely smiling now, but not in a friendly way.

Goggle-eyed, Jonathan stared at him. "How—how did you know?" he asked in his normal voice.

"Oh, I've seen all the tricks," Smilin' Steve told him. "I've got to give you kids credit, though. Most of the boys just call me up on the day of the party and try to convince me that the dance has been canceled. Once someone did tell me that there'd been a plague outbreak at the school. Sons of terrorists. Now, *that's* a new approach!"

Smilin' Steve leaned back comfortably in his seat.

"But hey, guys!" he said. "I just know you're gonna love it once you're there! Trust me, guys."

"Can you at least make sure there aren't any slow dances?" Bob blurted out.

Smilin' Steve's smile became even broader. "Oh, no. Believe me, dudes, a few nice ballads with that special lady in your arms will make the evenin' just fly by. Don't you worry about a thing. Now I've got to make some phone calls. Okay? Thanks for stoppin' by."

"So *now* what do we do?" Larry asked bitterly as they walked out of the offices.

"We think of something else, that's what," Bob told him. "Okay, Plan A didn't exactly work out. But that doesn't mean we can't come up with a great Plan B!"

Chapter Five

Plans B, C, D...

To all the oParrents of th Hollis Elemntary School SiXth GradersD: we wuld lik to imform you that the Dance hab been canclled. Anyone wh shoes up will recie8ve a failinGG grade. Also, smu]strmy ejp fprdm y nr;orbr ,r djpi;f tr,pbr yjrot vjo;f gtp, dvjpp;/ Thank you. Sincerly. Wilfriend Haypence.,

Proudly, Louie handed the smudged, tattered piece of paper to Bob. "Here's Plan B for you," he said triumphantly. "This ought to fool them. I'm a pretty good typer, don't you think?"

"Typist, you mean," Bob said absently, staring at the letter. He could hardly believe so many mistakes could have made it onto a single piece of paper.

"Uhhh, Louie, what's this part here?" he asked, pointing to the last lines.

A worried frown creased Louie's brow as he studied the letter. "Hey, uhhh, I'm not sure. . . . Oh, yeah! It's supposed to say, 'Any parent who doesn't like it can just remove their kid from school permanently.'"

Louie sighed gustily. "I guess I'll have to re-type it."

"Well, yes," Bob said. "And remember, Mr. Haypence's name is Wilfred, not Wilfriend. And you said 'shoes up' instead of 'shows up.' And—"

"Oh, that's just technical stuff!" Louie said impatiently. "As long as I have to retype it anyway, I'll just fix all the mistakes."

And probably make just as many new ones, Bob thought to himself. Aloud, he said only, "Hang on a sec, Louie. This letter's a great idea, but I'm not sure it'll work. I mean, how are you going to get it mailed?"

"What do you mean?" Louie looked puzzled. "I'll just send it to all the sixth-grade parents, of course!"

"But that's a lot of people," Bob pointed out. "And we don't have those little computerized name-and-address stickers they always use on the envelopes when they mail stuff to the parents. So the letters won't look as though they really come from the office."

"No big deal. So I address them by hand!" Louie said brightly. "I can just put a little note on each envelope that says the computer-envelope thingy broke down. And while I'm at it, maybe I should make the letter even scarier. How about if I say that any kid who shows up at the dance will be *killed*? What do you think?"

Bob was getting a headache, a bad headache.

"You know, Louie," he said after a long pause, "I hate to see you have to do so much work on this. Why don't we hold off on this letter until we see if we can come up with something a little easier. You know, something that won't take quite as long."

"Yeah," Louie said glumly. "Maybe you're right."

"But Rocky, you'll *die* if you don't eat!" gasped Tiffany in horror.

It was lunchtime of the next day, and a shocked group of sixth-graders was standing around Rocky in the lunchroom.

They were shocked because, for the first time in Hollis history, Rocky wasn't at the head of the lunch line. He wasn't even *in* the lunch line. Instead, he was leaning exhaustedly back in a chair at one of the tables, and his face was as white as a sheet.

"I'm totally prepared to die," Rocky told Tiffany weakly. "I'm on a hunger strike."

"A hunger strike! Why?" asked Bonnie. "What are you striking about?"

"The dance!" Rocky murmured, his forehead beaded with sweat. "And I won't eat again until the dance is called off!"

"Oh, give me a break," Bonnie said scornfully. "You're going to *starve* yourself just because you don't want to go to a dance?"

"Uh-huh."

"And how long has this been going on?" Bonnie asked.

"I just started," Rocky mumbled. He coughed weakly. "But I tell you, I'm suffering."

"Wow! A ten-minute hunger strike," said Bonnie sarcastically.

"Don't make fun of him, Bonnie!" Bob said. "He's a . . . a freedom fighter!" He gave Rocky a comforting pat on the shoulder. Rocky hadn't told him about this plan—Plan C, Bob guessed it should be called—but Bob couldn't help being impressed by it. The thought of Rocky's going without food for more than five minutes would shake up a lot of people.

Unfortunately, Jennifer Stevens wasn't one of them. "You might as well just get yourself measured for your coffin," she informed Rocky angrily. "This dance isn't going to be called off just because some stupid kid starves to death!" And with that, she flounced away back to the lunch line.

Rocky sat up indignantly for a second. Then, remembering that he was supposed to be weak and frail, he sank back in his seat again. "She'll be sorry she said that," he said. "When Jennifer Stevens sees my poor, wasted form being carried out of the lunchroom on a stretcher, she'll wish she had been nicer to me while I was still alive."

And with that, he slid out of his seat onto the floor and lay there, motionless.

Tiffany burst into tears.

"What's the matter?" came Ms. Weinstock's voice. She peered anxiously over the shoulders of the kids surrounding Rocky.

"Rocky's dying!" Tiffany moaned. "He's starving himself to death!"

"Why?" Ms. Weinstock asked in amazement, and a blubbering Tiffany filled her in.

Was Bob imagining things, or had the ghost of a smile flickered on Ms. Weinstock's face?

"Mrs. Carlson!" she called. Mrs. Carlson was everyone's favorite lunch lady.

In seconds, Mrs. Carlson was there. "We have a hunger striker here," Ms. Weinstock told her.

"Any suggestions on how to bring him out of his rapid decline?"

"No problem!" Mrs. Carlson answered. She darted back to the kitchen and quickly returned with a plate in her hand.

On the plate was a cheeseburger.

Mrs. Carlson knelt down next to Rocky and held the plate under his nose. "Kind of like smelling salts," she remarked in an undertone.

Rocky's nostrils began to twitch, and his eyelids flickered. He slowly pulled himself up to a sitting position, and then he reached a trembling hand out to the plate.

"Rocky, wait!" Bob cried.

"I can't," said Rocky. And he ate the cheeseburger in three bites.

All the color flooded back into his face. "Do you have any more of those?" he asked Mrs. Carlson sheepishly. "I guess I just can't handle skipping a whole meal like that."

"Boy, they haven't wasted any time putting up the posters!" Bob commented the next morning as he and Diego walked down the hall toward Mrs. Doubleday's room.

The publicity committee had been working hard; there was a poster about every three inches for the whole length of the hall. But the poster Bob was looking at now was especially awful. It was made of hot pink posterboard trimmed with lots of golden tinselly fringe. In the center was an elaborate painting of a dancing couple. Neither member of the couple would have been particularly comfortable at the Hollis Elementary School dance, though, because they looked like they were both about forty-five years old and they had really long legs and incredibly short arms. They both wore big idiotic smiles.

Under the happy couple were painted these words:

HOLLIS ELEMENTARY SCHOOL'S
FIRST ANNUAL DANCE
COME ONE COME ALL FOR FUN, ROMANCE,
AND DELICIOUS PUNCH AND COOKIES!
IN THE GRAND BALLROOM! (THE LUNCHROOM.)

While Bob was thinking what a stupid poster it was, Larry and Louie Watson, the Human Demolition Team, came striding by. As Larry passed the poster, he suddenly stumbled. His arms flailing, he grabbed wildly at the poster, ripping it off the wall as he fell to the ground with an enormous crash.

The same thing happened with the next poster when Louie passed it, and to the one after that when Larry passed it, and the next one.

"I can't believe it," Bob marveled. "It *looks* like

an accident, but they're really doing it on purpose!"

Diego whistled with admiration.

But it wasn't really fair to destroy the posters, Bob thought. "Hey, guys!" he called. "You can't do that!"

The twins whirled around. "Oh, it's you," Louie said in relief.

"Chill out," Larry told him. "We're just having . . . uhh, what's it called? . . . freedom of expression! It's protected by the Constitution."

"Yeah, that's right!" Louie put in.

Bob sighed. "Never mind," he said.

The twins continued on their path of destruction. "I guess that was Plan D. We've got to come up with something else, Diego. Something not so . . . not so . . ."

"Ridiculous?" Diego supplied. Bob nodded.

"I've been thinking about it," said Diego slowly, "and I may have come up with something." He grinned. "Get all the guys together on the playground after school, and I'll tell you all about it!"

"Bob, what's the matter?" asked Ms. Weinstock in alarm. It was lunchtime.

"I—I don't know, Ms. Weinstock!" Bob gasped. "It feels like the floor just started shaking or something!"

51

Plan E was underway.

Bob had just gone through the lunch line. He'd paid for his food, grabbed a straw and a napkin, and then, in a really spectacular move, he'd suddenly tumbled to the floor, spilling the entire contents of his lunch tray all over the place. (Lunch that day was something called Tofu Burger Delight—grayish-purple patties made without a shred of meat. They were a new invention of Ms. Weinstock's. And, Bob reflected, if nothing else, Plan E provided a convenient way of ditching a meal he had no intention of eating in the first place.)

"Ms. Weinstock, maybe it's an earthquake! We should all get out of here before the whole building collapses!" It was Tiffany, of course.

"It didn't feel exactly like an earthquake," Bob said. It hadn't felt like anything at all. He'd been making it up. "It was more like . . . oh, I don't know . . . a weak place in the floor or—"

Crash! At the other end of the room, Jonathan Matterhorn skidded to the floor right into a bunch of chairs. "Ow!" he cried, rubbing his head.

In yet another corner of the room, Rocky Latizano began quivering in his chair.

"Ms. Weinstock, Ms. Weinstock!" he bellowed. "I can't make my chair stay still!"

"Oh, no!" Tiffany moaned. "There's a poltergeist in here! Ms. Weinstock, you have to call an exorcist!"

Before Ms. Weinstock could answer, Larry and Louie Watson tipped forward out of their chairs and fell headlong into their plates. And then Junior Smith, who was walking toward the drinking fountain, suddenly flipped over backward and began flopping around.

"Help!" he screamed. "I can't walk. The floor's giving waayyy!"

"Hey, what's going on here? Oh, no! It's happening to Diego, too!" Now Ms. Weinstock looked almost as frightened as Tiffany, which was saying a lot.

Diego was lurching toward Ms. Weinstock like a sailor on a pitching ship. "There's some kind of dangerous vibration in this room!" he gasped. "Are you sure the supports under this floor are okay?"

A frightened silence fell over the lunchroom.

"I don't know anything about the floor supports!" Ms. Weinstock said, rushing toward the wall phone. "I'm calling Mr. Haypence. We'd better evacuate this lunchroom immediately!"

"Good idea!" called Rocky. "And you'd better call off the dance, too!"

Ms. Weinstock stopped in her tracks.

Thanks a lot, Rocky, thought Bob grimly.

Slowly, Ms. Weinstock turned to face Rocky,

whose chair had mysteriously calmed down when she'd turned her back.

"Say that again, Rocky?" she asked.

"Well, uh, you should call off the, uh, dance if the floor's so— Oops!" Rocky suddenly remembered his chair. Shooting a guilty look at Bob, he began shaking twice as hard as before. "Oh, no! It's started up again!" he yelled.

Ms. Weinstock gave him a long, cold stare. "Hmmm," she said finally. "Don't you think it's a little strange that none of the *girls* are having this trouble? Maybe the boys' imaginations are just a little hyperactive today. I don't think we'll bother Mr. Haypence after all. Bob, could you please clean up the mess you made, since you seem to have started this whole thing?"

Bob sheepishly got to his feet—and slipped on his smashed Tofu Burger Delight. Down he went again, right onto his left ankle.

A sharp pain shot up the whole length of his leg. "Ouch!" he yelped. "Ms. Weinstock, this time I've really hurt myself!"

"*Sure* you have," Bonnie said from a nearby table.

"But look at my ankle!" Bob begged. "It's swelling up!"

"It's just a sprain," said Bob's doctor half an hour later, "but it's a bad one. I'm afraid you'll have to take it easy for a while, Bob. I want you on crutches until this heals."

Crutches! No one could be expected to dance in crutches!

A wide grin spread across Bob's face. *I can't believe it!* he thought jubilantly. *I won't have to go to the dance after all!*

"Oh, no, that's terrible!" Mrs. Kelly said. "How long will he need them?"

"Well, kids heal fast," Dr. Talpey told her. "But he probably won't be able to walk on his own again for at least two weeks."

Mrs. Kelly brightened. "Oh, that's not so bad."

Two weeks, Bob was thinking. *In two weeks, I'll be all back to normal. Just in time for . . .*

The Hollis sixth-grade dance.

Chapter Six

Bob! It's for You!

Just as the Kelly family sat down to dinner that night, the telephone rang.

"Never fails," Bob's father said with a sigh. He pushed his chair back, but Lynn was already out of her seat and dashing to the phone with squirrel-like speed.

"Kelly residence. Lynn Kelly speaking," Lynn announced crisply into the phone. "How may I help you?"

She listened for a few seconds, and burst into shrieks of laughter. "Bob!" she caroled. "It's for you! It's a giiiiirrrrrl! Bob has a girlfriend! Bob has a girlfriend!"

"Shut up, Lynn! And put that phone down!" Bob reached for his crutches. Then he hobbled across the dining room toward the phone.

"Now, Lynn, come and sit down," said Mrs. Kelly. "Bob is getting to be a big boy. He needs to talk to his friends in privacy." She turned to Bob with a big smile. "Don't talk too long, honey," she said. "You know how much you hate cold stew."

What Bob *really* hated was the thought of whoever was on the line overhearing everything his family was saying. It was a good bet that everything they'd said had made it into the telephone loud and clear. Gingerly, he picked up the receiver.

"Hello?"

"Hi, Bob! It's Jennifer. Jennifer Stevens, you know?"

Bob's stomach turned to lead.

"Jennifer! What do you want? I mean . . . uh . . . how are you?"

"Just fine." As always, Jennifer got right to the point. "I'm calling about the dance." Bob's leaden stomach now turned to cement.

"The—the—the dance?" Bob stammered. "Uh, what dance?"

"The one at school! Like what else have we all been working on for so long?"

"Oh, that dance!" Bob gave an extremely feeble imitation of a laugh. "Well. Uh, well . . . *that* dance is still weeks and weeks away!"

"Just three weeks," Jennifer said quickly.

"Uh, Jennifer, I can't really talk on the phone right now," Bob mumbled. "See, we're eating dinner, and—"

"Bob, it's fine to talk!" his mother broke in loudly. "You just go right ahead and finish your conversation."

Bob clapped his hand over the receiver. "Quit spying on my phone calls!" he whispered.

"Oh but, sweetheart..." his mother began to protest.

Bob shot her a murderous glance and turned back to the telephone. "Sorry, Jennifer," he said. "Uhh...that was my mom and, uhh, I'll have to call you back later or something. Parents, you know."

"But I heard your mother say it's okay!" Jennifer began. "And I just want to ask you—"

"Gotta go!" Bob said quickly. "Well...uh... nice talking to you, Jennifer. See you tomorrow!"

Click! went the receiver as Bob hung up.

"Hey, thanks, you guys!" he burst out as he hobbled back toward his chair. "You've just managed to totally embarrass me—"

"In front of your girlfriend?" Lynn cut in sweetly.

"She's *not* my girlfriend!" Bob shouted as he pulled out his chair and tried to reposition his sprained ankle on the pillows. "She's just this bloodsucking, boy-crazy vampire who—"

"Robert Kelly!" said his mother. "That's no way to talk about one of your classmates!"

"But Mom, you've never even *met* Jennifer!"

"I certainly have. I remember her from your kindergarten class. She always wore the most darling little pinafores." Mrs. Kelly looked wistfully at Lynn, whose camouflage fatigues were even grubbier than usual.

Lynn glugged down her glass of milk, burped loudly, and wiped her mouth on the back of her hand.

Mrs. Kelly sighed. "Anyway, Bob, I'm sure Jennifer Stevens is still a lovely girl."

"You won't think she's so lovely when you hear that she's asking me to go to the dance with her," Bob said darkly.

"Why not?" his mother asked cheerfully. "It sounds fun. I bet you two will have a great time!"

Bob didn't even bother answering that. "But Mom, what about Bonnie? I didn't want to go to this thing in the first place, but at least I figured Bonnie would be the one asking me. She'll have a fit when she finds out that *Jennifer* asked me first!"

"Well, honey, that's really Bonnie's problem," said Bob's mother. "If she wanted to ask you to the dance, she should have done it."

"You know what they say about early birds

and worms," added Mr. Kelly in a jovial voice.

No one ever asks the worm what he *thinks about it*, Bob thought glumly.

It was the morning after Jennifer's phone call, and Bob was trying to get Diego's attention.

"Diego!" Bob called in a loud whisper. "Hey, Diego! Is that you?"

Diego looked around. "What? What?" he said. "Bob? Is that you? *Where are you?*"

"I'm in here!" Bob whispered. "In the janitor's closet!"

The closet door swung open a crack, and Diego peered into the gloom. "Hey, weird, Bob!" he said loudly. "What are you doing in—"

"Sssssshhhhhhhhhhhhh!" Bob said frantically. "Listen, Diego. Do you see Jennifer anywhere out there?"

Diego cast a glance up and down the hall. "Nope. Why?"

Bob sighed with relief. "Come in here for a second, and I'll explain everything."

"But Bob, you can't *stay* in here!" Diego protested a few minutes later when Bob had finished.

"Diego, a man's gotta do what he's gotta do."

"But you're *not* a man," Diego pointed out. "And anyway, what you've gotta do is go to class, not hide under some sink all day."

"I'm not going to stay in here all day," Bob said. "Just until the bell rings. Then I'll run into Mrs. Doubleday's room at the last minute, so Jennifer won't get a chance to talk to me. And then, during lunch, I'll come back here. I'll only have to do it for about twenty more days, until the dance is over. What do you think?"

"I don't know," Diego said cautiously. "But I'll try to help keep her away from you. Maybe I can distract her or something."

The bell rang. "Don't wait for me," Bob said. "It's going to take me a while to get to class on these crutches. Anyway, it's better if I'm a little late. That way, Jennifer definitely won't get to talk to me."

Bob's plan had taken everything into account—except for one thing. It had never occurred to him that Jennifer might pass him a note instead. Not until the middle of Mrs. Doubleday's lecture on the history of rocks, when he looked up and saw her nudge Tiffany, point to him, and whisper something in a giggle.

Tiffany giggled, too. Then she passed the note to Lacey Melcher, who passed it to Mary Featherstone, who was starting to pass it to Bonnie when Rocky reached out and grabbed it out of her hand.

He read it. His shoulders began shaking with mirth. "Oh, boy," he whispered. "Your goose is cooked, Kelly." And he tossed the note onto Bob's desk.

"Hi, Bob!" the note said in curlicued handwriting. "Well? Can you go to the dance with me?"

Bob glanced uneasily at Jennifer, who was gazing expectantly at him. He pointed at Mrs. Doubleday, frowned in a concerned way, and shook his head slightly. He hoped that his expression would convey the message, "I can't possibly answer such a frivolous question during earth science."

Jennifer started to pout and the bell rang. "Oh, no!" Bob thought. "Lunchtime!"

Fortunately, Diego rushed to the rescue. "Hey, Jen!" he said, grabbing her on the way to the door. "I was wondering if you could explain the math homework to me."

Jennifer stared at him in astonishment. "But *you're* a math genius, Diego!" she said. "What do you need help with?"

"It's—it's, uhhh, just something about the numbers that I don't get." Diego's math book was already open, and he held it right up under Jennifer's nose. "See, right here, where there's that little two? Don't you think it kind of looks more like a five?"

Swiftly, Bob began to swing out of the room on his crutches. "Hey, Bob!" Jennifer called.

"Wait!" But by then, he was already out the door.

Unfortunately, the janitor's closet was locked when Bob finally reached it. So he had to be a lot cleverer than he'd been planning on. First, he had to pretend to choke on his lunch when Jennifer marched purposefully toward him in the lunchroom. (Diego elbowed her out of the way and gave Bob a fake Heimlich maneuver.) Then he had to spend recess playing monsters with a horde of first-graders who kept him surrounded more effectively than fifty bodyguards. And last he had to come up with a special project for art class.

"But Bob," said Ms. Bartlett, Hollis's art teacher, "don't you think it will be rather difficult to make a plaster cast of your own mouth? You'll have to hold your mouth still for so long, and you won't be able to talk.... Wouldn't you rather make something else out of plaster?"

"No, Ms. Bartlett," said Bob. "Uhh...I don't mind not being able to talk." Not being able to talk would mean not being able to answer at all if Jennifer asked him The Question again.

But once again, Bob hadn't counted on Jennifer's determination.

"Well?" she asked him about fifteen minutes later.

Bob winced in an I-wish-I-could-help-you way

and pointed at his mouth, which was now thoroughly encased in thick white goo.

"So just nod or shake your head!" said Jennifer impatiently.

Trying to look as fragile as he could, Bob reached for a piece of paper and gingerly wrote "It would crack the plaster mold" on it.

"But so you *can* write!" Jennifer exclaimed. "So, why don't you just write an answer?"

"Jennifer!" It was Ms. Bartlett. "Please come and clean up your plaster right now. You can't just leave it to harden on the table."

Bob heaved a sigh of relief. "I don't know why not," Jennifer grumbled. "Stupid messy old glop. I hate it!"

But she went over to her table to clean up, and the bell rang before she got another chance to talk to Bob.

I did it! Bob thought jubilantly as he headed out the door toward his mom's waiting car. (She had agreed to drive him to and from school for as long as he was on crutches.) *I managed to avoid her for a whole day! Now, if I can just keep it up for another twenty—*

"Bob?" Jennifer was standing out by the parking circle in front of the school.

"I figured you'd be getting a ride home," she said. "So what about it? Can you go?"

There was an expression on her face that Bob couldn't quite identify.

I think she's nervous! he thought incredulously.

It seemed impossible. Jennifer Stevens, *nervous?*

Well, Bob suddenly told himself, *you might be a little nervous if someone you'd asked to a dance had been dodging you all day long.* Then he sighed. *I really, really, don't want to go to this stupid dance*, he thought.

"I'd be happy to go with you, Jennifer," he heard himself say. "Thank you for asking me."

"You did just exactly the right thing!" his mother gushed later that night. "I'm proud of you, Bob. I know this dance isn't exactly your kind of thing, and—"

Brrrriiiiiiing! went the telephone. Lynn scrambled up from her chair.

"Bobbbyyy!" Lynn called seconds later. "Get your kissing machine ready! It's a *giiiiirrrrrl!*"

"Probably Jennifer calling about some stupid dance details," Bob said to himself. *Well, I guess I just have to put up with it.*

He hobbled over to the phone and picked it up. "Hi, Jennifer," he said.

"Jennifer?! This isn't Jennifer! It's *Bonnie!*"

"Oh! I mean, uh, hi, Bonnie! Uhh...how are you?"

"I'm fine. Thank you." She sounded stiff and distant.

"I was ... I guess I was just expecting someone else."

"Well, it's just me," said Bonnie.

There was a long, awkward pause.

"So how are you?" asked Bob again.

"Oh, I'm fine. And I was wondering ... I know you think it's really dumb—and so do I—but ... well, would you mind going to the dance with me?"

Chapter Seven

Girl Trouble Times Three

"HIT THE FLOOR!" yelled Lynn. She jumped into Bob's bedroom and fired off a few quick rounds with her new semiautomatic machine gun.

Although it was just a toy, it sounded exactly like the real thing. It was seven-thirty in the morning, and Bob was still asleep. But not many people can stay asleep when they think they're being fired on, and Bob was no exception. With a shriek of terror, he flew out of the bed and straight into the air.

"*Aaaaaaagh!*" he yowled. "My ankle!" Once again, Bob had come down ankle-first!

Mrs. Kelly had heard the thud, and she was

upstairs in seconds. "What happened? Lynn, what did you do?" she gasped.

"She only shot at me in cold blood and re-sprained my ankle, that's all!" Bob shouted. "Look!" He jabbed his foot into the air.

His ankle was puffing out and turning blue all around the edges of the bandage. It also hurt like heck.

"Oh, dear," Mrs. Kelly said. "I guess we'll have to call the doctor. Lynn, what on earth got into you?"

"But, Mom," Lynn whined. "You *said* to wake up Bob! And you know how hard he is to wake up, so I had to—"

"You certainly didn't have to go *this* far," snapped Mrs. Kelly. "Go right into your room and stay there until it's time to leave for the bus. No arguments! Bob, honey, you just hang on a minute while I go call Dr. Talpey."

The minute his mother was out of sight, Bob lowered himself gingerly to the floor, crawled to his doorway, and stuck his head out the door. "I'll get you for this, Lynn," he hissed across the hall.

"You can't!" Lynn wailed from her bedroom. "You can't hurt a poor little seven-year-old!"

Bob laughed grimly. "I have no problems with hurting a seven-year-old, Lynn, when it's you.

And this time I'm really going to . . ."

At that moment, they both heard Mrs. Kelly coming back up the stairs. "Mom, Bob's trying to hurt me!" Lynn called out in a weak, pitiful little voice.

Bob vaulted across the room and back into his bed. Afterward he never knew quite how he'd done it, but when his mother came back in, Bob was lying in the same position she'd left him in. His ankle hurt agonizingly now, but that was a small price to pay for not being spotted out in the hallway.

"Oh, Lynn, what nonsense," Mrs. Kelly said crossly. She put a dishpan full of ice water by Bob's bedside. "It's quite clear to me who's done the hurting *this* morning. Now, Bob, Dr. Talpey said all you need to do is ice your ankle for a few minutes and it will be back to normal. I mean, back to normal for a sprained ankle. So you just stay here, and I'll run down and get your breakfast. No, Lynn, I will *not* get any breakfast for you! I want you to just stay in your room quietly, young lady!"

She disappeared down the hall, and Bob gingerly eased his foot into the agonizingly icy water.

Even on good days, weekday mornings in the Kelly household were pretty chaotic. But even by Kelly-household standards, this morning had been especially complicated—so much so that Mrs. Kelly was still wearing her bathrobe when the time came for her to drive Bob to school. That was why Bob insisted that his mother drop him off at the crossroads leading to the school rather than taking him all the way up to the front door.

And that was how he happened to meet up with Bonnie, who was walking to school alone. She arrived at the crossroads just as Bob did.

"Morning, Bonnie!" Mrs. Kelly called. She gave a cheery wave and pulled away from the curb.

Bonnie grimaced politely in return, but to Bob she said nothing at all. She just stared at him for a second, stepped off the curb, and continued walking toward school. "Hey, wait!" Bob shouted, hobbling after her as fast as he could on his crutches.

"Hey, Bonnie, you know I didn't want this to happen, right?" he called after her.

Bonnie stopped right in the middle of the street and whirled around to face him. "Well, then, why did you say yes when Jennifer called you?" she demanded in a hurt-sounding voice.

"What was I supposed to say?" Bob asked still swinging toward Bonnie on his crutches. "She called me before you did! I'm not going out with her or anything!"

"Hah!" Bonnie replied. "You probably will be soon."

"Listen, I only sprained my ankle because I was trying to get out of going to the dance..."

"And that's another thing," Bonnie cut in. "You guys have all been acting like such babies about this dance!"

"Wait a minute, Bon! You didn't like the idea of the dance, either! Why are you getting mad at me?"

"Maybe I didn't like the idea, but at least I didn't spend all my time trying to wriggle my way out of it! What's the big deal? It's just a dance, and it wouldn't kill you guys to act a little bit mature for once!"

Just then, Bob stepped a little too hard on his ankle, and the pain pushed him over the edge. Suddenly, he was furious—with Jennifer, with Bonnie, with all the people who'd made the awful Hollis Elementary sixth-grade dance happen.

"Oh, yeah," he sneered. "It's so mature to play dress-up!" Raising his voice about two octaves, he trilled, "We're just so *excited* to be having a big dance and a deejay and—"

"I take it back," Bonnie interrupted. "You haven't been acting like babies. You *are* babies!"

"Will you get out of the road, kids?"

Startled, Bob and Bonnie turned to see a furious-looking man poking his head out of his car window. Behind him was a long line of honking drivers.

"Sorry, sir," Bob muttered. He leaned over on his crutches to pick up his knapsack, and realized that he couldn't quite reach it. Silently Bonnie picked it up and handed it to him. Then she turned and stomped away again. His face flaming, Bob swung along after her.

After that, Bob and Bonnie stopped talking to each other. It wasn't that much of a change, Bob told himself. The dance had made it pretty hard for boys and girls to talk to each other normally anyway, and Bob hadn't been walking to school because of his ankle. "I don't care," Bob muttered to himself. "Good riddance and all that junk."

Still, he couldn't help feeling kind of weird when he heard that Bonnie had asked Diego to go to the dance with her.

"You don't mind, do you?" asked Diego after school one day. The two boys were standing at Bob's locker.

"No!" Bob answered quickly. "Why should I?"

"Well...uh...you guys are sort of friends, that's all," said Diego. "I just didn't know if..."

"Actually, I wouldn't really say Bonnie's much of a friend anymore," Bob said casually. "She's just too cranky. Around me, anyway."

"How's Jennifer?" Diego asked after a second.

Bob made a face. "Same as always, I guess."

To Bob's relief, Jennifer actually hadn't pestered him too much since she'd asked him to the dance. Maybe all she had wanted was to be sure she had someone to go with.

But on the Wednesday before the dance, Jennifer was waiting when Bob went to his locker after school.

"Hi, Bob. Only three days until the big event!" she greeted him.

"Right," Bob answered without much enthusiasm. "So I guess we'd better be careful to get all our studying done ahead of time, huh? In fact, I think I'll hurry right home and really buckle down to—"

"Oh, there won't be any time for homework over the next couple of days!" Jennifer said solemnly. "At least, I'm not planning on it. I mean, take a look at all the stuff I have to do!" She pressed a sheet of pink paper into Bob's reluctant hands.

"LIST OF THINGS FOR JENNIFER TO DO!!!!" she had written across the top in her flowery script.

Bob studied the list.

1). Rent tuxedo for B. K.

("That's you," Jennifer explained unnecessarily.)

2). Find dress for J. S.

("That's me.")

3). Corsage. (Wrist or pin-on? Ask B. K.)
4). Boutonniere for B. K. Rosebud or carnation?
5). Rent limo
6). TELL B. K. ABOUT MY HOUSE

"What's a boutonniere?" Bob asked at last.

"A little flower guys wear in the buttonhole of their jacket," Jennifer told him seriously. "What you get depends on what color your tux is."

"Tux. Right," said Bob dazedly. "And what's this about your house?"

"Oh, yeah. You're invited to my house for an hour or so before the dance. My parents are hiring a photographer."

"But Jennifer, I can't rent a tux and a limo and everything!" Bob protested. "I can't afford it, and I don't think my parents will want to—"

"Don't worry, Bob," Jennifer said. "It's all been taken care of. *My* parents are paying for everything. Including my corsage."

She smiled at him. "I mean, they want this to be a perfect, perfect evening for me, you know? So let's go rent you a tuxedo!"

Chapter Eight

Jackets, Bras, and Ants

"But Mom, why do I have to come to the store with you? Any outfit you like will be fine with me!"

Bob's mother gave him an exasperated look. "Bob! How am I supposed to tell whether it fits or not unless you're there? You should be glad you're *not* renting a tuxedo. That's a lot harder than picking out a plain old jacket and pants and shoes. Now let's just go out to the car."

Bob had flatly refused to rent a tuxedo with Jennifer.

"I *know* your parents would pay for it," he had told her. "But I'm not going to do it. I refuse to be the only guy at this dance who looks like a total geek." Something in the tone of his voice must have done the trick.

"Well, you don't have to get *mad* about it," Jennifer said sulkily. "I'm not going to force you to do it. If you want to look like a scarecrow at the most important social event of the whole sixth grade, I guess I can't stop you. Now, if you don't mind, I'm going to pick out *my* dress for the dance."

Then Jennifer stomped away down the hall.

Bob thought he was home free. But when he got home, he discovered that his mother had also been making clothes plans for him.

"You've been needing a new jacket for a long time," she greeted him as he walked into the kitchen, "and this dance gives us the perfect reason to get you one! And we'll get you some new dress pants and a pair of nice shoes, too."

"Why can't I just wear my jeans to the dance?"

"Because you can't," his mother said simply.

And that was why Bob found himself walking into the Better Boys department behind his mother.

The sales clerk who walked up to them with a great big smile on his face was wearing a name tag that said "Mr. Frisbee." He was a portly, maroon-faced man wearing a shiny dark-blue suit and very pointy shoes. "Dork shoes," Bob muttered. He noticed that Mr. Frisbee was practically rubbing his hands with delight as he headed toward them.

You can tell he's thinking, "Oh, great! I'll be able to unload anything on *these* suckers," Bob thought.

But, of course, Mr. Frisbee didn't say that. Instead, he bowed slightly and purred, "Good afternoon. How may I be of assistance?"

"We're looking for a formal outfit for my son," said Mrs. Kelly briskly. "A jacket, pants, and shoes."

"Ah. Excellent. And your son is how old?"

"Twelve," Bob said sullenly. He hated it when people talked about him like he wasn't there.

"I'm sure I can find something very, very special for the young gentleman," said Mr. Frisbee. "Now, let's just take a look and see what we've got to work with...."

He narrowed his eyes and scrutinized Bob for a second.

"There's a touch of the nautical about you, young man. I think we've got just the thing for a young seafarer like you." And he pulled a jacket off the rack next to him.

Bob eyed it in horror.

The jacket was double-breasted, with huge brass buttons that were shaped like little anchors. It had white piping around the lapels.

78

"I'm sorry," Bob heard himself saying, "but I think I need something a little more, you know, regular."

"Absolutely," Mrs. Kelly agreed.

Without a word, Mr. Frisbee headed to another rack. He returned holding another jacket.

"Now, *this*," said Mr. Frisbee, "is perfect for an adventurous young man, which, if I may say so, you seem to be."

It was bright red with a leopard-print pattern and metallic gold lapels.

"My son's not a lion tamer!" Mrs. Kelly exclaimed, shielding her eyes. "Could you please show us something a little . . . quieter?"

"Ah, so the two of you have more . . . uh . . . conventional tastes," said Mr. Frisbee in a disappointed voice. "Well, we have a full range of the less exciting garments as well. What colors would you be thinking of? A nice, soft pale apricot, perhaps?" he asked hopefully.

"No, I think a nice plain navy," said Mrs. Kelly firmly. "Or perhaps green."

Mr. Frisbee perked up again. "Green! An excellent suggestion! Green will pick up the highlights in . . . in . . ."

Yes, Bob thought. *Please go on, Mr. Frisbee. What part of my face, exactly, are you going to say green brings out the highlights in? My nice green cheeks? My nice green lips or teeth?* He grinned ferociously at the salesman.

"Green is a flattering shade to all complexions," Mr. Frisbee finished weakly.

"You've got to be kidding!" Bob protested when Mr. Frisbee brought out a jacket whose sleeves practically scraped the floor.

"The sleeves are perhaps a little long," Mr. Frisbee conceded, "but boys your age always need to have their clothes altered. I'm sure your mother is handy with a needle."

"Not exactly," put in Mrs. Kelly from the counter, where she was looking at socks.

Somehow, Bob ended up with an outfit that fit reasonably well. But he still hated it. Could things possibly get any worse?

"Is that your son sitting out there? He looks uncomfortable."

"Oh, he's okay," came Mrs. Kelly's voice.

Bob sank a little lower in his chair. He'd been sitting outside the fitting room for twenty minutes, ever since Mrs. Kelly had dragged him to the dress department, "so I can try on just a couple of things." To make things even worse, the fitting room was next to the lingerie section.

"Mommy, what's that boy doing in here?" came a sudden, piercing voice. Bob turned around and saw a little girl about four years old staring at him.

"Maybe he's waiting for his mommy, Marcelline," ventured the girl's mother tiredly.

"Do boys wear bras?" asked Marcelline in the same penetrating voice.

"Shh, honey! Of course they don't."

"Well, then why is he sitting in a chair that's all *surrounded* by bras?"

"My mom didn't come out for another *hour*," Bob told Diego.

Diego whistled sympathetically. "Boy, she really put you through the ringer, didn't she? Now, where's the molasses?"

"Right here." Bob handed him the jar.

"And the ant farm?"

"Here you go."

"Okay. Now we just spread the molasses across the sheet like this, and we're in business."

It was Thursday afternoon, and Bob was free to spend the afternoon doing the thing he most wanted to do: get back at Lynn. Ever since she had scared him so badly that he'd hurt his ankle again, he had been determined to get revenge.

A few minutes ago, Mrs. Kelly had dragged Lynn, kicking and screaming, to her weekly piano lesson. "Soldiers don't *need* to play piano!" Lynn had shouted as Mrs. Kelly dragged her out the door. Bob knew they'd be away for the whole afternoon. Lynn's piano teacher was the kind who makes people start over whenever they make a mistake, and Lynn pretty much played *only* mistakes. Bob had plenty of time to put his plan into action.

He had enlisted Diego's help, and the two of them had just finished stripping the blankets and top sheet off Lynn's bed. Now they were carefully painting the end of the bottom sheet with molasses.

"Okay, I think that's enough," said Diego. "Now, for the ants."

"Where did you get these ants, anyway?" Bob asked.

"I bought them at a scientific supply house. It's a great place. They've got all kinds of neat animals there. You know, for experiments and dissections and stuff. Actually, these ants kind of give me an idea about the dance . . . ," Diego added in a thoughtful voice.

"What do you mean?"

"Oh, nothing," Diego said vaguely. "I have to think about it some more. Maybe I'll tell you about it later."

"Okay," Bob said. "What are you going to do with the ants now? Just dump the whole farm into the bed?"

"Oh, no." Diego sounded shocked. "That would be much too crude. No, what we do is put the ant farm under the bed. Then we make the bed up again so it looks completely, utterly normal. After a couple of hours, the ants will start sort of trickling up the string. So, by the time Lynn goes to bed, most of them will be in there with her. But she won't realize it for a while, since all the molasses will be at the foot of the bed. Do you get my drift, Bob?"

Bob nodded admiringly. "What about the tape player?" he asked. Along with the ant farm, Diego had brought along a tiny tape player.

"Well, first we've got to record some kind of message on it. Then I'll attach the timer so it will start playing at midnight." Diego handed the tape player to Bob. "Here, you can do the message."

Bob cleared his throat and pressed the Record button.

"Lynn, Lynn," he wailed in a ghostly whisper. "You have been very wicked. You have been cruel to your brother. You must be *punished....*"

Diego grinned as he disappeared under the bed, string in hand.

"Do you hear the dripping?" Bob wailed on. He clicked his tongue a few times. It was the only driplike sound he could think of on such short notice. "That is *blood* dripping, Lynn. Blood from the ceiling above you, falling down onto your bed...."

"Say something about the ants," Diego whispered.

Let's see, Bob thought rapidly. *The tape's set for midnight. By then, Lynn will have found the ants, and her bed will have been remade, so...*

"Do you remember the aaaannnnntttss?" he moaned. "The ones you *thought* you had gotten rid of? Don't you feel them again now? Just a few of them, crawling around your feet? They've come back! And these are not ordinary ants, Lynn. They're meat-eating ants! They're starting to nibble your toes right now. And in a few hours, you won't have any legs left—just bones. Then they'll start in on your fingers, and then ... A-HA-HA-HA-HA-HA-HA!"

Bob had always been good at demonic laughter.

Now he clicked off the tape recorder. "That ought to take care of Lynn," he said with a big, wicked grin.

The next morning, as Lynn came into the kitchen, Mrs. Kelly stared at her curiously. "Why, honey," she said. "What's going on? Are you feeling okay?"

Lynn was wearing a flowered pink dress that was about three years old and very tight. "I'm okay," Lynn said in a small voice.

"But, dear, where are your ... your ..."

Machine guns and grenades? Bob thought with silent satisfaction. He smothered a giggle.

"I'm not going to be in the army anymore," Lynn announced.

"Why, honey, that's wonderful!" Mrs. Kelly said. "But, I mean, why not?"

"Something happened to me last night," Lynn said in a low, serious voice. "See, Mom, a demon came to my bedroom, and he...he warned me! He said if I kept being in the army, blood would drip down on me and ants—real ants—would come and eat me alive! Then he sent all these ants crawling into my bed, and...and..."

"Now, now, honey," Mrs. Kelly said, patting Lynn on the arm. "You know your father and I would never let a demon get you!" She shot Bob a curious glance. "But maybe it is best if you do, uh, quit the army for a while. In fact, why don't I take you to the mall and buy you some nice new clothes? Maybe some new dresses or shoes or a new winter coat?"

Lynn sighed. "Okay." There was a long pause, then she added, "Will you buy me a doll, too?"

"I suppose." Mrs. Kelly sounded as if she were in shock.

Bob got up from the table. "I've got to get to school," he announced.

"Bye, dear," his mother said, briefly giving

him another strange look. Then she actually grinned at him.

Bob didn't grin back. He was too depressed. The big dance was only two days away.

Chapter Nine

The Big, Big, Big, Big Night

"Well, Bob, what do you think?"

Bob's mother had just dropped him off at Jennifer's house. He hadn't even gotten through the front door before Jennifer came sweeping grandly down the stairs dressed in some kind of long green thing. That's what it looked like to Bob, anyway—a long, green thing with a bunch of bows or something sticking out all over the place and some big hunks of extra material at the shoulders and waist.

"It's very nice," he choked out.

Jennifer clearly expected more of a reaction. "But what do you think about the peplum?" she asked. "I mean, it's not too much, is it?"

What's a peplum? Bob thought frantically.

"Uhhhh...it's very nice, too," he said cautiously.

Just then, a woman who could only be Jennifer's mother came into the front hall. She grabbed Bob by the shoulders and gave him a big kiss on the cheek.

"I've got to get a picture of you!" she trilled. "Oh, Bobby, you look just adorable. You and Jennifer will be the cutest couple at the dance! I'm so glad we hired a photographer. Now we'll all be able to look back and remember this moment *forever*!" Bob seriously thought he might throw up. "Come out back when you're done primping," she went on, as she swirled out of the hallway.

Bob guessed the dreaded photographer was "out back."

Jennifer winced and glanced over at Bob. "Mom always has such an attack about everything," she said. "I guess we'd better go out there." She sighed.

She walked off through the living room and out the sun room into the backyard. Bob shuffled gingerly along behind her.

"Oh, isn't this..." Bob couldn't think of a single way to finish the sentence.

"This" was a white wicker arch about twenty feet tall outlined in tiny Christmas-tree lights. It had been looped and twined and festooned with hundreds and hundreds of pink and white roses.

Mrs. Stevens stood next to a glum-looking photographer who was holding a huge camera. "Isn't it adorable?" she asked proudly. "I designed it myself. Just look at all those tiny little lights . . ."

"Mom, I'd like to get to the dance sometime tonight," Jennifer interrupted.

"Of course, darling," Mrs. Stevens said instantly. "Now, I think it would be really special to have you two hold hands and march through the trellis while Mr. Tivol takes your picture."

Bob resolutely crossed his arms over his chest. It was bad enough that he had to go to this stupid dance, but he was NOT going to hold hands with Jennifer. Her mother could bring in the Terminator, and it wouldn't do any good. No way.

Mrs. Stevens must have realized this. Suddenly she said, "Well, don't you two look nice just standing there together! Well! What a lovely picture!" The photographer snapped a few pictures of Bob and Jennifer—Bob looking sort of like Chief Sitting Bull except he was standing, and Jennifer looking like she was about to be crowned Miss America.

Then Bob stood off to the side while Mr. Tivol took about a hundred pictures of Jennifer. Jennifer holding her corsage and looking at it, Jennifer clasping her hands and gazing up at the sky, Jennifer kissing her mother good-bye. Finally, it was time to get into the Stevenses' car so that Mr. Stevens could drive Jennifer and Bob to the dance.

As the car pulled out of the driveway at last, Jennifer sighed blissfully. "I bet people will be so jealous when they see us that they'll just throw up," she said.

"I'm sure they will," Bob said quietly.

"It looks great, doesn't it?" asked Jennifer.

"Yeah, sure, I guess," Bob replied.

The Decorating Committee had really gone crazy. Crepe-paper streamers were streaming from every possible place. A huge mirrored ball hung from the ceiling, casting bits of rainbowy light everywhere. Someone had cut out dozens of messy-looking construction-paper stars and stuck them up all over the walls. And the floor was covered with a whole sandbox worth of glitter. Bob could feel it grinding around under the stiff soles of his squeaky shoes.

"Hi, Bob! Hi, Jennifer! Doesn't this place look spectacular?"

Tiffany Root rushed up to Bob and Jennifer, dragging a reluctant-looking Jonathan Matterhorn along behind her. And behind him were Bonnie and Diego.

"I only hope this glitter won't cause problems," Tiffany said. "I hope no one slips on it."

But the glitter was only a slight annoyance

compared to something Bob had just realized: He was the only boy in the lunchroom who was dressed up.

None of the other girls was wearing a long dress, either. Bonnie, Tiffany, and all the rest of the girls Bob could see were dressed in normal dresses—nice, but not formal. And most of the boys weren't even wearing dress pants. They all had on jeans.

Bob wished he could disappear. "I guess you didn't want to tell me we were going to be the only ones who look like geeks, huh?" Bob hissed.

Jennifer shrugged. "We look nicer than everyone else. I think you should feel happy about that."

"I couldn't agree more," came a booming voice from behind them. It was Mr. Haypence, wearing an awful tuxedo that looked like a Mr. Frisbee Special, too. It was pale, pale blue with peach-colored stripes. A fountain of ruffles cascaded down the front of the shirt, and there was even a ruffle around the hem of Mr. Haypence's pants. The sight of those ruffles made Bob feel a lot better.

I guess there are worse things than shoes that squeak, he thought to himself, *like having a tux like Mr. Haypence's*.

But then he discovered that there were even worse things than that! The principal put his hand on Bob's shoulder. "In fact, you and Jennifer look so splendid that I'm going to ask you to open the dance for us," he said.

"O-open the dance?" Bob asked.

"That's right. You two will be the first couple out there on the floor." And before Bob could say a word, Mr. Haypence signaled to Smilin' Steve.

He winked at Bob and put on the first record.

This isn't happening, Bob thought desperately.

"It's the cha-cha," Jennifer gushed. "My favorite! Let's go."

She seized Bob's hand and dragged him to the center of the floor.

Then—just as she was about to put her hand on his shoulder—Jennifer's eyes widened, and she screamed.

"BOB! YOU'RE ALIVE!"

Chapter Ten

The Little Dance That Couldn't

"Of course I'm alive!" Bob replied in amazement. "What are you talking about?"

"Something's wiggling around your shoulder!" Jennifer's voice rose to a hysterical pitch. "Oh, no! Oh, no! It's a frog!"

Startled, Bob looked down at his shoulder. There *was* a frog sitting on it—a little green one. It was blinking its goggly eyes as though it, too, was wondering how it had gotten there. Bob reached up to grab it—but the frog was quicker. It leaped off his shoulder and plopped to the floor at Jennifer's feet.

"GET AWAY FROM ME, YOU HORRIBLE THING!" she screamed, and turned to run.

Then she stopped short. There was another

frog behind her. Three of them, actually.

In fact, Bob suddenly noticed that there were frogs all over the lunchroom floor. They were hopping confusedly around in what looked like a grotesque frog version of the cha-cha.

Did all those frogs come off me? Bob wondered in amazement.

Now Tiffany Root started screaming, too. "Help! Help!" she screeched. "They have rabies! They'll bite us! We're all going to die!"

"They'll get on my dress!" Jennifer howled. "I'm getting out of here!"

"No, don't!" Tiffany wailed. "You'll squash them, and that will be horrible. . . ." And she and Jennifer began to scream together.

Boy, this is quite a duet, Bob thought. Then the duet turned into a symphony. Screams were coming from every corner of the room.

Diego caught Bob's eye and grinned at him. Suddenly, Bob remembered their conversation when they were setting up the ant trap in Lynn's bed. *So Diego brought these frogs in*, Bob thought. *He really is a genius!*

"DO NOT MOVE! REMAIN CALM!" Mr. Haypence boomed out. Smilin' Steve clicked off the record. "We do not want to harm the frogs or each other," Mr. Haypence went on more quietly in the sudden silence. "If you will all wait a moment—"

"Hey! They're coming out of the waterfall!"

That was Louie Watson. He was kneeling down next to the ornamental waterfall and peering inside it with an amazed expression. "There's a whole mess of them in here!" he called. "I'll get them out for you, Mr. Haypence!"

"No, Louie, don't!" said Mr. Haypence quickly. But it was too late. Louie's twin Larry went over to help, and together the Human Demolition Team plunged their arms into the water.

"Wait a sec," Louie said. "There's some kind of pipe back on the wall here."

"Don't touch it!" yelled Mr. Haypence. But once again, he was too late. With Larry's help, Louie yanked the pipe out of the waterfall.

PSSSSSSSSSSSSSSSSHHHHHHHHH-HHHHHHH!

A massive geyser of water shot up from the base of the waterfall where the pipe had been. And within seconds, the sixth grade was soaked.

Gallons of cold water came raining down on them. Water swept across the slick tile floor in torrents and streamed down the walls. From somewhere in the lunchroom, Bob could hear Mr. Haypence howling.

"The pipe! Put the pipe back! It's hooked up to the draaaaaaaain!"

This is like being in a disaster movie! Bob

thought as he stumbled across the floor toward the waterfall.

Bob threw himself down on his knees next to Louie and grabbed half of the pipe. With his free hand, he groped around the base of the waterfall until he could vaguely feel the drain where the pipe was supposed to fit.

"Push the pipe down here!" he shouted to Louie. "It's like screwing in a garden hose!"

Except that about a thousand gallons of water per second was shooting out of the drain. With all their strength, he and Louie and Larry slowly, agonizingly slowly, screwed the pipe into place.

Instantly, as if nothing had happened, the waterfall began its gentle, murmuring flow again.

At last the lunchroom was quiet—wet, but quiet. The frogs were gone, washed away—who knew where?—by the enormous torrents of water.

Mr. Haypence passed a trembling hand over his hair. A little rivulet of water flowed down onto his collar. "That was—that was—" he began falteringly. He stopped in mid-sentence and sat on one of the crepe-paper-festooned cafeteria chairs.

Bob glanced around the lunchroom. People were starting to stir now, but no one knew quite what to do next. Except for Rocky.

"You know, all that exercise really gave me an appetite!" he said cheerfully.

As everyone watched, he walked over to the refreshment table and surveyed it for a second.

The plates that had once held Oreos now held mounds of blackish-gray glop. The plates that had been piled high with sandwiches were now piled high with what could only be described as melted bread. (Of course, the baloney that had been inside the sandwiches was still intact. It would take more than a few tons of water to dissolve baloney, Bob realized.) And what had formerly been potato chips now were mashed potatoes.

Rocky dipped his finger into the pile of dissolved Oreos and scooped up a fingerful, which he popped into his mouth. "Hey, this stuff is good!" he exclaimed. "How about some punch?"

He leaned toward the punch bowl, picked up the ladle, and began to pour himself a ladleful of punch.

A frog leaped out of the ladle, teetered uncertainly on the edge of the table, and then jumped back into the punch bowl.

Without hesitating, Rocky drained his cup of punch. "Tastes great!" he said happily. "Can I pour anyone else a cup?"

"No, you cannot."

It was Jennifer—a very angry Jennifer. Her

hair was plastered all over her face, her green gown hung limply around her like thirty bushels of seaweed, and she'd lost one of her shoes.

She lurched squashily up to Bob and glared at him. "This is all your fault!" she hissed. "If you hadn't had that frog on your shoulder, none of this would have happened!"

"Hey, Jennifer, I don't know where that frog came from! I can't help it that it was on my shoulder!" Bob protested, but he couldn't help laughing a little as he said it, and that really sent Jennifer over the edge.

"I should never have asked you to the dance, you crupid steep!" she shouted. "I mean, you stupid creep! You're just a total baby! You don't even know what a social life is!" And with that, Jennifer stormed out of the lunchroom, slamming the heavy door behind her. As she did so, the drenched flounce of the fabric around her waist got caught in the door and tore away.

"There goes her peplum," Bonnie murmured.

"Oh, so *that's* what a peplum is," said Bob. "I couldn't figure it out."

He grinned at her, and she grinned back.

Slam! went another far-off door. Jennifer was gone.

Mr. Haypence stood up slowly, turned and faced the rest of the sixth-graders. All the air seemed to have gone out of him. "I think we should cancel the dance," he said. He took off his glasses and rubbed the bridge of his nose tiredly.

Bob suddenly felt bad. He told his conscience, *Leave me alone.*

But his conscience wouldn't.

I already felt sorry for Jennifer, and look where that got me! he told his conscience. But it wouldn't shut up. Mr. Haypence looked too disappointed.

Bob stepped forward and took a deep breath. "We don't need to cancel the dance, Mr. Haypence," he said. "Why don't we reschedule it?"

"WHAT! NO WAY!" bellowed Rocky Latizano. In his shock, he inhaled a piece of popcorn and began to cough.

"He's choking! He needs the Heimlich maneuver!" shouted Larry Watson. He rushed up to Rocky, grabbed him under the ribs, and gave a mighty squeeze. It was too bad that he knocked over the refreshment table in the process.

"Don't worry, Mr. Haypence. We'll clean it up," said Bob before Rocky could get his breath back. "But back to the dance. I'm sure Diego would be glad to help me plan it. Right, Diego?"

Diego gulped a few times. He gave Bob a pleading look. Then he took a deep breath.

"Sure I would. And maybe Jonathan will help, too. And I'll track down those frogs."

I knew it! Bob thought. *I knew Diego had brought those frogs in here!*

But Bob didn't say that, of course. "You know," he said instead, "a bunch of us are—are kind of friends with the deejay. I bet we could persuade him to come back without too much trouble."

That would be a first for Smilin' Steve, anyway, Bob told himself, *sixth-grade boys trying to persuade him to come to a dance.*

"And—and we could make some really great refreshments," he finished. "Maybe Rocky could be in charge of that."

Rocky perked up immediately. "Sure thing!" he said.

Leaving Rocky mumbling something about man-sized refreshments, Bob turned to Mr. Haypence. "So what do you think?" he asked the principal.

Mr. Haypence had miraculously reinflated over the past five minutes. Now, even in his ridiculous tuxedo, with his glasses all askew on his nose, he looked like himself again.

"Bob, my fellow, I see I underestimated you," he boomed. "Your school spirit is very commendable. Clearly, you've just been too modest to let it show all this time...."

"Well...uh..." Bob faltered.

"I thought so!" Mr. Haypence said triumphantly. "Well, I'm proud of you, Bob, and I'm sure that the boys will come up with a very successful dance. And your kind offer of cleanup help would be most...uh...helpful. Any other volunteers?"

Bonnie stepped forward.

"Why I did it, I'll never know," she said the next morning, surveying the sodden lunchroom with dismay. "We're going to be here all day, Bob!"

"Well, that'll give us time to plan the dance," said Bob. "After all, we've got to get all the details taken care of before Jennifer gets her claws into it."

Bonnie smiled. "I'm sorry I got so cranky about her," she said. "It's too stupid."

"I agree," Bob said wholeheartedly.

"But maybe we could walk there together?" Bonnie suggested.

"Okay. No dancing together, though. I don't think I could stand it."

Bonnie's grin was even wider.

It's where everything happens!
by Ann Hodgman

___#1: NIGHT OF A THOUSAND PIZZAS 0-425-12091-0/$2.75
It all started with the school lunchroom's brand new, computerized pizza
maker. Instead of one-hundred pizzas, the cook accidentally programmed
it to make one thousand! What can the kids do? Have you ever tried to
get rid of a thousand extra-large pizzas?

___#2: FROG PUNCH 0-425-12092-9/$2.75
This time the principal has gone too far. Ballroom dancing lessons. UGH!
Even worse, he's planned a formal dance. Now the sixth grade is
determined to fight back. When they unleash their secret weapon in the
lunchroom, things will go completely bonkers!

___#3: THE COOKIE CAPER (On sale in June)
　　　　　　　0-425-12132-1/$2.75
The kids want to sell their baked cookies to raise money for the class
treasury. But where will they find a kitchen big enough? The lunchroom!
The cookies turn out to be so amazing the kids at Hollis get to be on TV,
but the baking business turns out to be more than *anybody* needed!

One day Allie, Rosie, Becky and Julie saved a birthday party from becoming a complete disaster. The next day, the four best friends are running their own business...

The Party Line

by Carrie Austen

___#1: ALLIE'S WILD SURPRISE 0-425-12047-3/$2.75
Allie's favorite rock star is in town, but how will she get the money for a concert ticket? When the clown hired for her little brother's birthday party is a no-show, Allie finds her miracle! Before you can say "make a wish," the girls are in the party business--having fun and getting paid for it! Can The Party Line make Allie's rock concert a dream come true?

___#2: JULIE'S BOY PROBLEM 0-425-12048-1/$2.75
It's hard to get a romance going with the cute Mark Harris when his best friend, Casey Wyatt, is an obnoxious girl-hater. Then, in the misunderstanding of the century, The Party Line gets hired to give a party for Casey. When Casey finds out, it's all-out war.

___#3: BECKY'S SUPER SECRET 0-425-12131-3/$2.75
Becky is putting together a top-secret mystery party and she'll need her three best friends to help her do it in style. The only problem is: Becky hasn't exactly told them yet that they're going to help. Can Becky pull off the surprise party of the year? (On Sale June '90)

___#4: ROSIE'S POPULARITY PLAN 0-425-12169-0/$2.75
It's just Rosie's luck to get paired with Jennifer--the weird new girl--for an English project. Next, Jennifer's mom thinks it would be a great idea if The Party Line threw a birthday party for Jennifer. The rest of the girls will need some serious convincing! (On Sale July '90)